Praise for *New York Times* bestselling author

ELIZABETH LOWELL

"This author delivers pure, undiluted excitement."
Jayne Ann Krentz

"Lowell brilliantly mingles danger, deception,
and desire . . . romantic suspense at its best."
Booklist

"Elizabeth Lowell has long set a standard
of excellence for thrillers that never stint
on either romance or suspense . . ."
BookPage

"Romantic suspense is her true forte."
Minneapolis Star-Tribune

Books by Elizabeth Lowell

Contemporary

Blue Smoke and Murder • Innocent as Sin
The Wrong Hostage • Whirlpool • The Secret Sister
Always Time to Die • Color of Death
Death is Forever • Die in Plain Sight
Running Scared • Moving Target
Midnight in Ruby Bayou • Pearl Cove
The Ruby • Jade Island
Amber Beach • Diamond Tiger

Historical

This Time Love • Eden Burning
Remember Summer • To the Ends of the Earth
Where the Heart Is • Winter Fire
Desert Rain • Autumn Lover
A Woman Without Lies • Only Love
Forget Me Not • Enchanted
Beautiful Dreamer • Lover in the Rough
Forbidden • Untamed
Only You • Only Mine • Only His

ELIZABETH LOWELL

FORGET ME NOT

AVON

An Imprint of HarperCollinsPublishers

Forget Me Not was previously published in an altered form by Silhouette Books in 1984.

AVON BOOKS
An Imprint of HarperCollins*Publishers*
10 East 53rd Street
New York, New York 10022-5299

Copyright © 1984 by Ann Maxwell; 1994 by Two of a Kind, Inc.
Excerpt from *Death Echo* copyright © 2010 by Two of a Kind, Inc.
ISBN 978-0-380-76759-5
www.avonromance.com

First Avon Books paperback printing: December 1994

Avon Trademark Reg. U.S. Pat. Off. and in Other Countries, Marca Registrada, Hecho en U.S.A.
HarperCollins® is a registered trademark of HarperCollins Publishers.

Printed in the U.S.A.

20 19 18 17 16

for my sister
Susan Mills
port in many storms

1

WHEN THE PHONE RANG, Alana was almost relieved. Though it was before dawn, she was wide awake. Since she had come back from Broken Mountain, she had slept very little, and never peacefully.

Kicking aside the tangled sheets, Alana turned toward the phone. It was too early for anyone she knew on the West Coast to be up and about. That meant it was probably her brother in Wyoming calling to see how she was.

Calling to see if she remembered what had happened on Broken Mountain.

"Hello," Alana said, keeping her voice steady with an effort.

"Sis? Is that you?"

"Hi, Bob. How's Merry?"

"Counting the weeks until February," said Bob, laughing. "If she gets much bigger, we'll have to put her in a stall with the brood mares."

Alana smiled at the thought of petite, blond Merry tucked into one of the heated stalls Bob kept for his prize mares.

"Better not let Merry hear you say that," Alana warned.

"Hell, it was her idea." Bob paused, then said, "Sis?"

Alana's hand tightened on the phone. She had heard that tone before, little brother to big sister, a smile and affectionate wheedling.

He wanted something from her.

"When are you coming home?" Bob asked bluntly.

Alana's heart began to beat too fast. She didn't know how to tell her brother that she was frightened by the thought of returning to the ranch where Broken Mountain rose steeply, mantled in ice and darkness.

Before her last trip to Broken Mountain, Alana had loved the ranch, the mountains, the silence, the heights, and the clouds swirling overhead. She had loved the memories of Rafael Winter—Rafe reflected in every lake, every fragrant forest, sunsets and sunrises sweeping across the land like fire, the wind's keening harmonies echoing the music Rafe had made on his harmonica.

Alana had come to love the land even more

because she and Rafe had been part of it, lovers suspended between sky and mountains, more beautiful than either, timeless, burning with the sun.

But now those mountains terrified Alana.

Now the memories of Rafe were a brittle, cutting armor that she pulled around her like the colors of dawn, hoping to drive away the horror and darkness that crawled up out of the abyss of those six missing days.

"I don't—" Alana began.

Her brother interrupted before she could refuse.

"I've already talked to your agent," Bob said cheerfully. "He told me you've refused to accept any concerts and won't even look at the songs he sends to you."

"Yes, but— "

Bob kept talking.

"So don't tell• me how busy you are," he said. "If you're writing songs again, you can write them just as well here. Better. You always did your best work here."

With a conscious effort, Alana loosened her grip on the phone. She had no more excuses, so she said nothing.

"Sis? I need you here."

"Bob, I don't think—" Alana began.

Then her voice broke.

"Don't say no," Bob said urgently. "You don't even know what I want yet."

And you don't know what I want, Alana thought rebelliously. You've never even asked if I want something.

The words went no further than Alana's thoughts, a silent cry of need. Yet even as the cry echoed in her mind, she recognized its unfairness.

What she needed, Bob couldn't provide. She needed warmth and reassurance, safety and a man's hard strength standing between her and the abyss, protecting her until she knew what had happened and could protect herself once more.

She needed love waiting instead of terror. She needed a dream to banish a nightmare.

She needed Rafael Winter.

But Rafe was just a dream. The nightmare was real.

With a deep breath, Alana gathered herself and set about living in her new world just as she always had lived. Alone, depending only on herself.

She had done this many times before, the deep breath and the determination to do the best she could with what she had, no matter how little that seemed to be when the nightmare descended like a storm.

"What do you want?" Alana asked softly.

"You know cash has always been a problem with the ranch," Bob said quickly. "Land poor, as they say. Well, Merry and I had this idea for a classy—and I mean *classy*—dude operation. High-country fishing safaris for people who can pay high prices."

Alana made a neutral sound.

"We had it all planned, all lined up, all our

ducks in a row," Bob said. "Our first two customers are very exclusive travel agents. Their clientele list reads like *Who's Who*. Everything was going great for us, and then . . ."

"And then?" Alana prompted.

"Merry got pregnant," Bob said simply. "I mean, we're both happy, we've been trying for two years, but . . ."

"But what?"

"Dr. Gene says Merry can't go on the pack trip."

"Is that a problem?"

"Hell, yes. She was going to be our cook and entertainer and general soother, take the rough edges off. You know what I mean, sis."

"Yes. I know."

It was the same role Alana had played in the family since she was thirteen and her mother died, leaving behind three boys, a devastated husband, and a daughter who had to grow up very quickly. That was when Alana had learned about reaching down into herself for the smile and the touch and the comfort that the people around her needed. She had rebuilt the shattered family as best she could, for she, too, needed the haven and the laughter and the warmth.

"It will really be more like time off than a job," coaxed Bob.

Alana heard the coaxing, but it didn't move her nearly as much as the disturbing thread of urgency beneath the soft tone.

"Riding and fishing and hiking in the high country just like we used to do. You'll love it, sis! I just know it. A real vacation for you."

Alana throttled the harsh laugh that was clawing at her throat.

Vacation, she thought, shuddering. In the mountains that nearly killed me. In the mountains that still come to me in nightmares.

Oh, God, that's some vacation my little brother has planned for me!

"Sis," Bob coaxed, "I wouldn't ask if I didn't really need you. I don't have anywhere else to turn. The pack trip is all set and the two dudes are here. Please?"

Unexpectedly, a vivid memory of Rafe came to Alana. . . . Late summer, a narrow trail going up Broken Mountain, a lame horse, and a saddle that weighed nearly as much as she did. She had been leading the horse, dragging the saddle, and watching the silent violence of clouds billowing toward a storm. At fifteen, she knew the dangers of being caught on an exposed ridge in a high-country cloudburst.

Without warning, lightning had come down so close to her that she smelled the stink of scorched rock. Thunder came like the end of the world. Her horse had screamed and reared, tearing the reins from her hand. Then the horse's lameness had been overridden by terror. The animal had bolted down the mountainside, leaving her alone.

She, too, had been terrified, her nostrils filled with the smell of lightning and her ears deafened by thunder. Then she had heard someone calling her name.

Rafe had come to her across the talus slope,

riding his plunging, scrambling horse with the strength and grace she had always admired. He had lifted her into the saddle in front of him and spurred his horse back down the slope while lightning arced around the mountain.

Sheltered in a thick growth of spruce, she had waited out the storm with Rafe, wearing his jacket and watching him with the eyes of a child-woman who was more woman and less child with every breath.

On Broken Mountain Alana had found first fear, then love, and finally horror.

She wondered if there was another balance to be discovered on Broken Mountain, opposites joined in harmony, freeing her from nightmare.

The possibility shimmered through Alana like dawn through night, transforming everything.

"Sis? Say something."

Alana was appalled to hear herself take a deep breath and say calmly, "Of course I'll help you."

She didn't hear Bob's whoop of victory, his assurances that he wouldn't tell any of the dudes that she was the famous singer Jilly, his gratitude that she was helping him out. She didn't hear anything but the echoes of her own terrifying decision to go back to Broken Mountain.

As though Bob sensed how fragile Alana's agreement was, he began speaking quickly.

"I've got you booked on the afternoon flight

to Salt Lake. From there, you're booked on a little feeder flight into the airport here. Got a pencil?"

Bemused, Alana stared at the phone. The simple fact that Bob had thought to take care of the details of her transportation was so unusual as to be overwhelming. It wasn't that Bob was thoughtless; he was very considerate of Merry, to the point that he was almost too protective.

Alana, however, had always been taken for granted in the manner that parents and older siblings often are.

"Sis," Bob said patiently, "do you have a pencil? He'll skin me if I louse this up."

"He?" asked Alana as she went through the drawer in her bedside table looking for a pencil. "Who will skin you alive?"

There was a static-filled silence. Then Bob laughed abruptly.

"The travel agent who made the arrangements," he said. "Who else? Ready?"

"Hold your horses," Alana muttered.

She found a pencil, grabbed a credit card receipt, turned it over, and wrote down the flight numbers and times.

"But that's today!" she protested.

"Told you we needed you."

"That's not much warning, little brother."

"That's the whole idea," Bob muttered.

"What?"

"Nothing. Just be sure you're on that plane or my butt is potato salad."

"Bob," Alana began.

"Thanks, sis," he said quickly, talking over her. "You won't regret it. If anyone can pull it off, he can."

"Huh?"

Alana felt as though she was missing half the conversation, and the most important half at that.

"He who?" she asked.

"*Damn*," Bob said beneath his breath.

"The travel agent?" Alana guessed.

"Yeah, the travel agent. He's something else," said Bob dryly. "See you tonight, sis. 'Bye."

Before Alana could say good-bye, the line was dead.

She stood and stared at the receiver clenched in her hand. Silently she asked herself why she had agreed to do something that terrified her.

She was a fool to let warm memories of Rafe Winter lure her back to the icy source of nightmare. She didn't even know if Rafe was in Wyoming. In the past, Rafe's job had taken him all over the world. His time at the Winter ranch had been limited to a few weeks now and then.

It had been enough, though. Alana had learned to love Rafe and to accept his absences. She had learned to live for the day when he would come home and marry her and she would never cry for him at night again.

And then Rafe had died.

Or so the Pentagon had said.

The phone began to make whooping noises, telling Alana that the receiver had been off the hook too long. She hung up and stared at the phone.

It was deep red, like the flowers in the Spanish tile that covered the kitchen counters. Red, like the wildflowers that grew high on the mountain slopes.

Red. Like blood.

"Did I see Jack die on Broken Mountain?" Alana whispered. "Is that what my mind refuses to remember?"

With a shudder, she jerked away from the bright red telephone.

Rubbing her arms to chase away the chill that had been with her since Broken Mountain, Alana walked quickly to the closet. She pulled on jeans and an old cotton blouse. From habit, she buttoned the blouse completely, concealing the delicate gold chain that Rafe had given her years before.

As always, Alana's fingertip lingered on the tiny symbol of infinity that was part of the chain.

Love ever after, love without end.

A beautiful dream.

Reality was six days missing from her life and a nightmare whose end she was still trying to find.

Slowly Alana walked into the kitchen. With hands that wanted to tremble, she plugged in the coffeepot, scrambled two eggs, and buttered a piece of toast. She forced herself to eat and drink, to clean up after herself, to do all the things normal people did.

An untidy stack of papers on the kitchen counter caught Alana's eye. Unhappily she looked at them. She should read the song sheets her agent had sent over. New songs. Solo material for the sole survivor of the Jack 'n' Jilly duo.

Alana should read the music, but she wouldn't, for she no longer could sing.

That was the most bitter loss, the most unbearable pain. Before Broken Mountain, she had been able to draw songs around her like colors of love chasing away the gray of loneliness and the black of despair.

Alana had taken her love for a man she believed was dead and transformed that love into song. Singing had been her greatest pleasure, her reason for living after she was told that Rafe was dead.

Jack Reeves hadn't loved her, but she had always known that. Nor had Alana loved him. Theirs had been a business marriage, pure and simple. Jack loved fame and Jilly loved singing.

Now Jack was dead and Jilly could sing only in her dreams. And in her dreams it was Rafe's harmonica that accompanied her, not Jack's flawless tenor.

Awake, she had no music in her.

It wasn't stage fright. Even now, Alana wasn't afraid of being in front of people. Nor was she afraid of the savage doggerel that would be running through the fans' minds as they watched her.

Jack 'n' Jilly
Went up the hilly

To fetch a pail of vodka.
Jack fell down
And broke his crown,
And Jilly lost her mind.

Alana had listened to it all before, read it in print a hundred times, heard it whispered. She could face that.

But she couldn't face opening her lips and feeling her throat close with terrible finality, as though there were no more songs in her now and never would be again. Nothing but screams and the silence of death.

Uneasily Alana looked around, barely recognizing her surroundings. Even though she had lived in the Oregon apartment for three weeks, the place was neither comfortable nor familiar to her. It certainly wasn't as real to her as the nightmare about Broken Mountain.

But then, nothing was.

Abruptly Alana walked toward the wall of glass that opened onto a small patio. She stood near the glass, trying to shake off the residue of nightmare and death, fear and mistakes, and most of all a past that was beyond her ability to change.

Or even to understand.

"I'll remember what happened someday," Alana whispered. "Won't I?"

2

TAKING A RAGGED BREATH, Alana forced herself to look at the dawn that was etching the room in shades of rose and vermilion, gold and translucent pink. The September sun's radiant warmth was like a miracle after the endless hours of night.

Alana found herself staring at her reflection in the glass as she often had since Broken Mountain, searching for some outer sign of the six-day gap in her memory. Nothing showed on the outside. She looked the same as she had before she had gone up the mountain with the worst mistake of her life—her singing partner, Jack Reeves.

The singing hadn't been the mistake. The

marriage of convenience had. He had always pushed for more. She had always wished for less. He had wanted a reconciliation. She had wanted only an end to a marriage that never should have begun. So they had gone up Broken Mountain together.

Only one of them had come back.

No visible marks of the ordeal in the mountains remained on Alana's five-foot, five-inch body. Her ankle had healed. It ached only when it was cold. The bruises and welts and cuts were gone, leaving no scars. She no longer had to diet to fit into the slender image demanded by the public. Since Broken Mountain, her appetite was gone.

But it wasn't something that showed.

Alana leaned forward, staring intently at her nearly transparent reflection in the sliding glass door. Everything still looked the same. Long legs, strong from a childhood spent hiking and riding in Wyoming's high country. Breasts and waist and hips that were neither large nor small. Her skin was a golden brown. Nothing unusual. Nothing at all.

"Surely something must show on the outside," Alana told her reflection. "I can't just lose my singing partner and six days of my life and wonder about my sanity and not have any of it show."

Yet nothing did.

Though Alana's eyes were too dark, too large, too haunted, her mouth still looked as though it was curved around a secret inner smile. Her hair was still black and glossy, divided into two thick braids that fell to her waist.

Alana stared at her braids for a long moment, realizing for the first time that something about them made her . . . uneasy.

She had never particularly liked having long hair, but she had accepted it as she had accepted the nickname Jilly, both necessary parts of the childlike image that audiences loved to love. The image went with her voice, clear and innocent, as supple and pure as a mountain stream. . . .

Water rushing down, cold, and darkness waiting, lined with rocks, ice and darkness closing around, clouds seething overhead, lightning lancing down, soundless thunder.

Fear.

It was too cold, no warmth anywhere, only fear hammering on her, leaving her weak.

She tried to run, but her feet weighed as much as the mountains and were as deeply rooted in the earth. Each step took an eternity. Try harder, move faster, or get caught.

She must run!

But she could not.

She was broken and bleeding, screaming down the night, running, stumbling, sprawling, and then lifted high, she was falling, she spun and screamed, falling. . . .

Alana's heart beat wildly, responding to the fragment of nightmare turning in her mind.

"Stop it!" she told herself fiercely, seeing the

reflection of her terror in dawn-tinted glass and sliding black shadows.

She took several deep breaths, bringing herself under control, telling herself that she had to stop treating her nightmare as though it was real. It wasn't.

The nightmare was simply a creation of her mind as it dealt with the horror of Jack's death in a mountain storm, and her own near death from exposure and the fall that had left her bruised and beaten.

That was what Dr. Gene had told Alana, and she had trusted his gravelly voice and gentle smile for as long as she could remember. He had said that her amnesia, while unusual, was not pathological. It was a survival reflex. When her mind felt she was strong enough to remember the details of her husband's death and her own suffering as she clawed her way down Broken Mountain, then she would remember.

And if she never remembered?

That, too, was all right, he had assured her. Alana was young. She was healthy. She could go out and make a new life for herself.

Alana's lips twisted bitterly as she remembered the conversation. It had been easy for Dr. Gene to say. He wasn't the one whose mind was turning six missing days into endless nightmares.

It wasn't that Alana missed her dead husband. She and Jack had been two very separate people bound together by the accident of perfect harmony. That was enough for a successful singing career. It wasn't enough for a successful marriage.

Yet sometimes Alana couldn't help feeling that maybe, just maybe, if she had done something different, Jack might have been different. If she had tried harder or not so hard. If she had been weaker or not quite as strong. If she had cared for Jack more or pitied him less . . .

Maybe it could have worked for the two of them.

But even as the thought came, Alana knew it was a lie. The only way she might have loved Jack was if she had never met Rafe Winter, never loved and lost him; Rafe, with his laughter and his passion and his gentle, knowing hands.

She had loved Rafe since she was fifteen, had been engaged to him when she was nineteen. And they had become lovers when she was twenty.

Rafael, dark hair and amber eyes glowing, watching her change as he touched her. Her fingers had looked so slender against the male planes of his face, the sliding sinew and muscle of his arms. His strength always surprised her, as did his quickness, but she had never been afraid with him. Rafe could hold her, could surround her softness with his power, and she felt no fear, only a consuming need to be closer still, to be held tighter, to give herself to him and to take him in return.

With Rafe there had only been beauty.

Then, four years ago, the Pentagon had told Alana that Rafael Winter had died. They had told her nothing more than that. Not where her fiancé had died. Not how. Certainly not why. Just the simple fact of his death.

It was a fact that had destroyed Alana. Never again would the lyric beauty of Rafe's harmonica call to her across the western night. Never again would her voice blend with that of the silver instrument that sang so superbly in Rafe's hands. She had sung with Rafe for pleasure and had known no greater beauty except making love with him, bodies and minds sharing an elemental harmony that surpassed everything, even song.

Alana had been empty after Rafe's death. She had cared for nothing. Even life. When the minutes and hours without Rafe had piled up one by one, dragging her down into darkness, she had turned instinctively to a singing career as her only salvation, her only way to hold on to the love she had lost.

Singing meant Jack Reeves, the man she had sung with in all the little cafés and fairs and roadhouses, the man for whom singing was a business rather than a pleasure. Jack had measured Alana's vulnerability, her desperation, and then he had calmly told her that there would be no more duets unless she married him and left the high plains for the high life in the city.

Alana had resisted marriage, wanting no man but the one who was dead.

Then the hours without Rafe had heaped into the hundreds, a thousand, fifteen hundred . . . and she had agreed to become Jack's wife

because she must do something or go insane.
Rafe was dead. There was nothing left but the
singing career that Jack had badgered Alana
for even while Rafe was alive.

So Alana had left the high plains and mountains of Wyoming, hoping that in another part
of the world she wouldn't hear Rafe in every
summer silence, sense him in every moonrise,
feel his heat in the warmth of the sun.

She had married Jack, but it was a marriage
in name only. With Jack Reeves there had been
nothing but an emptiness Alana had tried to
fill with songs.

Then, a year ago, she had been told that Rafael Winter was alive.

Rafe wasn't the one who told her. Rafe had
never called her, never written, never in any
way contacted the woman he once had said he
loved.

Now it was Jack who was dead, killed four
weeks ago by the wild country he had de-
spised. Alana had been with Jack on Broken
Mountain when he died. She didn't remember
it. Those six days were a blank wall.

Behind that wall, fear seethed and rippled,
trying to break free.

Alana closed her eyes, unable to face their
dark reflection in the glass door. Rafe was
dead and then not dead. Jack was dead now
and forever.

Her love for Rafe, undying.

With a small sound, Alana closed her eyes,
shutting out her reflection.

"Enough of that," she told herself sharply.

"Stop living in the past. Stop tearing yourself up over things you can't change."

She opened her eyes, confronting herself in yet another reflection, another window dawn hadn't yet made transparent. She looked like a mountain deer caught in the instant of stillness that precedes wild flight. Long brown limbs and brown eyes that were very dark, very wide, wild.

A black braid slid over Alana's shoulder and swung against the glass as she leaned forward. She brought the other braid forward over her shoulder, too. It was a gesture that had become automatic; when her braids hung down her back she pulled them forward.

That way if she had to run suddenly, the braids wouldn't fly out behind her, twin black ropes, perfect handles for something to grab and hold her and *lift her up, trapped, weightless, falling, she was falling—*

Alana choked off the scream clawing at her throat as she retreated to the kitchen. Her reflection looked back at her from the window over the kitchen sink.

Without looking away from her reflection, Alana groped in a nearby drawer. Her fingers closed around the handle of a long carving knife. The honed blade glittered as she pulled it out of the drawer.

She lifted the knife until the blunt side of the blade rested against her neck just below her chin. Calmly, deliberately, she began slicing through her left braid. The severed hair fell soundlessly to the floor. With no hesitation, she went to work on the right braid.

When Alana was finished she shook her head, making her hair fly. The loose, natural curls that had been imprisoned beneath the weight of the braids were suddenly set free. Wisps of hair curved around her face, framing it in soft, shiny black. Her brown eyes glowed darkly, haunted by dreams.

Abruptly Alana realized what she had done. She stared at the long black braids on the floor, the steel knife in her hand, the reflection in the window that no longer looked like Jilly.

The knife dropped to the floor with a metallic clatter.

Alana stared at herself and wondered if she had finally gone crazy.

She ran from the kitchen to the bedroom. There she pulled her few things out of drawers and off hangers, packing haphazardly. It didn't matter. Most of her clothes were still in L.A. or at the ranch, left there in anticipation of weeks spent with her brother and Merry.

Alana had been too frightened to go back to the ranch and pack after she had fled from the hospital. She had simply run to Portland, a city she had never lived in, hoping to leave the nightmare behind her.

It hadn't worked.

As Alana packed, she kept looking at the bedroom telephone. She wanted to call Bob, say that she had changed her mind, and then hang up before he could object.

Yet each time she reached for the phone, she

thought of Rafael Winter, a dream to balance her nightmare. She used memories of Rafe like a talisman to draw the terror from her six missing days.

The greatest pleasure and the greatest horror in Alana's life had both taken place on Broken Mountain. Perhaps they would simply cancel each other, leaving her free to go on with her life. Neutral, balanced.

No memories of the man she had loved, or of the husband she had not. No memories of the lover who had died and then come back, or of the husband who had died and would never come back.

Rafe, who came to her in dreams.

Jack, who came to her in nightmares.

When Alana finally picked up the phone, it was to call a nearby beauty salon and make an appointment to have her hair styled. The utterly normal activity reassured her.

By the time Alana got on the airplane, she felt more calm. Tonight she would be home. If nightmares stalked her, it would be down the familiar corridors of her childhood home rather than the strange hallways of a rented apartment.

She held to that thought as she switched planes in Salt Lake City and settled in for the flight to Wyoming. When the flight attendant offered her a newspaper, she took it automatically. As she flipped through the pages, a headline in the entertainment section caught her eye: *Jack 'n' Jilly's Last Song*.

Though Alana's stomach tightened just at

the headline, she knew she would read the article. She had read everything written about Jack's death, even the most sleazy imaginings of the yellow press. She would read this article too, because she could not help herself.

It had been a month since Jack's death. A month since the gap in Alana's memory had appeared. She kept hoping that someone, somewhere, would know more about Jack's death than she did, that a word or a phrase in an article would trigger something in her mind and the six days would spill through, freeing her from nightmare.

Or sending her into a more terrifying one.

There was always that possibility lurking in the twisting shadows of Alana's mind. Dr. Gene had suggested that there could be horrors Alana didn't imagine, *even in her nightmares.*

Amnesia could be looked at in many ways. Gift of a kind God. Survival reflex. Fountainhead of horror. All of them and none of them. But fear was always there, pooled in shadows, waiting for night.

Maybe Dr. Gene was right. Maybe she would be better off not remembering.

Impatiently Alana shoved the unwelcome thought away. Nothing could be worse than not trusting her own mind, her own courage, her own sanity.

Since her mother had died, Alana had always been the strong one, the one who saw what had to be done and did it. Then Rafe had died and Alana had been destroyed.

Music was her only solace after Rafe died.

With music she wove glowing dreams of warmth, of his laughter, and of a love that could only be sung, not spoken.

With song, Alana had survived even Rafe's death.

She could do whatever she had to. She had proved that in the past. Somehow, she would prove it again. She would survive.

Somehow.

Alana shook out the paper, folded it carefully, and began to read.

The first part of the story was a review of the Jack 'n' Jilly album that had just been released. The rest of the article was a simple recital of the facts of Jack's death.

A month ago, Jack and Jilly Reeves had gone on a pack trip in the Wyoming backcountry. An early winter storm had caught them. They had tried to get out, but only Jilly had made it. Jack had been killed in a fall. Somehow Jilly had managed to hobble down the mountain on a badly wrenched ankle until she had reached a fishing cabin and radioed for help.

Even so, she had nearly died of exposure. The experience had been so traumatic that she had no memory of the time she spent crawling down the mountain.

Hysterical amnesia, brought on by husband's accidental death, said the doctor. Apparently Sheriff Mitchell had agreed, for the autopsy listed the cause of Jack's death as a broken neck sustained in a fall.

Accidental.

Nothing new. Nothing unexpected. Nothing

to fill the horrifying gap six days had left in Alana's mind. Yet still she reread the article, searching for the key to her amnesia.

She didn't find it. She was neither surprised nor disappointed.

As the plane slid into its landing pattern, Alana sat up and nervously ran her fingers through her hair. Her head felt strange, light, no longer anchored by dense black braids. The stylist had transformed the remnants of her knife-cut hair into a gently curling cap that softened but didn't wholly conceal the taut lines of Alana's face. The result was arresting—glossy midnight silk framing an intelligent face that was haunted by loss and nightmare.

The small commercial plane touched down with a slight jerk. A few eager trout fishermen got off before Alana, trading stories of the past and bets for the first and biggest fish of the future.

Reluctantly she stood up and walked slowly down the narrow aisle. By the time she descended the metal stair, her baggage had already been unloaded and placed neatly beside the bottom step. She picked up her light suitcase and turned toward the small building that was the only sign of habitation for miles around.

Behind her the aircraft began retreating. It moved to the head of the runway, revved hard, and accelerated, gathering speed quickly, preparing itself for a leap into the brilliant high-plains sky.

Alana reached the building as the plane's engines gave a full-throated cry. She set down her bag and turned in time to see the aircraft's wheels lift. It climbed steeply, a powerful silver bird flying free. She listened until the engines were no more than a fading echo and the plane only a molten silver dot flying between the ragged grandeur of the Wind River and Green River mountain ranges.

For a moment, Alana closed her eyes. Her head tilted toward the sky, catching the surprising warmth of Wyoming's September sun. The wind was rich with scents of earth and sagebrush. Not the stunted, brittle sagebrush of the southwestern desert but the thick lavender-gray high-country sage, bushes as high as her head, higher, slender shapes weaving patterns against the empty sky.

A clean wind swept down from the granite heights, carrying sweetness and the promise of blue-green rivers curling lazily between rocky banks, of evergreens standing tall and fragrant against the summer moon, of coyotes calling from the ridge lines in harmonies older than man.

Home.

Alana breathed deeply, torn between pleasure and fear. She heard footsteps approaching across the cement. She spun around, her heart beating heavily. Since Broken Mountain, she was terrified if anything approached her unseen.

A man was walking toward Alana. The sun was at his back, reducing him to a black silhouette.

As he walked closer, he seemed to condense into three dimensions. He was about seven inches taller than she was. He had the easy stride of someone who spent as much time hiking as he did on horseback. His jeans were faded. His boots showed the scuff marks peculiar to riding. His shirt was the same pale blue as the sky.

Hair that was a thick, rich brown showed beneath the rim of his black Stetson. His eyes were the color of whiskey. His lips were a firm curve beneath a silky bar of mustache.

With a small sound, Alana closed her eyes. Her heart beat wildly, but it sent weakness rather than strength coursing through her. She was going crazy, hallucinating.

Storm and cold and terror, falling—

"Alana," he said.

His voice was gentle, deep, reaching out to her like an immaterial caress.

"Rafael?" She breathed raggedly, afraid to open her eyes, torn between hope and nightmare. "Oh, Rafe, is it really you?"

3

R AFE TOOK ALANA'S ARM, supporting her. Only then did she realize that she had been swaying as she stood. His warmth and strength went through her like a shock wave. For an instant she sagged against him.

Then she realized that she was being touched, *held*, and she wrenched away. Since Broken Mountain she was terrified of being touched.

"It's really me, Alana," said Rafe, watching her intently.

"Rafael—" Alana's voice broke as emotions overwhelmed her.

She extended her fingers as though she

would touch him, but did not. With an effort that left her aching, she fought down the tangle of emotions that was closing her throat. She was being torn apart by conflicting imperatives.

Run to him. Run from his male presence.

Be held by him. Fight not to be held by a man.

Love him. Feel nothing at all because the only safety lay in numbness.

Remember how it felt to be loved. Forget, forget everything, amnesia spreading outward like a black balm.

"Why are you here?" Alana asked in a ragged voice.

"I've come to take you home."

Inexplicably the words all but destroyed Alana.

With a small sound, she closed her eyes and struggled to control herself. Coming here had been a mistake. She had wanted a dream of love to balance a nightmare of terror. Yet Rafe was real, not a dream.

And so was terror.

Alana clung to the shreds of her control, wondering what had happened during those six missing days that had left a black legacy of fear. And most of all, she wondered if the nightmare would ever end, freeing her, letting her laugh and sing again . . . or if she would simply give up and let the black balm of amnesia claim all of her mind. All of *her*.

Rafe watched Alana, his eyes intent. When

he spoke, his voice was casual, soothing, utterly normal.

"We'd better get going," he said. "I'd like to beat the thundershower back to the ranch."

He bent to take Alana's suitcase from her nerveless fingers. With the easy movements of a mountain cat, he straightened and walked toward a Jeep parked a few hundred feet away.

Alana watched, her hand resting on the high neck of her burgundy silk blouse. She took a deep breath, still feeling the warmth of Rafe's hand on her arm as he had supported her. Just that. Support. Help. There was nothing to fear in that.

Was there?

Motionless, her heart beating rapidly, her dark eyes wide, Alana watched Rafe turn back toward her. The slanting, late-afternoon sun highlighted the strong bones of his face and made his amber eyes glow. As he turned, his shirt stretched across his shoulders, emphasizing the strength and masculine grace of him. His jeans fit the muscular outline of his legs like a faded blue shadow, moving as he moved.

Alana closed her eyes, but she could still see Rafe. He was burned into her awareness with a thoroughness that would have shocked her if she had any room left for new emotions. But she didn't.

She was still caught up in the moment when he had turned back to her, light brown eyes burning, mouth curved in a gentle male smile.

That was Rafe. Male. Totally. She had forgotten, even in her dreams.

Rafe hesitated as though he wanted to come back to Alana, to stand close to her again. But he didn't move. He simply watched her with whiskey-colored eyes that were both gentle and intent, consuming her softly, like a song.

"It's all right, Alana." Rafe's voice was as gentle as his smile. "I've come to take you home."

The words echoed and reechoed in Alana's mind, sending sensations sleeting through her. Cold and wind and snow, fear and screams clawing at her throat. Pain and terror and then . . .

It's all right, wildflower. I've come to take you home.

She had heard words like those before, and something more, other words, incredible words, dream and nightmare intertwined.

Without knowing it, Alana whimpered and swayed visibly, caught between hope and terror, dream and nightmare.

"What?" Alana demanded breathlessly, her heart beating faster, her voice urgent. "What did you say?"

Rafe watched Alana with a sudden intensity that was almost tangible.

"I said, 'I've come to take you home.' "

He waited, but Alana simply watched him with wide, very dark eyes. His expression shifted, gentle again.

"Bob threatened to have my hide for a saddle blanket if I didn't get home before Merry fell asleep. And," added Rafe with a smile, "since she falls asleep between coffee and dessert, we'd better hurry."

Alana watched Rafe with eyes that were dazed and more than a little wild.

"That wasn't what you said before." Alana's voice was as tight as the hand clutching her throat. Her eyes were blind, unfocused.

"Before?" asked Rafe, his voice intent, hard, his topaz eyes suddenly blazing like gems. "Before what, Alana?"

It was dark, so dark, black ice around her, a glacier grinding her down until she screamed and tried to run, but she couldn't run because she was frozen and it was so cold.

Alana shuddered and swayed, her face utterly pale, drained of life by the savage nightmare that came to her more and more often, stalking her even in the day, stealing what little sanity and peace remained.

Instantly Rafe came to her, supporting her, his hands warm and strong. Even as she turned toward his warmth, fear exploded in her. She wrenched away with all her strength.

Then she realized that it hadn't been necessary. Rafe hadn't tried to hold her. She was reacting to something that hadn't happened.

"I—" Alana watched Rafe with wild, dark eyes. "I don't—I'm—"

She held out her hands helplessly, wondering how to explain to Rafe that she was drawn to him yet terrified of being touched, and that above all she thought she was losing her mind.

"You're tired," Rafe said easily, as though Alana's actions were as normal as the slanting afternoon light. "It was a long flight. Come on. Bob and Merry are waiting for you like kids waiting for Christmas morning."

Rafe turned back to the suitcase, picked it up, and walked toward the Jeep. Before he arrived, a man got out of a Blazer and approached Rafe.

As Alana walked closer, she recognized Dr. Gene. He smiled and held out his arms to her. She hesitated, fighting against being held, even by the man who had delivered her, who had attended to all of her childhood ills, and who had cried in frustration at her mother's deathbed. Dr. Gene was as much a member of her family as her father or her brothers.

With an effort of will that made her tremble, Alana submitted to Dr. Gene's brief hug. Over her head, the doctor looked a question at Rafe, who answered with a tiny negative movement of his head.

"Well, it's good to have you back, " said Dr. Gene. "No limp, now. You look as pretty as ever, trout."

"And you lie very badly," said Alana.

But she smiled briefly at hearing the pet name from her childhood. Even so, she stepped back from the doctor's hug. Her haste was almost rude, but she couldn't help herself. That was the worst part of the nightmare, not being able to help herself.

"The only thing that was ever pretty about me was my voice," Alana said.

"No pain?" persisted the doctor. "How's your appetite?"

"No pain," she said evenly, ignoring the question about her appetite. "I don't even use the elastic bandage anymore."

And then Alana waited in fear for the doctor to ask her about her memory. She didn't want to talk about it in front of Rafe.

She didn't want to talk about her memory at all.

"You cut your hair," said Dr. Gene.

Alana raised her hand nervously, feeling the short, silky tendrils that were all that remained of her waist-length braids.

"Yes." And then, because the doctor seemed to expect something more, she added, "Today. I cut it today."

"Why?" asked Dr. Gene.

The doctor's voice was as gentle as the question was blunt.

"I . . ." Alana stopped. "I was . . . I wanted to."

"Yes, but why?" he asked.

The doctor's blue eyes were very pale, very watchful beneath the shock of gray hair and weathered forehead.

"The braids made me . . . uneasy," said Alana.

Her voice was tight, her eyes vague, frightened.

"Uneasy? How?" asked Dr. Gene.

"They kept . . . tangling in things." Alana

made a sudden motion with her hands, as though she were warding off something. "I . . ."

Her throat closed and she could say nothing more.

"Alana's tired," Rafe said, his voice quiet and very certain. "I'm going to take her home. Now. Excuse us, Dr. Gene."

Rafe and Dr. Gene exchanged a long look. Then the doctor sighed.

"All right," Dr. Gene said, his voice sharp with frustration. "Tell Bob I'm trying to get some time off to go fishing."

"Good. The Broken Mountain camp always has a cabin for you."

"Even now?"

"Especially now," said Rafe sardonically. "We may disagree on means, but our goal is identical."

Alana looked from one man to the other. "Goal?"

"Just a little fishing expedition in the high country," Rafe said, turning to her. "The good doctor prefers to drown worms. I, on the other hand, prefer to devise my own lures."

Dr. Gene smiled briefly. "Bet I catch more trout than you, Winter."

"I'm only after one trout. A very special one."

Alana wondered about the currents of emotion running between the two men, then decided she was being overly sensitive. Since Broken Mountain, she jumped at sighs and shadows and saw conspiracy and pursuit where there was nothing behind her but night and silence.

Dr. Gene turned to Alana. "If you need anything, trout, I'll come running."

"Thanks."

"I mean it, now," he added.

"I know," she said softly.

He nodded, got back in his Blazer, and drove off with a backward wave.

Rafe handed Alana into the Jeep truck and climbed in himself. She watched him covertly the whole time, matching memories with reality.

The Rafe Alana saw was older, much more controlled than in her memories. When he wasn't smiling, his face was hard, almost frightening in its planes and angles. Yet he still moved with the easy strength that had always fascinated her. His voice was still gentle, and his hands were ... beautiful. It was an odd way to describe anything as strong and quick and callused as a man's hands, yet she could think of no better word.

Not all masculine hands affected Alana like that. Sometimes she saw hands and terror sleeted through her.

"We're lucky today," said Rafe as he guided the Jeep expertly over the rough field that passed as the parking lot.

"Lucky?" said Alana, hearing the thin thread of panic in her voice and hating it.

"No rain so far. It rained a lot the last few days."

Alana tried to conceal the shudder that went

through her at the thought of lightning and thunder, mountains and slippery black ice.

"Yes," she said in a low voice. "I'm glad there isn't a storm."

"You used to love storms," said Rafe quietly.

Alana went very still, remembering one wild September afternoon when a storm had caught her and Rafe while they were out riding. They had arrived at the fishing cabins, soaked and breathless. He had peeled her wet jacket off her, then her blouse, and his hands had trembled when he touched her.

Closing her eyes, Alana tried to forget. The thought of being touched like that by Rafe made her weak with desire—and all but crazy with fear, dream and nightmare tangled together in a way she could neither explain nor understand.

But if Rafe remembered the September storm when he had undressed and caressed Alana until there was only fire and the hushed urgency of their breathing, his memories didn't show in his face or in his words.

"We had a good frost above five thousand feet last week," continued Rafe. "The aspen leaves turned. Now they look like pieces of sunlight dancing in the wind."

He looked quickly at Alana, seeing the lines of inner conflict on her face.

"You still like aspen, don't you?" Rafe asked.

Alana nodded her head, afraid to trust her voice. Mountain aspen, with its white bark and quivering, silver-backed leaves, was her favorite tree. In fall, aspens turned a yellow as pure as ... *sunlight dancing in the wind*.

A sideways glance told her that Rafe was watching her with intent, whiskey-colored eyes.

"I still like aspen," said Alana.

She tried to keep her voice normal, grateful for the safe topic. The present, not the past. The past was more than she could handle. The future was unthinkable. Just one day at a time. One hour. A minute. She could handle anything, one minute at a time.

"Even in winter," Alana added, her voice little more than a whisper, "when the branches are black and the trunks are like ghosts in the snow."

Rafe accelerated down the narrow, two-lane blacktop road. He glanced for a moment at the magnificent granite spine of the Wind River Mountains, rising on his left.

"Be a while before there's real snow in the high country," he said. "The frost put down the insects, though. Then it turned warm again. Trout ought to be hungry as hell. That means good fishing for our dudes—guests," he corrected immediately, smiling to himself. "Nobody likes being called a dude."

"*Our* dudes?" asked Alana slowly, watching Rafe with eyes so brown they were almost black.

Sunlight slanted through the windshield, intensifying the tan on Rafe's face and the richness of his dark brown mustache, making his eyes almost gold. His teeth showed in a sudden gleam of humor, but his expression said the joke was on him. He answered her question with another question.

"Didn't Bob mention me?"

"No," said Alana, her voice ragged. "You were a complete surprise."

Rafe's expression changed.

For an instant Alana thought she saw pain, but it came and went so quickly that she decided she had been wrong. She was being too sensitive again. Overreacting. Yet she still wanted to touch Rafe, to erase the instant when she sensed that she had hurt him and didn't even know how.

The thought of touching Rafe didn't frighten Alana. Not like being touched did. For an instant she wondered why, but all that came to her was . . . nothing. Blank.

Like those six missing days.

"Looks like we'll have to do it the hard way," Rafe said softly.

His voice was an odd mixture of resignation and some much stronger emotion in his voice, something close to anger.

Before Alana could speak, Rafe did.

"Bob and I are partners."

"Partners in what?" Alana asked.

"The dude—*guest* ranch. The cottages and fishing water are on Lazy W land. My land. The horses and supplies belong to Bob. He's the wrangler, I'm the fishing guide, and you're the cook. When Dr. Gene shows up," added

Rafe with a crooked smile, "he'll be the chief worm dunker."

Stunned, Alana could think of nothing to say. She would be going up Broken Mountain with Rafael Winter. Dream and nightmare running together, pouring over her, drowning her in freezing water.

She sat without moving, letting the sunlight and the landscape blur around her, trying to gather her fragmenting thoughts.

No wonder Bob didn't say anything to me about Rafael Winter, Alana thought unhappily. If I'd known that Bob had a partner, I might have let the partner bail Bob out of the mess.

Especially if I knew that the partner was Rafael Winter.

It was all Alana could do to handle the recent past, amnesia and accident and death. Bob should have known that she couldn't handle a present that included Rafe.

A year ago Bob had told her that Rafe was still alive. Then Bob had taken her letter to Rafe's ranch. Bob had come back with the letter unopened, *Deceased* written across the envelope's face—written in Rafe's distinctive hand.

Bob had seen Alana's pain and anger, then her despair. And now he was asking her to go up Broken Mountain with Rafael Winter, to confront the past love and loss all over again. And the present nightmare.

Alana shuddered and tried to think of nothing at all.

"Alana," began Rafe.

Somehow she was certain that he was going to talk about the past, about dying but not quite, about surviving but not wholly, about her and Jack and an envelope with a "dead" man's handwriting across its face, tearing her apart.

She wasn't strong enough for that. Not for the past. Not for anything but this minute. Now.

"Bob and Tom Sawyer have a lot in common," Alana said quickly, her voice as strained as it was determined. "Don't go near either of them if a fence needs painting. Unless you like painting fences, of course."

Rafe hesitated, visibly reluctant to give up whatever he had wanted to say. But Alana's taut, pale face and haunted eyes persuaded him.

"Yes," Rafe said slowly. "Bob could charm the needles off a pine tree."

Relieved, Alana sat back in the seat again.

"The only thing that ever got even with Bob was the hen he poured jam on and then dumped in the middle of eight half-grown hounds," Alana said. "That hen pecked Bob's hands until she was too tired to lift her head."

Rafe's laughter was as rich as the slanting sunlight pouring over the land. Alana turned toward him involuntarily, drawn by his humor and strength, by the laugh that had haunted her dreams as thoroughly as the scent of evergreens haunted the high country.

"So that's how Bob got those scars on his

hands," Rafe said, still chuckling. "He told me it was chicken pox."

Alana's lips curved into a full smile, the first in a long time. "So it was, after a fashion."

She glanced up at Rafe through her thick black lashes and caught the amber flash of his eyes as he looked away from her to the road. For an instant her heart stopped, then beat more quickly. He had been watching her.

She wondered if he was comparing the past and present as she had. And remembering.

"How did Bob talk you into painting his fence?" Alana asked quickly, wanting to hear Rafe talk, his voice deep and smooth and confident, like his laughter.

"Easy. I'm a sucker for fishing. I spend a lot of my time in the high country chasing trout. Might as well make it pay."

"Land poor," murmured Alana. "Rancher's lament."

"I have it better than Bob," Rafe said, shrugging. "I'm not buying out two brothers."

Alana thought of Dave and Sam, her other brothers. Sam worked for a large corporation with branches around the world. Dave was a computer programmer in Texas. Neither brother had any intention of coming back to the ranch for anything other than occasional visits. Of the four Burdette children, only she and Bob had loved the ranching life.

Nor had Jack Reeves loved the ranching life he had been born into. He couldn't leave Wyoming fast enough. He had hungered for city streets and applauding crowds.

"Jack hated Wyoming."

Startled, Alana heard the words echoing in the Jeep and realized she had spoken aloud.

"He's dead," she added.

"I know."

Alana stared at Rafe.

"How—" she began.

Then she realized that of course Rafe knew. Bob must have told him. They were partners. But how much had Bob told Rafe? Did he know about her amnesia? Did he know about the nightmares that lapped over into day, triggered by a word or a smell or the quality of the light? Did he know she was afraid she was going crazy?

Did Rafe know that she clung to her memories and dreams of him as though they were a lifeline able to pull her beyond the reach of whatever terror stalked her?

As though Rafe sensed Alana's unease, he added quietly, "It was good of you to help Bob. It can't be easy for you so soon after your . . . husband's . . . death."

At the word *husband* Rafe's mouth turned down sourly, telling Alana that her marriage was not a subject that brought Rafe any pleasure.

But then, Rafe had never liked Jack. Even before Rafe had "died," Jack had always been urging Alana to pack up and leave Wyoming, to build a career where artificial lights drowned out the cascading stars of the western sky.

"Did Bob tell you how Jack died?" asked

Alana, her voice tight, her hands clenched in her lap.

"No."

Rafe's voice was hard and very certain.

Alana let out a long breath. Apparently Bob had told Rafe only the bare minimum: Jack had died recently. Nothing about the amnesia or the nightmares.

She was glad Bob had told Rafe something. It would explain anything odd she might do. Jack was dead. Recently. She was a widow.

And when she slept, she was a frightened child.

The Jeep jolted off the pavement onto a gravel road. The miles unwound easily, silently, through a land of gently rolling sagebrush and a distant river that was pale silver against the land. Nothing moved but the Jeep and jackrabbits flushed by the sound of the car.

There was neither fence nor sign to mark the beginning of the Broken Mountain Ranch. Like many western ranchers, Alana's grandfather, father, and brother had left the range open wherever possible. They fenced in the best of their breeding stock and let the beef cattle range freely.

Alana searched the land for signs of Broken Mountain steers grazing the high plains.

"Has Bob brought the cattle out of the high country yet?" asked Alana.

"Most of them. He's leaving them in the middle elevations until late September. Later if he can."

"Good."

The longer the cattle stayed in the high and middle elevations, the less money Bob would have to spend on winter feed. Every year was a gamble. If a rancher left his cattle too long in the high country, winter storms could close in, locking the cattle into certain starvation. But if the rancher brought his cattle down too soon, the cost of buying hay to carry them through winter could mean bankruptcy.

"Grass looks thick," Alana said.

She wanted to keep to the neutral conversational territory of ranching, afraid that if the silence went on too long, Rafe might bring up the recent past and Jack's death. Or, even worse, the far past. Rafe's death and resurrection, a bureaucratic error that had cost Alana . . . everything.

"I'll bet Indian Seep is still flowing," she said. "The hay crop must have been good."

Rafe nodded.

Alana's dark eyes cataloged every feature of the land—the texture of the soil in road cuts, the presence or absence of water in the ravines, the smoky lavender sheen of living growth on the snarled sagebrush, the signs of wildlife, all the indicators that told an educated eye whether the land was being used or abused, husbanded or squandered.

And in between, when Alana thought Rafe wouldn't notice, she watched his profile, the sensuous sheen of his hair and lips, the male lines of his nose and jaw. Rafe was too powerful and too hard to be called handsome. He was compelling—a man made for mountains, a man of strength and endurance, mystery and silence, and sudden laughter like a river curling lazily beneath the sun.

"Am I so different from your memories?" asked Rafe quietly.

Alana drew in her breath sharply.

"No," she said. "But there are times when I can't tell my memories of you from my dreams. Seeing you again, close enough to touch, *alive...*"

Alana looked away, unable to meet Rafe's eyes, regretting her honesty and at the same time knowing she had no choice. She had enough trouble sorting out truth from nightmare. She didn't have the energy to keep track of lies, too.

When the truck rounded the shoulder of a small ridge, Alana leaned forward intently, staring into the condensing twilight. A long, narrow valley opened up before her. A few evergreens grew in the long, low ridges where the land began to lift to the sky. The ridges soon became foothills and then finally pinnacles clothed in ice and distance.

But it wasn't the savage splendor of the peaks that held Alana's attention. She had eyes only for the valley. It was empty of cattle.

Alana sat back with an audible sigh of relief.

"Good for you, little brother," she murmured.

"Bob's a good rancher," said Rafe quietly. "There's not one inch of overgrazed land on Broken Mountain's range."

"I know. I was just afraid that—" Alana's hands moved, describing vague fears. "The beef market has been so bad and the price of feed is so high now and Bob has to pay Sam and Dave. I was afraid Bob would gamble on the land being able to carry more cattle than it should."

Rafe glanced sideways at Alana with the lightning intensity that she remembered from her dreams.

"Since when do people on the West Coast notice feed prices and the carrying capacity of Wyoming ranch land?" he asked.

"They don't. I do." Alana made a wry face. "People in cities think beef grows between Styrofoam and plastic wrap, like mushrooms in the cracks of a log."

Rafe laughed again, softly.

Alana watched him, feeling the pull of his laughter. Above his pale collar, sleek neck muscles moved.

She felt again the moment of warmth at the airport, the resilience of his muscles beneath her fingers before she had snatched back her arm. He was strong. It showed in his movements, in his laughter, in the clean male lines of his face. He was strong and she was not.

Distantly Alana knew she should be terrified of that difference in their bodies. Yet when Rafe laughed, it was all she could do to keep herself from crawling over and huddling next to him as though he were a fire burning in the midst of a freezing storm.

The thought of being close to Rafe both fas-

cinated and frightened Alana. The fascination
she understood; Rafe was the only man she
had ever loved. She had no reason to fear him.

Yet she did.

Rafe was a man, and she was terrified of
men.

The fear baffled Alana. At no time in her
life, not even during the most vicious argu-
ments with Jack, had she ever been afraid.

Am I afraid of Rafe simply because he's
strong? Alana asked herself silently.

She turned the thought over in her mind,
testing it as she had tested so many things in
the weeks since she had awakened in the hospital, six days and a singing partner lost.

It can't be something as simple as physical
strength that frightens me, Alana decided. Jack
was six foot five, very thick in the shoulders
and neck and legs. He never used his strength,
though, or even seemed to notice it. He did
only what was needed to get by, and not one
bit more.

Jack had been born with a clear tenor voice
that he had accepted as casually as his size,
and he disliked working with his voice almost
as much as he had disliked physical labor.

Alana had been the one who had insisted
on rehearsing each song again and again,
searching for just the right combination of
phrasing and harmony that would bring out
the levels of meaning in the lyrics. Jack had
tolerated her "fanaticism" with the same easygoing indifference that he had tolerated
crummy motels and being on the road three

hundred and fifty-two nights a year.

Then Jack 'n' Jilly had become successful.

After that, Jack would rehearse a new country or folk song only as long as it took him to learn the words and melody. Anything beyond that was Jilly's problem.

A year ago Alana had left Jack and come to Broken Mountain Ranch to think about her life and her sad sham of a marriage. When word of their separation had leaked to the press, record and concert ticket sales had plummeted. Their agent had called Alana and quietly, cynically, suggested that she continue to present a happily married front to the world. Fame was transient. Obscurity was forever.

That same afternoon, Bob had come back from a trip to the high country babbling about seeing Rafe Winter. Alana had written the letter to Rafe, seen Rafe's rejection condensed into a single harsh word: *Deceased*.

She had wept until she felt nothing at all . . . and then she had gone back to L.A. to appear as half of Country's Perfect Couple.

Until six weeks ago, when Alana had told Jack that the sham was over. Country's Perfect Couple was an act she couldn't handle anymore. He had pleaded with her to think again, to take a trip with him to the high country she loved, and there they would work out something.

"Did you miss the ranch?" Rafe asked quietly.

Alana heard the question as though from a great distance, calling her out of a past that was another kind of nightmare waiting to drag her down. She reached for the question, pulling it eagerly around her.

"I missed the ranch more than . . . more than I knew."

And she had. It had been like having her eyes put out. She had hungered for the green and silver shimmer of aspens, but saw only dusty palm trees. She had searched for the primal blue of alpine lakes set among the chiseled spires of mountains older than man, but found only concrete freeways and the metallic flash of cars. She had always looked for the intense green silences of the wilderness forest, but discovered only tame squares of grass laid down amid hot stucco houses.

All that had saved Alana was singing. Working with a song. Tasting it, feeling it, seeing it grow and change as it became part of her and she of it.

Jack had never understood that. He had loved only the applause and worked just hard enough to get it. Alana loved the singing and would work to exhaustion until she and the song were one.

"If you missed the ranch that much, why did you leave after Jack died?"

Alana realized that she had heard the question before. Rafe had asked it at least twice and she hadn't answered, lost in her own thoughts.

"Jack died there," she whispered. "On Broken Mountain."

She looked to the right, where the Green

River Mountains lifted seamed granite faces toward the evening sky. High-flying clouds burned silver above the peaks, and over all arched an immense indigo bowl, twilight changing into night.

"You must have unhappy memories," said Rafe quietly.

"Yes, I suppose I must."

Alana heard her own words, heard their ambiguity, heard the fear tight in her voice. She looked up and saw that Rafe had been watching her.

But he turned away and said nothing, asked no more questions.

He simply drove her closer and closer to the ramparts of snow and ice where Jack had died and Jilly had lost her mind.

4

I T WAS DARK BY THE TIME RAFE
turned onto the fork of the road that led to the
Broken Mountain ranch house. An autumn
moon was up, huge and flat and ghostly, balanced on the edge of the world. Clouds raced
and seethed, veiled in moonlight and mystery,
veiling the moon in turn.

The mountains were invisible, yet Alana
could sense them rising black and massive in
front of her. They comforted and frightened
her at the same time as childhood memories
and recent fear set her on an emotional seesaw
that made her dizzy.

Alana knew she had been at the ranch just
four weeks ago.

She knew she and Jack had ridden into the high country.

She knew Jack was dead.

She knew—*but she didn't*.

Alana had awakened in the hospital, bruised and cut, ice-burned and aching. And frightened. Every shadow, every sound, had sent her heart racing.

It had taken a huge effort of will to allow Dr. Gene to examine her. He had tried to explain the inexplicable in ordinary words, telling Alana that her fear was normal, the overreaction of someone who had never known physical danger, much less death. In time, her mind and body would adjust to the presence of danger, the nearness of death in everyday life. Then she would be calm again. Until then, Dr. Gene could prescribe something to help her.

Alana had refused the tranquilizers. She had seen too many musicians dependent on drugs. For her, chemical solutions were no solution at all.

But it had been tempting, especially at first.

The presence of Dr. Gene had unnerved Alana to the point of tears. Even Bob, her favorite brother, had seen Alana withdraw from any kind of physical touch, any gesture of affection he made. Bob had been hurt and very worried about her, his brown eyes clouded with conflicting feelings.

Then, on the third morning after Alana had awakened, she had quietly walked out of the hospital, boarded a plane, and flown to Portland, a place where she had never lived. She hadn't waited for Sheriff Mitchell to come back down off the mountain with Jack's body. She hadn't stopped to think, to consider, to reason. She had simply run from the black gap in her mind.

Portland was big enough for Alana to lose herself in, but not big enough to remind her of L.A. and her life with Jack. There·were mountains in Portland, but only in the distance.

Yet fear had run with Alana anyway. Though she had never before been afraid of flying, or heights, there had been a horrible moment of terror as the plane had left the ground.

Earth falling away and her body twisting, weightless, she was falling, falling, black rushing up to meet her and when it did she would be torn from life like an aspen leaf from its stem, spinning away helplessly over the void—

"It's all right, Alana. You're safe. It's all right. I've come to take you home."

Vaguely Alana realized that Rafe had parked the Jeep at the side of the road. She heard Rafe's soothing murmur, sensed the warmth of his hand over her clenched fingers, the gentle pressure of his other hand stroking her hair. She felt the shudders wracking her body, the ache of teeth clenched against a futile scream.

Rafe continued speaking quietly, repeating his words. They warmed Alana, words as undemanding as sunlight, driving away the darkness that gripped her.

Suddenly she turned her head, pressing her cheek against the hard strength of Rafe's hand. But when he would have drawn her closer, she moved away with a jerk.

"I—" Alana stopped abruptly and drew a deep breath. "I'm sorry. Something—" Her hands moved jerkily. "Sometimes I—since Jack—"

Alana closed her eyes. She couldn't make Rafe understand what she herself had no words to describe.

"Seeing death is always hard," said Rafe quietly. "The more sheltered you've been, the harder it is."

Rafe's hand stroked Alana's hair, his touch as gentle as his words, as his presence, as his warmth.

After a few moments Alana let out a long sigh, feeling the tentacles of terror loosen, slide away, the nightmare withdrawing. She turned her head and looked at Rafe with eyes that were no longer black with fear.

"Thank you," she said simply.

Rafe's only answer was a light caress across Alana's cheek as his hand withdrew from her hair.

He started the Jeep again and pulled back onto the narrow gravel road that led to the Burdette family house. Beneath the truck, the country began to roll subtly, gathering itself for the sudden leap into mountain heights.

The ranch house was on the last piece of

land that could be described as high plains.
Behind the ranch buildings, the country rose
endlessly, becoming ranks of black peaks
wearing brilliant crowns of stars.

Gradually, squares of yellow light condensed out of the blackness as the ranch house
competed with and finally outshone the
brightness of the stars. Dark fences paralleled
the road, defining corrals and pastures where
brood mares grazed and champion bulls
moved with ponderous grace. A paved loop
of road curved in front of the house before
veering off toward the barns.

As Rafe braked to a stop by the walkway,
the front door of the house opened, sending a
thick rectangle of gold light into the yard like
a soundless cry of welcome. Three quicksilver
dogs bounded off the porch, barking and bay-
ing and dancing as though the dewy grass
were made of icicles too sharp to stand on.

Rafe climbed out of the truck and waded
into the hounds with good-natured curses,
pummeling them gently until they had
worked off the first exuberance of their greet-
ing. Then they stood and watched him with
bright eyes, nudging his hands with cold
noses until each silky ear had been scratched
at least once. In the moonlight the hounds'
coats shone like liquid silver, rippling and
changing with each movement of their muscular bodies.

Alana slid out of the Jeep with a smile on
her lips and the hounds' welcoming song
echoing in her ears. She stood quietly, watch-

ing the dogs greet Rafe, feeling the cool breeze tug at her hair.

One of the hounds lifted its head sharply, scenting Alana. It gave an eager whine and scrambled toward her. Automatically Alana bent over to greet the animal, rubbing its ears and thumping lightly on its muscular barrel, enjoying the warm rasp of a tongue over her hands.

"You're a beauty," Alana said, admiring the dog's lithe lines and strength.

The dog nosed her hand, then the pocket of her black slacks, then her hand again.

"What do you want?" asked Alana, her voice carrying clearly in the quiet air.

"Vamp wants the crackers you spoiled her with the last time you were here," called Bob as he stepped out onto the porch, laughter and resignation competing in his voice.

Alana looked up blankly.

"Crackers?" she repeated.

She looked down at the dog. The dog watched her, dancing from foot to foot, obviously waiting for something.

"Crackers," said Bob, holding one out to Alana as he walked toward her. "I figured that you'd forgotten—er, I mean I figured that you wouldn't have any crackers on you, so I brought one."

"Vamp?" asked Alana.

She took the cracker and looked at the pale square as though she'd never seen one before. She held it out.

The hound took the tidbit with the delicate mouth of a well-trained bird dog.

"Vampire," Bob said, gesturing to the dog at Alana's feet. "You know, for all the sharp teeth she had as a pup."

The look on Alana's face made it clear that she didn't know the story behind the dog's name. Yet it was equally clear that Bob had told her the story before.

"*Hell,*" said Bob under his breath.

Then he hugged Alana and spoke so softly that only she could hear.

"Sorry, sis. It's hard for me to keep track of all the things you've forgotten."

Alana stiffened for an instant as her brother's arms held her. Then she forced herself to relax. She knew she must get over her irrational fear of human contact. The source of fear was only in her nightmares, a creation of her mind that had nothing to do with here, now, reality. Withdrawing would hurt Bob badly, just as she had hurt him at the hospital.

She returned the hug a little fiercely, holding on too tightly, releasing her brother too quickly. Bob gave her a troubled look but said nothing.

Until he saw her hair.

"What in God's name did you do to your hair?" Bob yelped.

"I cut it."

Alana shook her head, making moonlight run like ghostly fingers through the loose black curves of her hair.

"Why?" asked Bob.

"It seemed like a good idea at the time."

"But you've always had long hair."

His voice was surprisingly plaintive for a man who was just over six-and-a-half feet tall and nearly twenty-three years old.

"Things change, little brother," Alana said tightly.

"Not you, sis," Bob said, confidence in every word. "You're like the mountains. You never change."

Alana stood without moving, not knowing what to say. In that moment, she realized for the first time how much like a mother she was to Bob, how fixed in his mind as a port for every storm. Somehow she had given a continuity of love and caring to him that she had never found for herself after their mother died. And Rafe, who had died and then not died. But he had come back too late.

Like now. Too late, Alana thought. How can I tell Bob that there are no ports anymore, only storms?

"You're forgetting something, Bob," said Rafe, his voice easy yet somehow commanding.

"What? Oh. Yeah. Damn. I told you, Winter, I'm no—"

"Sisters are women, too," Rafe said, cutting across whatever Bob had been about to say. "Some sisters are even beautiful women."

Rafe's amber eyes flashed as he looked briefly at Alana. His smile reflected the light pouring out of the ranch house.

Bob cocked his head and looked at Alana as though she were a stranger.

"A matter of taste, I suppose," Bob said, deadpan. "She looks like a stray fence post to me. Didn't they have any food in Portland?"

Quietly Rafe looked from the graceful curve of Alana's neck to the feminine swell of breasts, the small waist, the firm curve of hips, the legs long and graceful.

"Burdette," Rafe said, "you're as blind as a stone rolling down a mountain."

Alana flushed under Rafe's frankly approving glance. Yet she was smiling, too. She was used to being told she had a beautiful voice. As for the rest, she had never felt especially attractive.

Except when she had been with Rafe and he had looked at her the way he was looking at her right now, smiling.

"I guess Rafe told *you*, baby brother," Alana said, glad that the words came out light, teasing. She smiled at Rafe. "I'll bet you ride a white horse and rescue maidens in distress, too."

Rafe's face changed, intent, watching Alana as though he was willing her to do . . . something.

The look passed so quickly that Alana thought she had imagined it.

"Wrong, sis," said Bob triumphantly, yanking her suitcase out of the back of the Jeep. "The horse Rafe rides is as spotted as his past."

Alana looked from Bob to Rafe, wondering what her brother meant.

What had Rafe done in the years before, and after, he was declared dead in Central America?

"Bob, you need a bridle for that tongue of yours," said Rafe.

His smile was narrow, his voice flat.

Bob winced. "Stepped in it again. Sorry. I'm not very good at forgetting. Or"—he looked apologetically at Alana again—"remembering, either."

She sighed. "You couldn't even keep secrets at Christmastime, could you?"

"Nope," Bob agreed cheerfully. "Not a one. In one ear and out the mouth."

Rafe made a sound that was halfway between disgust and amusement.

"There are times when I can't believe you're Sam's brother," Rafe said dryly.

Alana looked quickly at Rafe. Something in his voice told her that Rafe had seen Sam more recently than the times when Sam had hero-worshipped the older Rafe from afar.

"Have you seen Sam? I mean, lately?" Alana asked Rafe.

When Bob would have spoken, Rafe gave him a quelling look.

"We met in Central America," Rafe said, "when Sam was drilling a few dry holes. I haven't seen him in a while, though."

Alana's lips turned down.

"Neither have I," she said. "It's been years.

I was in Florida doing a concert the last time he came to the States."

"My brother the spook," said Bob. "Now you see him, now you don't."

"What?" asked Alana.

"Oops," said Bob.

What Rafe said was mercifully blurred by Merry's voice calling out threats to the husband who had let her sleep through Alana's homecoming.

"Honey," Bob said, dropping Alana's suitcase and racing toward the steps, "be careful!"

The dogs ran after Bob, yipping and yapping with excitement. Alana couldn't help laughing as Bob swept Merry off her tiny feet and carried her across the grass, swearing at the dogs every step of the way. Merry was laughing too, her face buried against Bob's neck as she squealed and ducked away from the long-tongued, leaping hounds.

Rafe put his fists on his hips and shook his head, smiling. He turned to Alana and held out his hand.

"Welcome to Broken Mountain Dude Ranch," he said wryly. "Peace and quiet await you. Somewhere. It says so in the fine print in the brochure."

"I'll hold you to that," murmured Alana.

Smiling, she rested her hand lightly on Rafe's, feeling the heat and texture of his palm as his fingers curled around hers. The touch sent both pleasure and fear coursing through her.

The instant before Alana would have withdrawn, Rafe released her hand and picked up her luggage. She went ahead quickly, opening the screen door for Rafe and for Bob, who was still carrying a giggling Merry.

The dogs stopped short at the threshold and begged silently, their amber wolf eyes pale and hopeful.

Alana looked toward Bob.

"No," he said firmly. "No weimaraners allowed."

"Not even Vamp?" Alana asked coaxingly.

"Sis," Bob said in an exasperated tone, "I told you the last time that I don't want to take a chance of Merry tripping over—"

Bob stopped abruptly, remembering too late that Alana had no memory of her last trip to the ranch.

"Sorry," said Alana tightly, closing the door. "I forgot."

"So did I. Again. *Damn.*"

Bob ran his fingers through his thick black hair in a gesture both sister and brother had learned from their father.

"Oh, Alana," Merry said softly, her pretty face stricken as she looked at her sister-in-law. "Bob didn't mean to hurt you."

"I know."

Alana closed her eyes and unclenched her hands.

"Where do you want the suitcase?" asked Rafe into the silence.

His voice was matter-of-fact, as though he hadn't sensed the undercurrents of emotion swirling through Alana. She knew better. With every instant she and Rafe spent together, Alana became more certain that he was intensely aware of everything about her.

"Alana is sleeping in the upstairs bedroom on the east corner," said Merry, wriggling in Bob's arms. "Put me down, you big moose. There's nothing wrong with my feet."

"Never mind," said Rafe. "I know where the room is. Don't climb any more stairs than you have to."

"Not you, too!" Merry rolled her blue eyes and pulled on her long blond hair in mock despair. "Why me, Lord? Why am I stuck with men who think pregnancy is an exotic kind of broken leg?"

Rafe smiled crookedly as he watched the tiny woman's halfhearted struggle in Bob's thick arms.

"Enjoy it, Merry," Rafe said. "Come diaper time, Bob will develop an exotic kind of broken arm."

"Slander," muttered Bob to Merry, nuzzling her cheek. "Don't believe a word of it."

"Believe it," said Alana. "Every time there were grubby chores to be done, Bob evaporated."

"Hey, not fair," he said, a wounded look on his face.

"Not fair or not true?" Alana asked wryly.

"I grew up after that carnivorous hen ate half my hands."

"Chicken pox," called Rafe just before he disappeared down the hall at the top of the stairway. "Remember?"

Bob groaned. "He's worse than Sam when it comes to keeping track of life's little lies. Mind like a steel trap. No fun at all."

Privately Alana thought it would be wonderful to have a mind that forgot nothing, held everything. If she knew about those six days, her nightmares would be gone.

Or maybe they would just move in and take over her days, too.

Maybe Dr. Gene was right. Maybe she wasn't ready to accept what had happened, at least not all of it, every little horrifying detail.

Height and ice and falling . . .

"You look tired, sis," said Bob.

He set Merry on her feet with exaggerated care and watched lovingly as she yawned, waved good night, and went back to the downstairs bedroom. He turned back to Alana.

"Want to go right to bed?" he asked.

Bob waited, but there was no answer.

"Sis?"

With a start, Alana came out of her thoughts. Her hand was against her neck, as though holding back a scream.

"Sis? What is it? Are you remembering?"

Alana forced herself not to flinch when Bob's big hand came down on her shoulder.

"No," she said, hearing the harshness of her voice but unable to make it softer. "I'm trying, but I'm not remembering anything."

"Where does your memory stop?" asked Bob hesitantly.

"California. I was packing to come here."

"Where does it begin again?"

"When I woke up in the hospital."

"Six days."

"Nice counting, baby brother," Alana said sardonically. Then, "I'm sorry. It's just . . . not easy. I don't know why I forgot, and I'm . . . afraid."

Bob patted Alana's shoulder clumsily, not knowing how to comfort the older sister who had always been the one to comfort him.

"I love you, sis."

Tears burned behind Alana's eyes. She looked up into the face that was as familiar to her as her own. Familiar, yet different. Bob was a man now, but in her memories he was so often a boy.

"Thanks," she whispered. "I love you, too."

Bob smiled almost shyly and squeezed Alana's shoulder. A frown passed over his face as he felt her slight body beneath his big hand.

"You're nearly as small as Merry," said Bob, surprise clear in his voice.

Alana almost laughed. "I'm three inches taller."

Bob dismissed the inches with a wave of his hand.

"That's not what I meant," he said. "I've always thought of you as . . . bigger. You know. Physically."

"And I've always thought of you as smaller. Guess we both have some new thinking to do."

"Yeah, guess so." Bob ran his thick fingers through his hair. "I've been thinking a lot

since Merry got pregnant. It's kind of scary."
Then he grinned. "It's kind of fantastic, too."

Alana smiled despite her trembling lips.

"You'll be a good father, Bob. Just like
you're a good rancher."

Bob's eyes widened slightly, showing clear
brown depths.

"You mean that, sis? About being a good
rancher, too?"

"You've been good to the land. It shows.
Rafe thinks so, too," she added.

Bob smiled with pleasure. "High marks
from both of you, huh? That means a lot to
me. I know how much you love the ranch.
And Rafe, well, he's a hard son of a bitch, but
he's working miracles with the Lazy W. It had
really gone to hell by the time his father had
that last stroke."

"How long has Rafe lived at the Lazy W?"

Bob looked uncomfortable, obviously remembering the time Alana had come for a
visit and he had told her that Rafael Winter
was alive.

"Bob?" Alana pressed.

"A couple of years," he admitted.

"All that time?" asked Alana.

Before, when she had known Rafe, loved
him, been engaged to him, his work had taken
him on long trips to unexpected places.

"He used to travel a lot," she added.

"Yeah. About four years ago he was . . . uh,
he had some kind of accident in some godfor-
saken place. And then his father died. Rafe has
stayed on the Lazy W the whole time since

then. Guess he's here for good. Unless something goes to hell overseas or Sam gets in trouble again and needs Rafe to pull his tail out of a crack."

"Sam? In trouble? How? And what could Rafe do about it?"

Bob laughed wryly. "Sis, Rafe would—"

"Bring Sam a toothbrush," said Rafe from the stairway.

Alana looked up. Rafe was leaning against the wall, his hands in his pockets, his shirt tightly across bunched shoulder muscles. For all his casual pose, she sensed that Rafe was angry about something.

Bob breathed a curse and an apology.

"I warned you, Rafe," Bob said. "I'm no damn good at—"

"Burdette." Rafe's voice cracked with authority. "Shut up. If you can't do that, talk about the weather."

There was a charged silence for a moment. Alana looked from Bob to Rafe and back again. Although her brother had five inches and fifty pounds on Rafe, Rafe didn't seem the least bit intimidated by the prospect of a brawl.

"Storm coming on," said Bob finally. "Should be thunder in the high country by midnight, rain down here before dawn. It's supposed to clear up at sunrise, though. Part of a cold front that's moving across the Rockies. Now, if you ask me, I think we should roust those sleeping dudes upstairs and leave for your lodge at dawn or as soon afterward as it stops raining."

"That," said Rafe distinctly, "is one hell of an idea. Do you suppose you can keep your feet out of your mouth long enough to sit a horse all the way to Five Lakes Lodge?"

"Didn't you know I'm a trick rider?" said Bob, his smile wide and forgiving.

"Who had chicken pox," retorted Rafe, but he was smiling, too.

"Now you got it," said Bob approvingly. "Keep that good thought until morning. And I'll practice biting my damned tongue. But only for a while."

"I'll hold you to it."

"Yeah. It goes both ways, Winter. Don't forget. I sure as hell won't. Goodnight."

Beneath the humor in Bob's voice there was something much harder.

Alana heard it, and she wondered if Rafe heard it, too.

And then she wondered why Bob, who was normally easygoing to a fault, was leaning on Rafael Winter.

5

R AFE SHOOK HIS HEAD AND
said something harsh under his breath as Bob
vanished. But Rafe was smiling when he
turned to Alana.

"How did you hold your own?" he asked.
"Sam and Bob together. My God. And Dave,
too. Boggles the mind."

"What did Bob mean about your 'spotted
past'?" asked Alana.

"Terrible work record," Rafe said laconically. "Moved around a lot. Remember?"

"And about Sam being in trouble?"

"He's not in trouble now."

"But he was?" persisted Alana.

"Everyone gets in trouble now and again."

Alana made an exasperated sound. "Am I permitted to ask about the dudes?"

Rafe's glance narrowed.

"Sure," he said. "Ask away."

"But will I get any answers?"

"Now I remember how you held your own with your brothers," Rafe said, smiling. "Stubborn."

"I prefer to think of it as determined."

"Good thing, determination."

Alana looked at Rafe's carefully bland expression, at the intelligence and humor that gave depth to his whiskey eyes, at the clean line of his lips beneath his mustache.

What she saw made her forget her unanswered questions. Rafe had taken off his hat, revealing the rich depths of color and texture in his hair. It was a very dark brown, with surprising gleams of gold, clean and thick and lustrous. No shadow of beard lay beneath his skin, which meant that he must have shaved before he picked her up at the airport.

The open collar of Rafe's shirt revealed hair darker than his mustache, more curly. Her glance went back to his forehead, where the rich brown hair had been combed back by his fingers.

Is it a memory or a dream, Alana asked herself silently, or did Rafe's hair once feel like winter mink between my fingers?

"What are you thinking?" he asked.

Rafe's voice was casual, as though he were asking the time.

Reflexively Alana responded to the offhand

tone, answering before she realized what he had asked or what her answer would reveal.

"Your hair," she said, "like winter mink . . . ?"

"Want to find out?"

"What?"

"If my hair feels like mink."

Rafe spoke as though it were a perfectly normal thing for Alana to do.

"Don't worry," he added softly. "I won't touch you at all. I know you don't want to be touched."

Rafe's voice was low, murmurous, as soothing as it had been in the Jeep when nightmare had overtaken Alana without warning.

"Go ahead and touch me," he said. "I promise I won't do anything but stand here. You're safe with me, Alana. Always. I'm the man who came to take you home."

Alana looked at the amber eyes and gentle smile while Rafe's voice surrounded her, caressing her. His hands were still in his pockets, his body was still relaxed. His posture told Alana that he understood and accepted her fear of being touched, held. Restrained.

"How did you know?" Alana asked, her voice trembling.

"That you didn't want to be touched?"

"Yes."

"Every time I touch you, you freeze. That's as good as words for me. Better."

Alana was caught by the emotion she sensed coiling beneath Rafe's surface calm.

He sent back my letter unopened, Alana

thought tensely. But did he dream of me, too? Is my coldness cutting him, making him bleed as I bled when my letter came back unopened?

Remembered grief ripped through Alana, shaking her.

That's in the past, she told herself harshly. I'm living in the present. Today, Rafe has shown me only kindness. And now I'm hurting him.

Alana wanted to hold on to Rafe, comforting both of them, but the thought of being held in return made her body tense to fight or flee.

"It isn't anything personal," she said in a strained voice.

"Are you sure it isn't something I've done?"

Alana looked at Rafe. His eyes were as clear as a high-country stream. Glints of gold and topaz mixed with the predominant amber color, radiating outward from the black pupil. He was watching her with strange intensity.

"I'm sure," she said, sighing, relaxing. "Very sure."

"Then what is it?" Rafe asked gently.

"I—I don't know. Since Jack died, I just don't like people touching me."

"Do you like touching people?"

"I—"

Alana stopped, a puzzled expression bringing her black brows together.

"I hadn't thought about it that way," she admitted.

Rafe waited, watching her.

And Alana watched Rafe, absorbing his silence and his restraint, the pulse beating slowly in his neck, the slide and coil of muscles across his chest as he breathed in the even rhythms of relaxation, waiting for her.

Slowly Alana's hand came up. He bent down to make it easier for her to touch him. Her fingers brushed over his hair lightly, hesitated, then quickly retreated.

"Well?" Rafe asked as he straightened, smiling. "Is someone going to skin me for a fancy coat?"

Alana laughed a little breathlessly.

"I'm not sure," she admitted. "It was so quick."

"Try again," he offered casually.

Alana climbed the stairs until she was on the same step as Rafe. This time her hand lingered as she allowed his hair to sift over the sensitive skin between her fingers. With a smile that was both shy and remembering, she lifted her hand.

"Better," Rafe said. "But you should take lessons from a professional furrier."

She made a questioning sound.

"Professionals rub the pelt with their palms and fingertips," said Rafe.

His glance moved from Alana's mouth to her glossy black hair.

"And they tease the fur with their breath," he said, "hold its softness to their lips, smell it, taste it, then gently slide the fur over their most sensitive skin."

Alana's breath caught. A shiver of pleasure spread through her at the thought of being touched so gently . . . by Rafael Winter.

"Do they really?" she asked.

"I don't know," Rafe admitted, his voice a teasing kind of velvet as he smiled down at her. "But that's what I'd do to you if you were a fur and I were a furrier."

Though Rafe hadn't moved any closer, Alana felt surrounded by him, by sensual possibilities that sent warmth showering through her.

Suddenly, vividly, memories from the times they had made love went through Alana's body like liquid lightning. She had spent so long trying to forget, yet the memories were as hot and fresh as though newly made.

Or perhaps her memories of Rafe's exquisite touch were merely hunger and dream entangled so thoroughly that truth was lost. Another kind of amnesia, more gentle, but just as filled with pitfalls in the present.

Yet Alana had just touched Rafe, and he had felt better than in her memories.

Rafe smiled as though he knew exactly what Alana was feeling. Before she could retreat, he pushed away from the wall and passed her on the narrow stairway without touching her. When he spoke his voice was no longer teasing, husky, intimate.

"Get some sleep," Rafe advised. "Bob and I weren't kidding about leaving at dawn. If you need anything, I'm in the room next to yours. Don't worry about making noise. The dudes are still on Virginia time. Sleeping like babes all in a row."

She stared at Rafe as he walked toward the living room.

"And Alana..."

Rafe turned back toward her, his face half in light, half in shadow, his eyes the radiant gold of sunset rain.

"Yes?" she asked.

"Don't be afraid. Whatever happens, I'm here."

Rafe vanished into the living room before Alana could answer.

Slowly she walked upstairs to her room, hoping at every moment to hear Rafe's footsteps behind her.

Only silence followed Alana to her bedroom.

The exhaustion of sleepless nights combined with the familiar background sounds of the ranch to send Alana into a deep sleep. She slept undisturbed until clouds gathered and thickened, stitched together by lightning and torn apart by thunder.

Then she began to sleep restlessly, her head moving from side to side, her limbs shifting unpredictably, her throat clenching over unspoken words.

Riding next to Jack, arguing.

He's angry and the clouds are angry and the mountains loom over me like thunder.

Spruce and fir and aspens bent double by the cruel wind. Wind tearing off leaves, spinning them like bright coins into the black void, and the horses are gone.

Screaming but no one can hear, I'm a single bright leaf spinning endlessly down and down and—

Cold, sweating, Alana woke up, her heart hammering against her ribs, her breath ragged. She looked at the bedside clock. Three-forty. Too soon to get up, even if they were leaving at dawn.

Lightning bleached the room, leaving intense darkness behind, trailing an avalanche of thunder.

Suddenly Alana felt trapped.

She leaped out of bed, yanked open the door, and ran into the hallway. She raced down the stairs and out onto the front porch. Incandescent lightning skidded over the land, separated by split seconds of darkness that were almost dizzying.

Frightened, disoriented, a broken scream tearing at her throat, Alana turned back to the front door.

A man came out, walking toward her.

At first Alana thought it was Rafe; then she realized that the man was too tall. But it wasn't Bob. The walk was different.

Lightning came again, outlining the man, revealing his pale hair, long sideburns, blunt nose, narrow mouth, and eyes so blue they were almost black.

Jack.

Past and present, nightmare and reality fused into a seamless horror. Helpless, terrified, shaken by thunder and her own screaming, Alana scrambled backward, hands flailing frantically, *running, scrambling, falling, and everywhere ice and lightning, thunder and darkness and screaming.*

Falling.

I'm falling . . . !

This time Alana could hear the screams tearing apart her throat. But it wasn't Jack's name she screamed as she spun toward the void.

It was Rafe's.

The front door burst open and slammed back against the wall. Abruptly Jack disappeared between one stroke of lightning and the next.

Shaking, holding on to herself, Alana told herself that Jack was a product of her imagination, a waking nightmare from which she would soon be freed.

Then she saw Jack laid out on the porch, Rafe astride him, Rafe's forearm like an iron bar across Jack's throat.

Panic exploded inside Alana, shards of ice slashing through her, paralyzing her. Jack was so much bigger than Rafe, as big as Bob, bigger, and Jack could be so cruel in his strength.

Then her paralysis melted, sliding away into darkness and lightning as Alana realized that Rafe was in control. It was Jack who was down and was going to stay that way until Rafe decided to let him up again.

Bob ran out onto the front porch, flashlight in one hand and shotgun in the other. He saw Rafe and the man beneath him.

"What in the hell—?" began Bob.

Then he saw Alana backed up against the porch railing, terror in every line of her face, her hands clenched around her throat.

"Sis? Oh, God!"

Bob started for her, holding out his arms.

Alana screamed.

Rafe came to his feet in a single powerful lunge. He stood between brother and sister.

"Don't touch her," Rafe said flatly.

"But—" began Bob.

Lightning flared again. Bob saw Rafe's face, hard and utterly savage. Without another word, Bob backed up.

Rafe turned with the same fluid power that he had used to come up off the porch floor. As he looked at Alana, his eyes burned with rage and regret. He ached to gather her in his arms, to hold her, to feel her melt and flow along his body as she accepted his embrace.

And he knew that was a dream, and she lived in nightmare. Broken Mountain was destroying their future as surely as his "death" once had.

"It's all right, wildflower," Rafe said quietly. "I won't let anyone touch you. Not even me."

Numbly Alana nodded, hearing the word *wildflower* echo and reecho in her mind, a name from the deep past, before Rafe had died and been reborn, killing her without knowing it.

Wildflower.

A name out of dreams.

A name out of nightmares.

"Bob," Rafe said without turning around, "pick up Stan and get the hell out of Alana's sight. *Now.*"

Bob had no desire to argue with the whiplike voice, the poised fighting stance, the muscles visibly coiled across Rafe's naked back, ready to unleash violence. Silently Bob bent over, levered the man called Stan to his feet, and dragged him into the living room.

The screen door banged shut behind them like a small crack of thunder.

Distant lightning came, revealing Rafe's face, harshness and yearning combined.

Alana blinked, half expecting Rafe to vanish.

He stayed before her, outlined by forked lightning, a man both lean and powerful, wearing only jeans, and regret was a dark veil across his features.

Instinctively Alana swayed toward him, needing the very comfort that her mind wouldn't let her take.

Rafe stood without moving, looking at her slender body shaken by shudders of cold and fear, his own private nightmare come true. He would have put his arms around her, but he knew that she would only scream again, tearing both of them apart.

In the end, Rafe could not help holding out his hand to Alana. It was a gesture that asked nothing, offered everything.

"Hold on to me, wildflower," he said softly. "If you want to."

With a small sound, Alana took Rafe's hand between her own. She held on to him with bruising intensity. He didn't object. Nor did he so much as curl his fingers around hers. She took a shuddering breath, then another, fighting to control herself.

"I thought—" Alana's voice broke.

She bent over, pressing her forehead to the back of Rafe's hand. He was as warm as life itself, flowing into her, giving her peace. She swallowed and spoke without lifting her head.

"I thought he was J-Jack."

Rafe's left hand hovered over Alana's bent head, as though he would stroke her hair. Then his hand dropped to his side and remained there, clenched in a fist.

He was afraid to touch her, to frighten her and rend the fragile fabric of trust being woven between them.

"Stan is one of the dudes," Rafe said quietly, but emotions turned just beneath the smooth surface of his voice, testing his control. "Stan is big, like Jack was. And blond."

Alana shuddered and said nothing.

"If I had known that the first time you saw Stan it would be in the lightning and darkness, a storm, like Broken Mountain—" Rafe didn't finish. "I'm sorry, wildflower. For so many things."

But the last words were said so softly that Alana wasn't sure she had heard them at all. For a moment longer she clung to Rafe's hand, drawing strength and warmth from him, the nightmare draining away, fading like thunder into the distance.

Slowly Alana's head came up. She drew more deep breaths, sending oxygen through a body that had been starved for it, paralyzed by fear to the point that she had forgotten to breathe. Gradually the shuddering left her body, only to return as shivers of cold rather than fear.

For the first time she realized that she was wearing only a thin silk nightshirt, which the icy rain had plastered across her body. The vivid orange cloth was nearly black where water had touched it, as dark as her eyes looking up at Rafe.

Alana shivered again, and for an instant Rafe held his warm hand against her cheek. A single fingertip traced the black wing of her eyebrow with such exquisite gentleness that she forgot to be afraid. Tears stood in her eyes, magnifying them. Tears flowed down silently, tears as warm as Rafe's hand.

With dreamlike slowness, Alana turned her face until her lips rested against his palm. When she spoke, her breath was another caress flowing over his skin.

"Thank you for understanding," Alana whispered.

Rafe's body tensed visibly as he fought his impulse to hold Alana, to turn her lips up to his own, to taste again the warmth of her, to feel her respond. He knew that if he reached for her she would retreat, terrified.

And that knowledge was a knife turning inside him.

Slowly Alana released Rafe's hand. For a moment he held his palm against her cheek, then he withdrew.

"I feel like such a fool," said Alana, closing her eyes. "What must that poor man think of me?"

"Stan thinks he was a real horse's ass to come barging outside after you in a storm, scaring you half to death," said Rafe, his voice like a whip once more. "He's lucky I didn't take him apart."

Alana made a sound of protest.

"It was my fault, not his," she said. "I'll have to apologize."

"Like hell. Stan will apologize to you, in good light, when you can see him clearly. *And then he will stay away from you.*"

Rafe's words were clear and hard, like glacier ice. Alana realized that he was furious, but not with her. He was enraged with Stan, because Stan had frightened her.

Then she realized that Rafe was also furious with himself, because he hadn't prevented her from being frightened.

"It wasn't your fault," whispered Alana.

"The hell it wasn't."

Then, before she could respond, Rafe was talking again.

"You're shivering. Are you ready to go back inside?"

Alana hesitated. The thought of seeing the man who looked so much like Jack disturbed her deeply. But she had no choice. She refused to spend the rest of her life at the mercy of her own fears.

She clenched her hands at her sides, took a deep breath, and lifted her chin.

"Yes, I'm ready," Alana said.

"You don't have to." Rafe's voice was gentle despite his tightly leashed anger. "I'll go in and tell Bob you'd rather not meet Stan right now."

"No. I've got to stop being so damned ... fragile."

"You've been through too much, too recently. You've been through more than anyone should have to bear. Don't be so hard on yourself. Ease up. Give yourself a chance to heal."

Alana shook her head.

She wasn't healing. The nightmare was getting worse, taking over more and more of her waking hours.

"Life goes on, Rafe. The biggest cliché, and the one with the most truth. I have to go on, too. I have to leave those six days behind me. *I have to.*"

For an instant Rafe closed his eyes, unable to bear either Alana's pain or her courage.

"Just like a wildflower," he whispered. "Delicate and tough, growing in the most difficult places."

He opened his eyes and held his hand out to her.

"Will you let me help you?" Rafe asked.

After a moment's hesitation, Alana put her hand in Rafe's. The warmth of his skin was like fire, telling her how cold her own body was.

"Thank you," Rafe said simply.

Then he opened the door and led Alana back into the living room, where her nightmare waited.

6

BOB AND STAN WERE SITTING in the living room, talking about storms and high-country trout. Both men looked up, then away, clearly not wanting to intrude if Alana needed privacy.

Rafe plucked a flannel shirt off a coatrack standing near the door, draped the colorful plaid folds over Alana, and turned toward the two men.

Instantly Stan stood up.

Alana took a quick breath and stepped backward until she came up hard against Rafe's chest. Over Alana's head, Rafe smiled coldly at the blond, muscular giant who was every bit as tall as Bob.

"Alana Reeves, meet Stan Wilson," said Rafe. "Stan, you'll understand if Alana doesn't want to shake hands. You have an unnerving resemblance to her recently deceased husband."

For a long moment, Rafe and Stan measured each other.

Stan nodded, a brief incline of his head that was almost an apology. Then his head moved slightly as he looked toward Alana.

At the sight of Stan's cobalt-blue eyes, Alana made a small sound. Like Jack. Just like Jack. Only the solid warmth of Rafe at her back kept her from falling into nightmare again.

"I'm sorry, Mrs. Reeves," Stan said. "I sure didn't mean to frighten you like that."

Relief uncurled deep inside Alana. The voice was different, entirely different, deeper, permeated by the subtle rhythms of the Southwest.

"Please call me Alana," she said. "And I'm sorry for—"

"You have nothing to apologize for," said Rafe, cutting across Alana's words. "Now that Stan is aware of the situation, I'm sure he won't take you by surprise again."

Rafe's voice was smooth and polished, steel hard, having no soft surfaces that might admit argument. His eyes were narrowed, watching Stan with the intensity of a cougar stalking deer.

Again, Stan hesitated before responding. Again, Stan nodded slightly, though his expression was as hard as Rafe's.

Alana looked from one man to the other and then to Bob, whom she feared would be worried about the fate of his dreams for a dude ranch. If Stan Wilson had an awful vacation at the Broken Mountain Dude Ranch, he would hardly recommend the place to his wealthy clients.

Yet Bob didn't look upset. He looked more like a man making bets with himself, and winning.

When Bob realized that Alana was watching him, he smiled at her.

"Some homecoming, sis," Bob said, shaking his head.

"Yes," she whispered. "Some homecoming."

Yawning, Bob looked at the wristwatch he always wore.

"Well, there's not much point in me going back to sleep," Bob said, stretching. "I'll start working on the pack string. Stan, you said you wanted to watch a real cowboy at work. Still game?"

The faint challenge in Bob's voice brought a smile to Stan's face.

Quickly Alana looked away. The smile was like an echo of Jack, charming and boyish. Stan was a very handsome man ... and Alana's skin crawled every time she looked at him.

It wasn't rational or fair to Stan, but it wasn't something she could control, either.

"I'll be glad to help you," drawled Stan, "seeing as how you're such a puny thing."

Bob looked startled, then laughed out loud. He clapped Stan on the shoulder and led him toward the kitchen. Bob's voice drifted back as the two huge men left the room.

"Merry left some coffee warming. We'll need it. And I've got a jacket that I think will fit you, seeing as how you're such a puny thing, too."

Listening, Alana realized that her brother liked Stan. That was different from before, from Jack. Bob hadn't liked Jack at all. None of the Burdettes had.

Alana heard Stan's laughter trailing back into the living room, laughter as charming as his smile. Yet, unlike the smile, Stan's laughter didn't remind Alana of Jack. Jack had rarely laughed, and never at himself.

Even so, she was glad that Stan was out of sight. It was unnerving to catch a glimpse of him out of the corner of her eye, blond shades of Jack stalking behind her. She let out a long sigh as the kitchen door slammed, telling her that the two men were on the way to the barn.

"Okay?" asked Rafe, feeling the deep breath Alana had taken and let out, for her back was still pressed against his chest.

Alana nodded. "He—he's nice, isn't he?"

Rafe grunted, a sound that told her nothing.

"Bob likes him," said Alana.

"They're a lot alike," Rafe said dryly. "Muscle and impulse in equal amounts and places."

"Between their ears?" suggested Alana.

"Sometimes." Rafe sighed. "Just sometimes."

Alana shifted her weight slightly. The movement reminded her that she was standing very close to Rafe, all but leaning on him. The contact didn't bother her. He wasn't touching her. She was touching him.

The difference was both subtle and infinitely reassuring. The warmth of Rafe's bare chest radiated through the flannel shirt and her damp silk nightshirt, a warmth as natural as the embers glowing in the living room hearth.

For an instant Alana wanted to turn and wrap herself in his warmth, chasing away the chill that had come the day they'd told her that Rafe was dead.

She shivered again, but not from cold.

"You should try to sleep a little more," Rafe said. "You're still on West Coast time."

He was so close to Alana that she felt the vibration of his chest as he spoke, the subtle movement of his muscles as he bent slightly toward her, and the brush of his breath over her ear. She closed her eyes, savoring a tactile intimacy that demanded nothing from her.

"I feel safer here with you," she said simply.

Alana felt Rafe's quick, subdued breath and realized what she had said. She tensed, knowing that if Rafe accepted her unintended invitation and put his arms around her, she had only herself to blame.

The worst of it was that part of her very much wanted his arms around her.

And part of her panicked at the thought of being held.

Suddenly Alana wondered if Jack had been

holding her when they fell, if that was why she froze at a man's touch.

Does my mind equate the act of being embraced with falling and terror and death? Alana asked herself silently.

She stiffened, listening intently, hoping to hear an inner voice say *yes* or *no*, hoping to tear the veil of amnesia and look upon just a few minutes of those six missing days.

The only answer, if answer it was, came in the sudden coldness of her skin, nausea turning in her stomach, her heart beating quickly, erratically.

"What's wrong?" asked Rafe, sensing the change in Alana. Then, sadly, "Does being close to me frighten you?"

"No, it's not that. I was thinking of Jack."

Behind Alana, Rafe's expression changed, tightening in anger and defeat. But his voice was neutral when he spoke.

"Did you love him?"

Alana closed her eyes.

"No," she said flatly. "I didn't love him."

"Then why did you marry him so fast? Not even two months after—"

Abruptly Rafe stopped speaking.

"They told me you were dead," Alana said, her voice ragged. "Music was all that was left to me. And that meant Jack, a voice to make angels weep."

"I'm sorry," said Rafe, stepping backward. "I had no right to ask."

Rafe's voice was neutral, distant, and Alana's back felt cold without his warmth. She spun around, suddenly angry, remembering the letter that had come back, Rafe's own handwriting telling her that he didn't want to say anything to her, not even good-bye.

"That's correct," Alana said tightly. "You have no right. You didn't even open my letter."

"You were another man's woman."

Rafe's voice was as opaque as his eyes, his mouth a thin line of remembered anger beneath his dark mustache.

"I never belonged to Jack. Not like that."

"You were his wife. Didn't that mean anything to you?"

"Yes," Alana said harshly. *"It meant you were dead!"*

Tears spilled suddenly down her cheeks. She spun away, wanting only to be alone, not to be torn between a past she couldn't change and a present that was trying to destroy her.

"Alana, please don't turn away."

Rafe's voice was gentle, coaxing, making subtle music out of her name. She knew without turning around that he was holding his hand out to her, asking her for something she could not give.

Trust. Caring. Warmth. Passion. Love. All the things she needed but no longer believed in. Not really.

Those things had been taken away from her once too often. She had survived her mother's death. She had survived her lover's death. She had survived her husband's death.

Now Alana was trying to survive a different

kind of death, a shattering loss of belief in her own strength, her own mind, her music. Now she was trying not to ask herself if it was worth it, any of it, if there was no end to fear and loss and death.

"I'm sorry, wildflower. I shouldn't have brought up the past. It's too soon. You're too close to what happened on Broken Mountain."

Rafe walked to Alana, not stopping until he felt the cool, rough flannel he had draped around her shoulders rubbing against his chest. She sensed his arm moving and held her breath, anticipating his touch, not knowing whether she would run or scream or stand quietly.

It was agony not to know, not to be able to trust anything, most of all herself.

"No," Alana said hoarsely, stepping away. "I can't take any more. Leave me alone, Rafe."

"Is it the letter? Is that what you can't forgive me for?" Rafe asked sadly.

"No. It's worse than the letter, although that was bad enough, losing you a second time . . ."

Alana's voice died.

"If not the letter, what?" Rafe said softly, urgently. "What have I done? *What are your memories?*"

At first Alana thought she wasn't going to tell him. Then words rushed out of her in a bittersweet torrent.

"After you, I couldn't bear another man's touch. God, how Jack hated you! You ruined me for any other man."

Rafe's face changed, all anger and urgency gone, only hunger remaining. He reached for Alana and could not help protesting when she flinched away.

"Alana. Don't. Please."

She turned and looked at Rafe with eyes that were wild and dark, shadows as deep as despair.

"Jack got even with me, though," Alana whispered. "Somehow he ruined me for any man at all. Even you!"

Alana turned and fled up the stairs, not stopping even when Rafe called out her name in a voice hoarse with emotion, a cry out of her dreams and nightmares.

She locked the bedroom door behind her and stared out the window until dawn came, bringing color and life to the black land. She watched the world change, born anew out of the empty night.

Just as the last star faded, she heard Bob's voice.

"Sis? You awake?"

Alana realized she was shivering, her skin icy, roughened by gooseflesh. Every muscle ached with the tension that hadn't left her since Broken Mountain. Now she faced another day like all the other days.

But not quite. This day would bring the exquisite torture of being close to the only man she had ever loved. So close and yet so very, very far away.

Dream and nightmare and nothing in between, no safety, no port in the unending, violent storm.

"Alana?"

"Yes," she said tiredly. "I'm awake."

"Don't sound so happy about it," teased Bob.

Alana tugged the flannel shirt more firmly around her, opened the door, and pulled her mouth into the semblance of a smile.

"Morning, little brother," she said, grateful that her voice sounded better than she felt. "Is it time for me to cook breakfast?"

"Nope. Merry's doing the honors this morning. I just came up to get your gear."

Alana gestured toward the small duffel bag on the bed.

"Have at it," she said.

"That's all?"

"This is a pack trip, right? I don't think the trees will care how I'm dressed," Alana said, shrugging.

"Er, right."

Bob gave his sister a sidelong glance, then asked softly, "Are you sure you're up to this?"

"What does that have to do with it?" asked Alana sardonically. "Ready or not, here life comes."

She smiled to take the sting out of her words, but she could tell from Bob's look that she hadn't been very convincing.

"It's okay, Bob. Not to worry. I'm doing fine. Just fine."

He hesitated, then nodded. "Like Dr. Gene says, Burdettes are survivors. And you're the toughest Burdette of all, sis. You taught the rest of us how to survive after Mom died."

Alana blinked back sudden tears.

"Would you mind very much if I hugged you?" she asked.

Bob looked startled, then pleased. Remembering Rafe's blunt instructions, Bob kept his arms at his sides while Alana gave him a hard hug.

"You're stronger than you feel," said Bob, patting her slender shoulder.

Alana laughed strangely and shook her head.

"I hope so, baby brother. I hope so."

"Are you—are you remembering anything now that you're home?" asked Bob in a rush. Then, "Damn, there I go! Rafe will nail my dumb hide to the barn if he finds out."

Alana stiffened at Rafe's name.

"What happens between me and my brother is none of Rafe's business."

Bob laughed. "Don't you believe it, sis. That is one determined man. Makes a pack mule look positively wishy-washy."

She looked narrowly at her brother.

"You don't resent Rafe, though, do you?" Alana asked.

Surprised, Bob stared down at Alana. His dark eyes, so like her own, narrowed as he measured the emotion on her face.

"Rafe is quite a man. I don't resent learning from him. Granted," said Bob with a smile, "he's a jealous son of a bitch. I thought he was going to fieldstrip Stan and feed him to the coyotes."

Alana blinked, seeing the previous night through Bob's eyes, a totally different view.

"Jealous?" she asked.

Bob snapped his fingers and waved his hands in front of her face.

"Wake up, sis. Stan wouldn't have minded, er, soothing you. And Rafe has made it pretty plain that . . ."

Shrugging, Bob shut up, his caution for once getting the better of his tongue.

"Rafe cares about you," Bob said, "and Stan is bigger, stronger, and better looking than Rafe. No surprise that Rafe's jealous."

"Stan's bigger," agreed Alana, "but it was Stan who ended up flat on his back. And there's more to looks than blond hair, bulging muscles, and a big smile. A lot more."

Bob grinned. "Does that mean you've forgiven Rafe for not opening your letter?"

Alana's face changed, darkness and grief clear on her features. Bob swore.

"Goddamnit, sis. I'm sorry. I'll never learn when to keep my big mouth shut."

"Sure you will," said Rafe from the doorway, "even if I have to pound the lessons into your thick skull one by one with a twenty-pound sledgehammer."

Alana spun around and saw Rafe lounging against the door frame, his rich brown hair alive with sunlight, his mouth hard and yet oddly sensual, his face expressionless except for the whiskey eyes burning with suppressed emotion.

Distantly she wondered how Bob could think that Stan was better looking than the utterly male Rafe.

And then Alana wondered how much of the conversation Rafe had overheard.

"Morning, Rafe," said Bob with a cheerful grin.

He turned and grabbed Alana's duffel off the bed, ignoring both of them.

Rafe simply looked at Alana. The flannel shirt she still wore was in shades of russet and orange and chocolate brown. The long tails came nearly to her knees, and the sleeve cuffs lapped over her fingertips, making her look very small, very fragile. Only in her face and in her movements did her strength show, a woman's strength made of grace and endurance.

A wildflower with pale cheeks and haunted eyes, watching him.

The sound of Bob unzipping Alana's duffel bag seemed very loud in the silence. He rummaged for a few seconds, muttered under his breath, and went to the closet where she had left her clothes after the last disastrous visit.

Bob ran a critical eye over the contents of the closet, then began pulling bright blouses and slacks off hangers. He hesitated between a scarlet dress and a floor-length indigo wraparound that was shot through with metallic gold threads.

"Which one of these travels best?" asked

Bob, looking over his shoulder at Alana.

With a start, Alana pulled her attention away from Rafe. She saw Bob in front of her closet, his arms overflowing with color and silk. In his large hands, the clothes looked exquisitely feminine, as intimate as French lingerie.

"What are you doing?" asked Alana.

"Packing for my big sister," Bob said patiently. "As cute as you look in Rafe's flannel shirt, that wasn't what I had in mind when I told the dudes we dressed for dinner. This is a classy operation, remember?"

Alana looked down at the big flannel shirt folded around her like a warm blanket.

Rafe's shirt.

The thought disturbed Alana. She had assumed that the shirt belonged to Bob.

"Sis? Anybody home?"

"Oh. Um, the dark blue one packs best."

Bob began folding the wraparound with more determination than expertise.

Alana started to object, then shrugged. Whatever Bob did to the silk could be steamed out at the other end. But when he went back to the closet for more clothes, and then more, she finally protested.

"How long are we staying on Broken Mountain?" she asked.

"As long as it takes," Bob said laconically, folding bright clothes.

"As long as what takes?"

"Finding out what—"

Abruptly Rafe's voice cut across Bob's.

"As long as it takes to convince the dudes that Broken Mountain is a good place to send clients. Right, Burdette?"

Bob gritted his teeth.

"Right," he said, folding clothes industriously. "I'm counting on your cooking to win them over, sis."

"But—" began Alana.

"But nothing," Bob said suddenly.

His dark eyes looked at Alana with a combination of affection and maturity that was new to him.

"You signed on for the duration, sis. Get used to the idea. No running out this time, no matter what happens. We'll come after you if you do. Right, Rafe?"

"Right," said Rafe, looking narrowly at Bob. "You're learning, Burdette."

"And not a sledgehammer in sight," pointed out Bob, smiling widely.

Rafe glanced at Alana and saw her baffled look.

"Better get dressed," Rafe said as he went back into the hallway. "Breakfast is getting cold."

Bob zipped up Alana's bag and left her standing in the room with a bemused look on her face.

"Hurry up, sis. Like Dad always used to say, 'You can't keep the mountain waiting.' "

The phrase from her childhood gave Alana a dizzying sense of déjà vu. She remembered her first pack trip up Broken Mountain. She had been only nine and wild with pride that her fa-

ther was taking her on a fishing expedition, just
the two of them together. It had been a wonderful time, full of campfires and long conversa-
tions while stars moved in slow motion
overhead like a silent, glittering symphony.

It hadn't been like that the last time, when
she and Jack had gone up the mountain.

Six days gone.

Six blank days poisoning past memories,
poisoning each day, poisoning her; Broken
Mountain looming over her with inhuman patience, waiting, waiting.

For what? Alana asked silently. For me to
die, too?

You can't keep the mountain waiting.

With a shudder Alana turned away from
her thoughts, dressed quickly, and went
downstairs. The thought of food didn't appeal
to her. She avoided the dining room, where
she heard laughter and strange voices, Stan's
and the woman whom Alana hadn't officially
met. She didn't feel up to meeting Janice Simp-
son right now, either.

Quietly Alana let herself out the front door,
then circled around to the barn where the pack
mules waited patiently.

There were five horses lined up at the hitch-
ing posts. One horse was a magnificent Appaloosa stallion. Two were good-looking bays,
their brown hides glossy in the sun. Of the two
remaining horses, one was as black as midnight and one was a big, dapple-gray gelding.

Alana went to the black mare and stood for
a moment, letting the velvet muzzle *whuff* over

her, drinking her scent. When the mare returned to a relaxed posture, accepting Alana's presence, she ran her hand down the animal's muscular legs and picked up each hoof, checking for stones or loose nails in the shoes.

"Well, Sid," Alana said as she straightened up from the last hoof, "are you ready for that long climb and that rotten talus slope at the end?"

Sid snorted.

Alana checked the cinch and stirrup length, talking softly all the while, not hearing Rafe approach behind her.

"Good-looking mare," said Rafe, his voice neutral.

Alana checked the bridle, then stepped back to admire the horse.

"Sid's a beauty, all right, but the best thing about her is the way she moves," Alana said. "She just flattens out those mountain trails."

"Sid?" Rafe asked, his voice tight.

"Short for Obsidian," explained Alana, returning to the bridle. "You know, that shiny black volcanic glass."

"Yes, I know," he said softly. "You say she has a good trail gait?"

"Yes," Alana said absently, her attention more on loosening the strap beneath the bit than on the conversation. "Riding her is like riding a smooth black wind. A real joy. Not a mean hair on her shiny hide."

"She didn't mind the talus?" continued Rafe in a voice that was restrained, tight with emotion.

"No. The gray didn't like it much, though," said Alana, rearranging the mare's forelock so it wouldn't be pulled by the leather straps.

"The gray?" Rafe asked.

"Jack's horse," she said casually, gesturing toward the big dapple-gray gelding. "It—"

Alana blinked. Suddenly her hands began to shake. She spun and faced Rafe.

"It balked," she said urgently. "The gray balked. And then Jack—Jack—"

She closed her eyes, willing the memories to come. All that came was the thunder of her own heartbeat. She made an anguished sound.

"It's gone!" Alana cried. "I can't remember anything!"

"You remembered something," said Rafe, his whiskey eyes intent. "That's a start."

"Jack's horse balked. Six seconds out of six days." Alana's hands clenched until her fingernails dug deeply into her palms. "Six lousy seconds!"

"That's not all you remembered."

"What do you mean?"

"Sid. You walked out here today and picked her out of a row of horses without any hesitation at all."

"Of course. I've always ridden—" Alana stopped, a startled look on her face. "I can't remember the first time I rode Sid."

"Bob bought her two months ago. He hadn't named her by the time you and Jack came up. You named her, Alana.

"And then you rode her up Broken Mountain."

7

THE FIRST HALF OF THE eight-hour ride to the fishing cabins on the Winter ranch wasn't strenuous. The trail wound through evergreens and along a small, boulder-strewn river that drained a series of lakes higher up the mountain. The air was vibrant with light and fragrance.

The horses' hooves made a soothing, subtly syncopated beat that permeated Alana's subconscious, setting up tiny earthquakes of remembrance beneath amnesia's opaque mantle.

Little things.

Simple things.

Sunlight fanning through a pine branch, stilettos of gold and quivering green needles.

The ring of a horse's steel-shod hoof against stone. The liquid crystal of a brook sliding through shadows. The creak of a saddle beneath a man's shifting weight.

The pale flash of blond hair just off her shoulder when Jack's gray horse crowded against Sid's side.

No, not Jack's horse, Alana corrected instantly. Stan's horse. Jack is dead and the sky over Broken Mountain is clear. No clouds, no thunder, no ice storm poised to flay my unprotected skin and make walking a treacherous joke.

There was sunlight now, hot and pouring, blazing over her, warming her all the way to her bones. She was hot, not cold. Her hands were flexible, not numb and useless. Her throat wasn't a raw sore from too many screams.

It was just rigid with the effort of not screaming now.

Deliberately Alana swallowed and unclenched her hands from the reins. She wiped her forehead, beaded with cold sweat despite the heat of the day.

She didn't notice Bob's concerned looks or the grim line of Rafe's mouth. When Rafe called for an early lunch, she thought nothing of it, other than that she would have a few minutes of relief, a few minutes longer before she had to face Broken Mountain's savage heights.

Alana dismounted and automatically loosened the cinch. She was a little stiff from the ride, but it wasn't anything that a bit of walking wouldn't cure.

Janice, however, wasn't as resilient. She groaned loudly and leaned against her patient horse. Rafe came up and offered his arm. Janice took it and walked a few painful steps. Alana watched the woman's chestnut hair gleam in the sun and heard Janice's feminine, rueful laughter joined by the deep, male sound of Rafe's own amusement.

Slowly the two of them walked back down the line of horses on the opposite side of the trail, coming closer to Alana, who was all but invisible as she leaned on Sid.

Envy turned in Alana as she watched Janice with Rafe. To be able to accept touch so casually. To laugh. To feel Rafe's strength and warmth so close and not be afraid. To remember everything.

Did Janice know how lucky she was? And did she have to cling so closely to Rafe that her breasts pressed against his arm?

Alana closed her eyes and choked off her uncharitable thoughts. Obviously Janice wasn't at all accustomed to riding. Her legs must feel like cooked spaghetti. Yet she hadn't complained once in the four hours since they had left the ranch.

Bob had demanded a brisk pace, wanting to reach Five Lakes Lodge on Broken Mountain before the late-afternoon thundershowers materialized. The hard ride hadn't been easy on the two dudes, who weren't accustomed either to riding or to the increasingly thin air as the trail climbed toward timberline.

But no one had objected to the pace. Not even Stan, who had good reason to be feeling irritable.

Stan, who had been first screamed at and then attacked with no warning, laid out flat, choking beneath Rafe's hard arm.

Blood rose in Alana's cheeks as she remembered last night's fiasco. She put her face against the smooth leather of the saddle, cooling her hot skin.

Stan came up on the other side of Janice and took her arm, supporting her. She smiled up at him in rueful thanks. The smile was vivid, inviting, a perfect foil for Janice's clear blue eyes. Stan smiled back with obvious male appreciation.

"I'll leave you in Stan's capable hands," said Rafe, withdrawing. "But don't go too far. We have to be back on the trail within half an hour."

The big blond man looked at the meadow just beyond the trees, where several trails snaked off in various directions.

"Which trail?" asked Stan.

"That one."

Rafe pointed toward the rugged shoulder of Broken Mountain, looming at the end of the meadow.

Janice groaned and rolled her eyes.

"Only for you, Rafe Winter," she muttered, "would I get on that damned horse again and ride up that god-awful trail."

Alana lifted her head and looked over Sid's back with sudden, intense curiosity. Janice's words, her ease with Rafe, everything about the two of them together added up to people who had known each other longer than a few hours. Stan, too, seemed familiar with Rafe, more like an old friend than a new client for Broken Mountain Dude Ranch.

As Janice and Stan hobbled off down the trail, Rafe smiled after them with a combination of affection and amusement. Alana watched both the smile and the man, and she wondered how well Rafe knew Stan and Janice.

Especially Janice.

As though Rafe sensed Alana's scrutiny, he looked up and saw the black of her hair blending perfectly with Sid's shiny hide. Other than her eyes and hair, Alana was hidden behind the horse's bulk.

"You know them," Alana said when she saw the whiskey eyes watching her. Her voice sounded accusing.

Rafe waited for a long moment, then shrugged.

"I used to travel a lot. The two of them were my favorite agents." He smiled swiftly, amused by a private joke. "We've done a lot of business together, one way or another."

"She's very attractive."

There was a question mark in Alana's eyes, if not in her voice.

Rafe glanced in the direction of Janice, now well down the trail, leaning on Stan.

"Yes, I suppose she is," said Rafe, his voice indifferent. Then he turned suddenly, pinning Alana with amber eyes. "So is Stan."

"Not to me."

"Because he reminds you of Jack?"

Alana thought of lying, then decided it was too much trouble. It was hard enough to keep dream separate from nightmare. If she started lying to herself and to Rafe, it would become impossible to separate the threads of reality from the snarl of amnesia and unreality.

"Stan isn't attractive to me because he isn't you."

Rafe's nostrils flared with the sudden intake of his breath. Before he could speak, Alana did, her voice both haunted and unflinching.

"But it doesn't matter that you're attractive to me and other men aren't," she said, her voice low, "because it's too late."

"No."

Rafe said nothing more. He didn't have to. Every line of his strong body rejected what she said.

Slowly Alana shook her head, making sunlight slide and burn in her black hair.

"I can't handle any more, Rafe," she said, a thread of desperation in her voice. "I can't handle you and the past and today, what was and what wasn't, what is and what isn't. Just getting through the days is hard enough, and the nights . . ."

Alana took a sharp breath, fighting to control herself. It was harder each hour, each minute, for her mind was screaming at her that with every moment, every foot up the trail to Broken Mountain, she came closer to death.

Her death.

It was irrational. She knew it. But knowing didn't stop the fear.

"Seeing you and then remembering the days before and knowing that it will never again . . ." said Alana in a rush.

Her breath came out raggedly, almost a sob. She closed her dark eyes, not wanting to reveal the hunger and fear and helplessness seething inside her.

"I just can't!" Alana said.

"No," countered Rafe, his voice both soft and certain. "I lost you once. I won't lose you again. Unless you don't want me?"

Alana made a sound that was halfway between a laugh and a sob.

"I've never wanted anyone else, for all the good that does either one of us," she said. "It wasn't enough in the past, was it? And it isn't enough now. *Even you can't touch me.*"

"It's been hardly a month," Rafe said reasonably. "Give yourself time to heal."

"I'm starting to hate myself," she said.

Alana's voice was husky with the effort it took to speak rationally about the panic that was turning her strength to water and then draining even that away.

"I'm a coward," she whispered. "Hiding behind amnesia."

"That's not true!"

Alana looked longingly at Rafe, an unattainable dream.

"Yes, it is," she said. "I shouldn't have come back. I'm getting worse, not better."

Rafe's face showed an instant of pain that made Alana catch her breath.

"Was it better for you in Portland?" he asked, his voice quiet, almost without inflection.

Slowly Alana shook her head.

"No. When I slept the nightmares came, more each time, and worse. I'd wake up and fight myself. Hate myself. That's why I'm here. I thought . . ."

Rafe waited, but when Alana didn't say any more, he asked, "What did you think?"

She took a deep, shuddering breath, then another.

"I thought there was something here for me, something that would help me to be strong again. Something that would . . ."

Alana's voice broke but she went on, forcing herself to tell Rafe what she had told no one else.

"Something that would let me sing again," she whispered.

Rafe wondered if he had heard correctly. Her voice was so soft, so frayed.

"What do you mean?" asked Rafe.

"I haven't sung since Broken Mountain. I can't. Every time I try, my throat just closes."

Alana looked at Rafe desperately, wondering if he knew how much singing meant to her.

"Singing was all I had left after you died," she said. "And now I can't sing. Not one note.

Nothing. You're alive now, and I can't bear to be touched. *And I can't sing.*"

Rafe's eyes closed. He remembered the sliding, supple beauty of Alana's voice soaring with his harmonica's swirling notes, Alana's face radiant with music and love as she sang to him.

He wanted to reassure her, protect her, love her, give her back song and laughter, all that the past had taken from her and from him. Yet everything he did brought Alana more pain, more fear.

She could not sing.

He could not hold her.

Rafe swore softly, viciously. When his eyes opened they were clear and hard, and pain was a darkness pooling in their depths.

"I'll take you back down the mountain, Alana. And then I'll leave you alone if that's what you want. I can't bear hurting you like this."

"Rafe," she said, catching her breath, touching his cheek with fingers that trembled. "None of this is your fault."

"All of it is," he said harshly. "I leaned on Bob to get you back here. Now you're here and everything I do hurts you."

"That isn't true," said Alana.

She couldn't bear knowing that she had hurt Rafe. She had never wanted that, even in the worst times after her letter had come back unopened.

"Isn't it?" Rafe asked.

He looked at her with narrow amber eyes.

His anger at himself showed in his lips, sensual curves flattened into a hard line.

"No, it isn't true," she whispered.

But words weren't enough to convince Rafe. Alana could see his disbelief in his grim expression. If she could have sung her emotions to him, he would have believed her, but she couldn't sing.

Hesitantly she lifted her hand to Rafe's face, the face that had smiled and laughed and loved her in her memories, in her dreams. He had always been a song inside her, even in the worst of times.

Especially then, when nightmare and ice avalanched around her, smothering her. He had given her so much, reality and dream and hope. Surely she could give something of that back to him now, when his eyes were dark with pain and anger at himself.

Alana's fingertips pushed beneath the brim of Rafe's Stetson until it tipped back on his head and slid unnoticed to the ground. Fingers spread wide, she eased into the rich warmth of his hair.

"You do feel like winter mink, Rafael," she murmured, giving his name its liquid Spanish pronunciation, making a love song out of the three syllables. "Rafael . . . Rafael. You feel better than in my dreams of you. And my dreams of you are good. They are what kept me sane since Broken Mountain."

Alana felt the fine trembling that went through Rafe, the outrush of his breath that was her name. For an instant she was afraid he would touch her, breaking the spell.

Instead, he moved his head slowly, rubbing against her hand like a big cat. He closed his eyes and concentrated on the feel of her fingers sliding deeply through his hair.

His sensual intensity sent a new kind of weakness through Alana, fire licking down her fingers and radiating through her body, fire deep inside her, burning.

Rafe's dense brown lashes shifted as he looked at Alana, holding her focused in the hungry amber depths of his eyes.

"I've dreamed of you," he said. "Of this."

Alana said nothing, for she could not. Her fingers tightened in his hair, searching deeply, as though she would find something in his thick male pelt that she had lost and all but given up hope of ever finding again.

Even when the sound of Janice and Stan walking back up the row of horses reminded Alana that she and Rafe weren't alone, even then she couldn't bring herself to withdraw from the rich sensation of his hair sliding between her fingers.

Bob's voice cut through Alana's trance.

"Twenty minutes to trail time, everyone," he called from the front of the line of pack mules. "If you haven't eaten lunch, you'll regret it."

Slowly, reluctantly, Alana released the silk and warmth of Rafe's hair. Just before her hand dropped to her side again, her fingertips paused to smooth the crisp hairs of his mustache, a caress as light as sunshine.

He moved his head slowly, sliding his lips over the sensitive pads of her fingers. When her hand no longer touched him, he bent swiftly, retrieved his hat, and settled it into place with an easy tug.

"Bob's right about food," Rafe said, his voice husky and warm. "You didn't have breakfast."

Alana shook her head, though it hadn't been a question.

"I forgot to pack lunch," she admitted.

"Merry packed enough for twenty in my saddlebag." Then, smiling, Rafe added in a coaxing voice, "Share it with me, Alana. Even wildflowers have to eat something."

Beneath his teasing was real concern. Alana was thinner than he had ever seen her. Too thin, too finely drawn, like an animal that had been hunted too long.

"Roast beef, apples, homemade bread, chocolate chip cookies . . ." he murmured.

Alana's mouth watered. She licked her lips with unconscious hunger.

"Sold," she said breathlessly.

She and Rafe ate in the shifting shade of a windblown pine. They sat side by side, almost touching, sharing his canteen. The mint-flavored tea Merry had made for Rafe tasted extraordinary in the clean mountain air.

Alana ate hungrily, enjoying food for the first time in weeks. Rafe watched her, smiling. This, too, had been part of his dreams. Alana and the mountains and him.

When everything else in his life had reeked

of death and betrayal, he had dreamed of her.

"Saddle up," called Bob.

Alana stopped, her hand halfway into the paper bag of cookies. Rafe scooped up the bag and handed it to her.

"Take them," he said, smiling.

"Are you sure? I don't want you to be hungry just because I was too stupid to remember my own lunch."

"There's another bag of cookies in there," Rafe assured her, gesturing to the saddlebags draped across his leg. "Apples, too."

He dug into the supple leather pouch and pulled out two apples.

"Here," he said. "One for you and one for Sid."

Rafe stood and pulled Alana to her feet with one hand, releasing her before she had time to be afraid.

"I'd better help Janice," he said. "She's going to be sore."

Alana winced slightly, flexing her legs.

"She's not the only one," Alana muttered. "Although, considering that it's been more than a year since I rode this hard, I'm not very sore at all."

Then Alana heard the echo of her own words. Her face changed, tension coming back to her in a rush.

"That's not true, is it?" she said, her voice raw. "It hasn't been a year. It's been less than a month. Why can't I remember?"

"Alana," said Rafe urgently.

He bent over her, so close that he could see

the pulse beating in her throat, smell the minty sweetness of her breath. Close but not touching her, afraid to hold her and bring back nightmares in place of dreams.

"Alana, don't. Clawing at yourself won't help you heal."

She drew several long, ragged breaths. Her eyes opened again, very dark but not as wild. She nodded almost curtly, then turned and went back to her horse, clutching a bag of cookies in one hand and two forgotten apples in the other.

The rest of the ride became a waking nightmare for Alana. It began with the first of the five Paternoster lakes, so named because they were strung out like beads on a rosary, shining circles of blue water joined by silver cascades.

The first, lowest lake was at six thousand feet and the highest was just above eight thousand. Pines grew down to the shores of the lower lakes, making dark green exclamation points against the silver-gray boulders that embraced the transparent water. The first lake was beautiful, reflecting the sky in endless shades of blue, serene and quiet.

And after one look, Alana felt fear rise and begin to prowl the corridors of her mind. She heard thunder belling from a cloudless sky, saw violent lightning in every golden shaft of sunshine, heard Jack's voice where nothing but ravens spoke from high overhead.

Gradually, without realizing it, Alana's hands tightened on the reins until Sid fretted, tossing her sleek black head. After a time, Alana's nervousness was reflected in Sid's actions. A line of foam grew around the steel bit. The horse's long, easy stride became a mincing walk. Streaks of sweat radiated from Sid's flanks despite the coolness of the air.

The pressure of Alana's hands on the bit increased by subtle increments until finally Sid stopped. But even then the pressure didn't decrease.

Sid shook her head repeatedly, seeking freedom from the bit.

"Alana."

Rafe's voice was soft and undemanding, despite the harshness of his expression as he watched Alana's blank, unfocused eyes. He leaned over and pulled forward slowly on the reins, easing them out of her rigid fingers. Gradually the thin leather strips slid free, ending the relentless pressure of the bit.

"It's all right, wildflower," murmured Rafe. "I've come to take you home."

Alana blinked and looked around with eyes that were still caught between nightmare and reality.

"Rafael . . . ?"

"I'm here."

Alana sighed and flexed hands that were cramped from the tension of hanging onto reins as though they were a rope pulling her up out of a nightmare. She started to speak, couldn't, and swallowed. The second time she tried, her throat no longer closed around her dead husband's name.

"Jack and I rode this way."

Beneath the shadow of the hat brim, Rafe's narrowed eyes looked like brilliant lines of topaz. He knew that the trail they were on was only one of three trails that led to Five Lakes Lodge. If Alana recognized this particular trail, she must be remembering at least parts of the six lost days.

"You're sure," said Rafe, no question in his voice.

She nodded stiffly. "The first storm began here."

"The first?"

"There were several, I think. Or was it just one long storm?"

She frowned intently, reaching for memories that vanished even as she touched them.

"I don't remember!" Then, more calmly, Alana said, "I don't remember."

She closed her eyes, hiding the shadows that haunted her.

When Alana finally opened her eyes again, she was living only in the present. Rafe and the two horses were waiting patiently. No one else was in sight.

"Where is everyone?" she asked.

"Over the next ridge. I told them we'd catch up later, if you felt well enough."

Distantly Alana wondered what the two dudes thought of her. A woman with strange moods. Hysterical.

Crazy.

The word kept ringing in Alana's mind, an interior thunder drowning out the rational words she kept trying to think of, to cling to.

"Am I crazy?" Alana wondered aloud, not realizing she had spoken. "Or does it matter? If sanity is terror, is there peace in madness? Or is there only greater terror?"

Abruptly Alana shuddered.

"You aren't crazy," Rafe said, his voice gentle and angry and sad. "Do you hear me, Alana? You aren't crazy. You've been beaten and terrified. You've seen your husband killed and you damn near died yourself. And then you were out of your head with shock and exposure. You've hardly eaten at all and slept even less since Broken Mountain."

Wide-eyed, Alana watched Rafe, feeling his words sink into her like sunlight.

"You aren't crazy," he said. "You're just at the end of your physical resources, driven right up to the edge of hallucination in order to keep reality at bay until you decide there's no choice but to face it."

Alana listened, heard the certainty of Rafe's voice, heard the state of her mind and body described so precisely in his deep tones.

"How did you know?" she asked achingly.

"It happens to people when they're pushed too hard, too long."

Slowly Alana shook her head. "Not to strong people. Like you. I used to think I was strong."

Rafe laughed. It was a harsh sound, almost cruel.

"Anyone can be broken, Alana. Anyone. I know. I saw it happen in Central America time and time again."

"Rafe," she whispered.

"They said that I died. For a long time I believed them. It was like dying, only worse. There was no end to it. And then it happened again here."

Alana searched Rafe's eyes and found emotions she had never seen in him before. Violence and hatred and a rage so deep it went all the way to his soul.

"What ... what happened in Central America?" asked Alana.

Rafe's expression changed, becoming remote, shutting down, shutting her out. The muscles in his jaw flexed and he spoke slowly, with a reluctance that told Alana more than his words.

"I've never told anyone. But I'll tell you. On Broken Mountain, I'll tell you. Unless ..." Rafe looked at her swiftly, concerned again. "Unless you want to turn back. I'll take you back, Alana. If that's what you want. Is that what you want?"

"I want to trust myself again, to trust my mind and my memory and my emotions," she said in a rush. "I want to be *me* again. And I want ..."

Rafe waited, an expression of restraint and longing drawing his face into taut planes and angular shadows.

"What do you want?" he asked softly.

"You," Alana said simply. "I was never more myself than when I was with you."

But even as she spoke, she was shaking her

head, not believing that what she wanted was possible.

Rafe held out his hand, palm up, not touching Alana but asking that she touch him. She put her palm lightly on his.

"I'm yours, wildflower," said Rafe. "I have been since I saw you on that exposed trail with a lame horse and lightning all around. You were brave then. You're even more brave now."

"I don't feel brave."

"You came back to Broken Mountain. You're honest with yourself, and with me. If that isn't courage, I don't know what is."

Rafe's voice was deep and sure, conviction reflected in every syllable and in the amber clarity of his eyes as he watched her, approving of her.

With fingers that shook slightly, Alana brushed away the tears that starred her eyelashes. Teardrops gleamed on her fingertips as she almost smiled at him.

"Thank you," she said.

"For telling the truth?" Rafe smiled sadly. "I have a lot more truths for you. But not now."

"What do you mean?"

"My truths wouldn't help you now. And that's what I want. To help you, and me. We'll heal each other and then the past will stay where it belongs. In the past. Memories, not nightmares."

Rafe held out his other hand, palm up.

Alana put her hand in his, felt the strong

pulse in his wrist beneath her touch, saw the glitter of tears transferred from her fingertips to his smooth, tanned skin. Unerringly, he found the pulse point of her wrists and rested lightly against it, savoring the strong flow of her life beneath his fingertips.

"Are you ready for the mountain?" asked Rafe softly.

Slowly Alana withdrew her palms, letting his touch caress her from wrists to fingertips.

"I'm ready," she whispered.

8

FOR THE REST OF THE TRIP, Rafe and Alana rode side by side when the trail permitted. When it didn't, Alana rode first. When pieces of the nightmare condensed around her, she looked over her shoulder to reassure herself that it was Rafe rather than Jack who followed her.

The fragments of nightmare and memory came unexpectedly, out of sequence, tormenting Alana because she couldn't be sure whether it was true memory or false nightmare that stalked her. When she heard Jack's voice raised in anger, she didn't know if it came from the far past or the recent past, or if the words were a creation of her own mind trying to fill in the six missing days.

Sometimes there was no doubt. The sound of wind through the aspens, the shiver of yellow leaves, the song sticking in her throat . . .

Those were real. Those she had heard before, seen before, felt before, and remembered only now. She and Jack had rested by the second lake, there, down by the glacier-polished boulder. They had drunk coffee from their individual canteens and watched trout fingerlings rise in the turquoise shallows.

Then the wind had come again, moving like a melancholy hand over the lake, stirring reflections into chaos, bringing the scent of the heights and storms boiling down.

Jack had watched the clouds seething around the lonely ridges. He had smiled. And he had said . . .

What had he said? Alana asked herself. Something about the land. Something. . . . Yes, that was it: *I always knew this country was good for something. I just never knew what.*

And then he had laughed.

Shivering, Alana drew an imaginary jacket around her shoulders. Sid stumbled slightly, jarring her into the present.

Alana loosened the reins, giving the horse more freedom. She looked over her shoulder. Rafe was there, riding the big Appaloosa stallion, his hat pulled low against the restless wind. She sensed his quick regard, his concern for her. She waved slightly, reassuring him that she was all right.

Other fragments of memory returned, hoofbeats following, wind twisting and booming between ridges, ice-tipped rain. An argument . . .

She and Jack had argued over something. The storm. And the fishing camp. She had wanted to stay at the Five Lakes Lodge until the storm passed. Jack had refused, even though the fishing camp's five buildings were deserted and looked as though they had been empty for years.

In the end Jack had won, but only because Alana couldn't bear to see the site of her greatest happiness standing blank-eyed and empty, cabin doors ajar and porches heaped with dead needles and random debris.

Everywhere she turned, she had seen shadows of Rafe. Every breath she drew had reminded her of the first time Rafe had made love to her, in the loft of the main cabin with a storm coming down, surrounding them. But she hadn't been afraid then. She had been an aspen shivering, and Rafe the mountain wind caressing her.

Sid snorted and shied as she came around the shoulder of an old landslide. Again, Alana was jarred out of the past. Bob was waiting there, riding the big bay mare that was his favorite.

"Everything okay?" asked Bob.

His dark glance roamed his sister's face, looking for and finding signs of strain.

"Yes," Alana said tightly.

"You don't look it," he said, blunt as only a brother can be.

"I'm remembering a few things. Little things."

"That's great!"

"Is it?" she countered quickly. Then, "Sorry. Of course it is."

"Have you told Rafe about remembering?"

Before Alana could answer, Bob was talking again, words rushing out in excitement and triumph.

"He was right!" Bob said, delight in every word. "He said you'd remember once you were here and knew it was safe. And neither doctor would let him go to Portland because—"

"*Burdette.*"

Rafe's whiplash voice stopped Bob's tumbling words.

Bob looked startled, then stricken. "Oh, God, I really stepped in it this time. Damn my big mouth anyway."

Rafe gave Bob a narrow glance that spoke volumes on the subject of loose lips and secrets.

Alana looked from Rafe to Bob, questions in her eyes, questions Rafe knew he would have to answer, questions whose answers she wasn't ready to hear. So he chose his truths and half-truths carefully.

"I told you I leaned on a few people to get you here," said Rafe.

Uncertainly, Alana nodded.

"When Merry couldn't be chief cook and tour guide, I thought of you," Rafe said. "It would be a perfect opportunity to get you back home, where you belonged."

Then Rafe looked toward Bob and spoke in a soft, cold voice. "Isn't that how you remember it, Burdette?"

"Rafe leaned like hell," Bob agreed, looking relieved. "Sis, you aren't mad, are you? I mean, about coming home? We just want what's right for you."

Alana sighed, caught as always by her affection for the brother who rarely had an unspoken thought.

"No, baby brother, I'm not mad. Maybe," she added, smiling crookedly, "I'm not even crazy."

Bob drew in his breath sharply. "Alana, what in hell gave you the idea that you were crazy?"

"What would you call it when someone runs scared from six missing days?"

"I'd call it shock," Rafe cut in smoothly. "Survival reflex. In a word, sanity."

He looked from Alana to Bob.

"Let's get to the camp," Rafe said. "That storm won't hold off forever."

There was an urgency in his voice that allowed no argument. He didn't want Alana to be caught in the open in a storm. Not now. She was off balance, easily startled, too tired. Too fragile.

She needed rest now, not a resurgence of nightmare and violence. It was enough that she had begun to remember. More than enough. He didn't want the past to rise up and rend the delicate fabric of trust binding her to him.

He didn't want her to remember too much, too soon. If she did, then he would lose her again. Only this time there would be no hope. She would be lost to him irrevocably, forever.

Don't remember all of it, wildflower, Rafe prayed silently. Not yet. Give us time to love again.

"Move it, Burdette," Rafe said aloud. "The storm won't wait much longer."

At Rafe's curt signal, Bob set a fast pace to the cabins. Rafe hoped that riding hard would keep Alana's mind in the present rather than in the nightmare he saw too often in her eyes.

Even after they reached the cabins, Rafe watched Alana without seeming to while she prepared supper. He saw no signs that the storm building outside the cabin was bothering her.

After dinner, Bob and Stan went to Janice's cabin for a round of poker and conversation. Alana didn't go. She spent as little time as possible near Stan.

Rafe, too, turned down the offer of cards. His excuse was the flies that needed to be tied for tomorrow's fishing. But he doubted Bob was fooled. He was certain Stan wasn't fooled. The cynical gleam in the big man's eyes said he knew Rafe wanted to be alone with Alana.

As Alana finished setting the table for tomorrow's breakfast, Rafe came back from turning off the generator for the night. He shrugged out of a yellow slicker that sparkled with rain. So far, the evening storm consisted mainly of fat drops randomly sprayed and distant mutters of thunder stalking elusive lightning.

Alana adjusted the wick on the kitchen light until it burned with a clear, steady glow. Rafe hung his slicker on a hook by the back door.

"Hope the dudes don't mind kerosene lamps," said Alana.

"So long as they can see the cards, they'll do just fine. Besides, it will nudge them into bed at a decent hour. Trout rise early. If you want to catch them, you'd better rise early, too."

Eyes the color of whiskey measured the signs of fatigue on Alana's face.

"You should think about going to bed," Rafe said.

"It's hardly even dark," she protested, despite the tiredness welling up in her.

She didn't want to be alone. Not yet. Not with lightning and thunder loose among the peaks.

"It won't be completely dark until nearly ten," Rafe said reasonably. "That's too late for you, if you're going to get up at five to cook breakfast. Tell you what, I'll do breakfast tomorrow. You sleep in."

"No," said Alana quickly. "You look like you haven't been sleeping too well, either. Besides, I came here to cook and that's what I'm going to do. If I get too tired, I'll take a nap tomorrow afternoon."

Rafe looked as though he was going to protest. Then he let out a long breath.

"Will the light bother you if I work down here for a while?" he asked.

Alana looked at the loft bedroom that was simply a partial second story. One "wall" of the room was a polished railing that prevented anyone from wandering out of bed and taking a fall to the living room floor. Curtains could be drawn across the opening of the loft, but that cut off the welcome currents of warmth rising from the hearth. Even though it was only the first week of September, the nights at sixty-three hundred feet crackled with the promise of winter.

"You won't bother me," said Alana. "I always sleep with the light on now."

Again, Rafe paused. Again, he said nothing, merely looked at Alana with eyes that saw everything, accepted everything, even her fear. Knowing that he didn't withdraw from or judge her gave Alana a small measure of acceptance of her own irrational feelings.

"Go to sleep, Alana. If you need anything, I'll be in the downstairs bedroom. So will Bob, unless he plays cards all night like a young fool." As Rafe turned toward the dining room, he added, "There's plenty of hot water for a bath."

The thought of a tub full of steaming water made Alana close her eyes and all but groan with pleasure.

"A hot bath. Damn. That's my idea of roughing it," she said emphatically.

Smiling, Rafe turned back to Alana. He leaned against the door between the living room and dining room.

"From what Dad told me, Mother and Grandmother felt the same way," Rafe said.

"How about you?"

"I'm not all that upset at having hot water," Rafe drawled. "Only thing that bothers me is that damn noisy generator. As for the rest, this is home for me. It took me a lot of years and pain to realize it, but it was worth it."

Slowly Rafe looked around the lodge, enjoying the vivid Indian blankets and brass camp lamps, the suede furniture and a fireplace big enough to stand in. Luxury and simplicity combined. The generator provided electricity for the refrigerator, the water pump, and the lights. The kitchen stove, which also heated water for the cabin, burned wood.

All that was lacking was telephone service. His father had taken care of that by adding a shortwave radio and a repeater on the nearby ridge. By tradition, though, the radio was reserved for emergencies.

Alana watched Rafe quietly, sensing his pleasure in his surroundings, a pleasure she shared. She had loved the Lazy W's lodge and cabins from the first time she saw them, when she and Rafe had raced a storm and lost. They had been drenched and laughing when they arrived.

They would have been cold, too, but the bright currents of passion that raced through them made a mockery of cold. He had started a fire in the hearth to dry their clothes. Then he had led her up to the loft and taught her about other kinds of fire, and the beauty that a man and a woman in love can bring to each other.

Alana blinked, coming back to the present, bringing with her part of the past's shimmering warmth. She saw Rafe watching her with hungry whiskey eyes, as though he knew what she had been thinking.

Or perhaps it was simply that Rafe, too, was remembering a storm and a loft and the woman he loved burning in his arms.

"I laid out your things in the bathroom," Rafe said.

"Thank you," Alana said, her voice almost husky.

Rafe nodded and turned away, leaving her alone.

The bath relaxed Alana, taking the soreness from her body and the tightness from her mind. When she pulled on the long, soft cotton nightgown and went up to the loft bedroom, Rafe was nowhere in sight.

The hearth fire was blazing hotly, ensuring that she wouldn't be chilled by the trip from the bathroom to bed. The bed itself had also been warmed. The metal warmer was still hot to the touch, the coals from the fireplace still glowing when she opened the lid. The covers had been turned down, inviting her to slide in and sleep deeply.

"Rafael," Alana said softly, though she

knew he couldn't hear. "Oh, Rafe, why does it have to be too late for us?"

There was no answer, unless the bed itself was an answer, a bridge between past and present, a promise of warmth and safety.

With a sigh, Alana discarded her robe and slid underneath the covers, pulling them up to her chin as she snuggled into the haven Rafe had so carefully prepared for her. Sleep came quickly.

So did dreams.

As the storm outside the cabin strengthened, dreams twisted into nightmares called by thunder and wind screaming from the ridge lines. A lake condensed around Alana . . . *a landscape subtly blurred, like water pushed by the wind. A glacier-polished boulder stood crookedly, laughing.*

Jack was laughing and the sound was colder than the wind.

Rain swirled, laughing, showing clear ice teeth, stirring water and rocks and trees until another lake condensed. Small, perfect, utterly real but for the shadows of terror flowing out of the trees.

Jack's arms reaching for her, his words telling her of desire and his eyes telling her of death. Jack holding her despite her struggles and then pain came, pain and terror and her screams tearing apart her world.

Alana woke with her heart pounding and her skin clammy. She was breathing in short, shallow bursts. She had recognized the third lake in her nightmare, but not the other lake, the beautiful lake surrounded by horror.

Jack, too, was new, unrecognizable, desire and death inextricably mixed. A raw nightmare, a horrible compound of today's memories and . . . what?

Truth? Imagination? Both? Neither? Alana asked herself frantically. Jack wanted me, yes, but only as the other half of Jack 'n' Jilly. He didn't want me as a woman.

And if he had, it wouldn't have mattered. I didn't want him. I never wanted any man but the one I loved and couldn't have. Rafael Winter. Jack didn't like it, but he finally accepted it—after I told him I would leave him if he ever touched me again.

Is that what we argued about on Broken Mountain?

Shivering, Alana wrapped her arms around her body and let reality condense around her once more. It was so long ago, all of it, on the far side of a six-day gap in her mind that might as well be eternity.

So far away and so futile. Jack was dead and she was not, not quite. She couldn't sing, she couldn't be touched, she couldn't love. But she was alive.

And so was Rafael Winter.

Lightning burst silently into the room, bleaching everything into shades of gray and a white so pure her eyes winced from it. Thunder came, but only slowly, telling of a storm retreating down the mountainside.

Taking a deep breath, Alana lay back once

more, trying to sleep. Even as her head
touched the pillow, she knew that it would be
futile. Her body was too loaded with adrenaline and the aftermath of nightmare to go back
to sleep right away.

She got up, barely feeling the chill. Her deep
green nightgown settled around her ankles.
The soft T-shirt material clung and flared as
she walked to the edge of the loft. The tiny
silver buttons that went from her collarbones
to her thighs sparkled like raindrops in the
muted light from the living room.

Below Alana, engrossed in the multicolored
materials spread before him on a table, Rafe
worked quietly. His back was to her, so she
couldn't see precisely what he was doing.

Alana hesitated long enough to be startled
by another burst of lightning. Then she went
quickly down the stairs. The battery-powered
clock over the mantel told her it was just after
eleven.

Though Alana would have sworn that she'd
made no noise, Rafe knew she was there.

"Take the chair that's closest to the fire,"
Rafe said without looking up from the small
vise in front of him.

Alana pulled out a chair and sat, careful not
to come between Rafe and the light radiating
from the kerosene lantern. He was focused on
a tiny hook held in a small vise. Silently, delicately, he tied an iridescent bit of feather to
the hook's shank using gossamer thread.

In the warm light Rafe's eyes were almost
gold, his lashes and hair nearly black. Horn-

rimmed half glasses sat partway down his nose, magnifying the work in front of him. Deft, tapered fingers handled special tweezers and dots of glue no bigger than the tip of a needle. He wound the thread once more around the shank of the hook, made a half hitch, tugged gently, and cut the thread.

"There are two schools of thought about fly-fishing," said Rafe as he picked up a delicate shaft of iridescent black feather. "One school is that you attract a trout by presenting it with something it's never seen before, something flashy but not frightening. Like this."

Rafe opened a small metal box. Inside were neat rows of flies, their sharp hooks buried in the wool fleece that lined the box. The fly that Rafe selected was nearly as long as his thumb. The colors were bright, a whimsical combination of blue, yellow, and rose that culminated in graceful silver streamers reminiscent of lacy wings.

"Now, Bob swears by this Lively Lady," Rafe said, neatly replacing the fly in its box. "And I admit to using it a time or two when the fishing was so bad I'd tried everything but a DuPont spinner."

"What's a DuPont spinner?"

"Dynamite," Rafe said dryly. "The Lively Lady is outrageous, but it's more sporting than shock waves."

"Does it work?" asked Alana, watching the play of light over the hair on the back of Rafe's hand.

"Only for Bob." Rafe smiled crookedly.

"The times I used it, you could hear the fish snickering all up and down the canyon."

Alana smiled and almost forgot to jump when lightning flicked again, washing the room with shards of white light. Rafe's deep, calm voice smoothed off the jagged edges of the night for her.

"What's the other kind of fly-fishing?" she asked.

"The kind that imitates natural conditions so exactly that the trout can't tell the difference," said Rafe.

His voice was casual yet reassuring, as though he sensed the fear that had driven Alana out of bed and downstairs to the table where he worked. He set aside the fly he had just tied and picked up a hook that already had been wound with mink-brown thread.

"Usually at this time of year, all you have left are larger, darker flying insects," Rafe said. "Most of the smaller bugs have all been killed off in the same frost that turned the aspens pure gold. I'm a little short on autumn flies, so I decided to do a few tonight."

As Rafe talked, his fingers searched delicately among the boxes. There were feathers and tiny, shimmering drifts of fur, as well as nylon and tinsel and Mylar threads of various thicknesses. It was as though he searched with his touch as well as his eyes, savoring the subtle differences in texture with skilled, sensitive fingertips.

There was no sense of hurry or frustration in Rafe's actions. If the thread he chose was stubborn or slippery, refusing to wrap neatly around the hook's shank, he didn't show any impatience. He simply smoothed everything into place and began again, his fingers sure, his expression calm, his mouth relaxed.

With eyes darker than the night, Alana watched Rafe's every movement. He had rolled up the sleeves of his navy-blue flannel shirt past his elbows. Dark hair shimmered and burned with gold highlights as his arms moved. Muscles tightened and relaxed, making light slide over his skin with each supple movement of his body. Beneath the skin, veins showed like dark velvet, inviting her fingers to trace the branching network of life.

"It's important to match environments precisely if you hope to lure a trout out of the depths of a lake or a river," said Rafe, tying a tiny bit of deep red feather to the body of the hook.

"Why?" Alana asked softly.

"It's so quiet down where they hide, safe and deepest blue. But being safe isn't enough for living things. They need more. They need to touch the sun. At least," Rafe added, smiling, "the special ones do."

Alana watched Rafe's face, her eyes wide and intent, feeling his words slide past the fear in her, sinking down into her core, promising her something for which she had no words, only a song that couldn't be sung.

"So my job is to tempt a special trout out of those safe, sterile depths," said Rafe. "To do that, I have to know what's happening around the fish. If dun-colored mayflies are flying, then a black gnat will be ignored by my special trout, no matter how beautifully the fly is tied or presented."

Deftly he added a radiant filament of black to the shank of the hook.

"You see," Rafe added softly, "my special trout is neither stupid nor foolish. It's unique and strong and wary. Yet it's hungry for the sun."

Tiny shafts of color shimmered as Rafe worked, feathers as fragile as they were beautiful. He handled them so gently that not a single filament was crushed or broken.

When he had taken whatever tiny contribution he needed for the fly he was making, his fingers smoothed the remaining feather, making each iridescent shaft into a graceful arch once more. Tufts of color curled and clung to his fingertips as though thanking him for understanding their delicacy and beauty.

Alana closed her eyes and let memories rise, welcoming them the way a flower welcomes sunlight. Rafe had touched her like that the first time, his strength balanced with his understanding of her innocence.

And she had responded, sighing and curling around him, clinging to his fingertips while his lips feathered across her breasts until she sang a love song that was his name. He had called to her in return, the exquisite beauty of his hands caressing her until she knew nothing but him, felt nothing but ecstasy shivering through her as she sang his name.

Then he had come to her like gentle lightning, moving deeply until she learned what it was to die and be reborn in the arms of the man she loved.

To be touched like that again, exquisitely . . .

Alana shivered deep inside herself, a tiny ripple that was reflected in the subtle color high in her cheeks.

Glancing up, Rafe saw the faint flush and rapid pulse beating just above the soft emerald neckline of Alana's nightgown. For an instant his fingers tightened and the color of his eyes became a smoky amber fire.

Then he forced himself to concentrate again on his work, knowing it wasn't time yet. He must be patient or he would frighten her back into the bleak safety of withdrawal from memory, from life.

From him.

Alana's brief, ragged breath sounded like fire flickering inside the glass cage of the kerosene lamp. She opened her eyes and watched Rafe, wanting to touch him, to savor the textures of his hair and skin as delicately as he was savoring the materials with which he tied flies.

Yet if she did, he would touch her in return and she would be afraid. Then she would despise herself for her fears.

"Dad never used flies," said Alana, her voice husky as she searched for a safe topic. "Worms or metal lures only. Spinning rods. That's what I was raised with."

"A lot of people prefer them," Rafe said.

His voice was calm, neutral, demanding nothing of her.

"But you don't?"

Rafe smiled slightly as he tied another tiny piece of feather onto the mink-brown body of the fly.

"I prefer the special fish, the shy and elusive one hiding deep in the secret places known only to trout," he said. "To tempt that trout out of the depths and into the sunlight will require all my skill and patience and respect."

He turned a feather, letting light wash over it from various angles, admiring the play of color.

"But wouldn't it be easier to fish down deep rather than to try and lure the trout to the surface?" asked Alana, watching Rafe intently.

"Easier, yes. But easy things have so little value."

Rafe looked up at Alana over the dark rims of his glasses. His eyes were gold, as hot as the flame burning in the lantern.

"The trout should want the fisherman," he said. "Otherwise it's a simple exercise in meat hunting. I want to create a lure so perfect that only a very special trout will rise to it."

"And die," Alana said, her voice almost harsh.

"No," Rafe said very softly. "My hooks have no barbs."

Alana's eyes widened. She looked at the hooks set out on the table, flies finished and half finished and barely begun. Each hook was a clean, uncluttered curve, not a single barb to tear at the flesh. She looked back up into Rafe's amber eyes and felt the breath stop in her throat.

"Would you like to learn how to fly-fish?" he asked.

While he waited for an answer, he turned a golden pheasant feather in the lamplight, making color run in iridescent waves over the shaft.

"I'd be all thumbs," said Alana.

Rafe laughed softly and shook his head. "Not you."

She held out her hands as though to convince him of her awkwardness. Slowly he ran the feather from her wrists to her palms to her fingertips, stroking her with the delicacy of a sigh, seeing her response in the slight tremor of her fingertips.

"Your hands are just right," Rafe said. "Graceful and long and very, very sensitive."

Alana's breath came in raggedly as she saw Rafe's expression. She knew that he was remembering being touched by her, the sensual contrast of her hands against the male contours of his body, the heat and pleasure she had brought to him.

"You'll enjoy it," continued Rafe softly. "I promise you."

"I—yes," Alana said quickly, before she could change her mind and be afraid again. "After breakfast?"

"After breakfast."

Rafe turned his attention to the hook in his

vise. He released the hook and carefully buried the sharp tip in the fleece-lined box.

"Can you sleep now," he asked, "or would you like me to sit next to your bed for a while?"

Then he looked up, catching and holding Alana's glance with his own.

"I wouldn't touch you unless you asked me to," Rafe said. "And I don't expect you to ask."

"I know," Alana said, her voice low.

And she did. She trusted him.

The realization sent a quiver of light through the dark pool that fear and amnesia had made in the depths of her mind.

"Would you mind staying with me?" she whispered. "For just a few minutes? I know it's childish—"

"Then we're both children," said Rafe easily, cutting across her words, "because I'd rather sit with you than be alone."

Alana brushed his mustache with her fingertips.

"Thank you," she breathed.

The touch was so light, it was almost more imagined than real. Yet she felt it all the way to her knees.

And so did he. His eyes were tawny, reflecting the dance of flame from the lamp.

"My pleasure," Rafe said.

Then he looked away from Alana, not wanting her to see his hunger.

"Go upstairs before you get cold," Rafe said. "I'll clean up here."

"Can I help?"

"No. It will just take a minute."

Alana hesitated, then turned away as Rafe began deftly sorting materials and stacking small boxes onto a tray.

But as soon as she no longer watched him, Rafe looked up, ignoring the brilliant materials at his fingertips. Motionless, entirely focused on Alana, he watched as she climbed up the narrow stairs to the loft.

The glossy black of her hair caught and held the lamplight like stars reflected in a wind-ruffled midnight lake. The green of her night-gown clung and shifted, revealing and then concealing the womanly curves beneath. Her bare feet looked small, graceful, oddly vulnerable beneath the swirling folds of cloth.

Silently, savagely, Rafe cursed Jack Reeves.

9

ALANA OPENED THE CAST-
iron stove door, using a pot holder that had
been crocheted by Rafe's grandmother. Inside
the belly of the stove, a neat pattern of wood
burned brightly, sending vivid orange flames
licking at the thick iron griddle above.

"So far, so good," Alana muttered.

She closed the door, adjusted the vent,
dipped her fingers into a saucer of water, and
flicked drops on the griddle. Water hissed and
danced whitely across the griddle's searing
black surface.

"Perfect."

The kitchen was washed in the golden
warmth of a kerosene lamp, for it was at least

147

half an hour until dawn. The smell of bacon and coffee permeated the lodge and spread through the crisp air to the other cabins, prodding everyone out of bed.

From just outside the kitchen door came the clean, sharp sound of Rafe splitting wood for the stove. It was a strangely peaceful sound, a promise of warmth and a reminder that Rafe wasn't far away.

The rhythm of a song began to sift through Alana's mind, working its way down to her throat. She hummed almost silently, not knowing what she did. It was only the barest thread of sound, more a hope of song than song itself.

Alana picked up the pitcher of pancake batter and poured creamy circles onto the griddle. When the bubbles burst and batter didn't run in to fill the hollows, she flipped each pancake neatly. Soon she had several stacks warming at the back of the stove next to the thick slices of bacon she had already cooked and set aside.

As she poured more batter onto the griddle, she sensed someone walking up behind her.

"I don't need any more wood yet, Rafe," Alana said, setting aside the pitcher as she turned around. "Not until I—*oh!*"

It was Stan, not Rafe, who had come up behind Alana. Reflexively she took a step backward, forgetting about the hot stove.

"Watch out!" said Stan, reaching toward her automatically, trying to prevent her from being burned.

Alana flinched away, bringing the back of her hand into contact with the cast-iron stove. She made a sound of pain and twisted aside, evading Stan's touch at the cost of burning herself again. Again, he reached for her, trying to help.

"Don't touch her."

Rafe's voice was so cold, so savage, that Alana almost didn't recognize it.

Stan did, though. He stepped back instantly. When his blue eyes assessed the fear on Alana's face, he stepped back even more, giving her all the room she needed.

"What in hell do you think you're doing?" demanded Rafe.

His voice was flat and low, promising violence. The stove wood he had carried inside fell into the wood box with a crash that was startling in the charged silence.

Though Rafe hadn't made a move toward Stan, the blond man backed up all the way to the door between the dining room and the kitchen before he spoke.

"Sorry," muttered Stan. "Bob and I thought Alana might need help with . . . whatever."

"Bob and you? Christ," snarled Rafe. "That's an idiots' duet if ever there was one."

Stan flushed. "Now look here, Winter."

"Go tell Bob that if Alana needs the kind of *help* that you had in mind, I'll be the first one to suggest it. Got that?"

Stan's mouth flattened, but he nodded his head curtly, accepting Rafe's command.

"That was your free one," Rafe said grimly. "Do you read me?"

Again, Stan nodded curtly.

Rafe turned his back on Stan and went to Alana. He held out his hand.

"Let me see your burn," Rafe said softly.

The change in his voice was almost shocking. Warm, gentle, reassuring, it seemed impossible that the words came from the same man who had flayed Stan to the bone with a few razor phrases.

"It's all right, wildflower," murmured Rafe. "I won't hurt you."

With a long, shuddering release of breath, Alana held out her burned hand to Rafe.

He looked at the two red bars where her skin had touched the stove and felt rage like raw lightning scoring his gut. Turning on his heel, he went to the refrigerator and pulled out a handful of ice. He dampened a kitchen towel, wrapped the ice, and held it out to Alana.

"Put this over the burns," he said gently. "It will take away the pain."

Numbly Alana did as Rafe said. Within seconds the pain from the seared flesh was gone.

"Thank you," she said, sighing. Then, "It seems that I'm always thanking you."

He took the spatula from Alana and scraped off the pancakes that had begun to burn.

"Funny," Rafe muttered, "it seems that I'm always hurting you."

"It wasn't your fault. It wasn't Stan's, either. It was my own foolishness," said Alana.

"Bullshit," Rafe said in a clipped voice.

He scraped charred batter off the griddle with short, vicious strokes.

"You wouldn't be here if it wasn't for me," he said, "and neither would Stan."

Alana was too surprised to say anything.

With a disgusted sound, Rafe threw the spatula onto the counter and turned to Alana. His eyes were nearly black with the violence of his emotions.

"Forgive me?" he asked simply.

"There's nothing to forgive."

"I wish to Christ that was true."

Abruptly Rafe turned back to the stove and began greasing the griddle.

"I'll finish cooking breakfast," he said.

"But—"

"Sit down and keep those burns covered. They aren't bad, but they'll hurt unless you leave the ice on for a while."

Alana sat on the kitchen stool and watched Rafe covertly. He cooked as he did everything, with clean motions, nothing wasted, everything smooth and sure. The stacks of pancakes grew.

By the time everyone was seated in the dining room, there were enough pancakes to feed twice as many people as were around the table. At least it seemed like that, until everyone began to eat. The altitude and crisp air combined to double everyone's appetite.

Even Alana ate enough to make her groan. At Rafe's pointed suggestion, Bob did the dishes. Stan insisted on helping, as did Janice.

Rafe set out fishing gear while Alana packed lunches.

There were still a few stars out when Rafe led the two dudes to a stretch of fishing water and gave advice on the most effective lures and techniques to use in the extraordinarily clear water.

When Bob turned to follow Rafe and Alana back up the trail, Rafe gave him a long look.

"I promised to teach Alana how to fly-fish," Rafe said. "For that, she definitely doesn't need an audience."

"I won't laugh," said Bob, his lips quirked around a smile. "Much."

"You won't laugh at all," Rafe said smoothly, "because you're not going to be around."

Bob looked quickly at Alana, but she shook her head. He shrugged and accepted the fact that he wasn't going fishing with his older sister.

"Oh, well," Bob said. "I promised Stan I'd show him how to use the Lively Lady. Bet we catch more than you do."

"You'd better," retorted Alana. "Rafe uses barbless hooks. If we're going to eat trout, it's up to you, baby brother."

"Barbless?" asked Bob, giving Rafe a swift look. "Since when?"

"Since I was old enough to shave."

"Hell of a way to fish," Bob said, turning away. "A man could starve."

"Fishing is more than a way to feed your rumbling gut," pointed out Rafe.

"Depends on how hungry you are, doesn't it?" retorted Bob over his shoulder as he walked down the trail.

"Or what you're hungry for," added Rafe softly.

He turned to Alana.

"Ready?" he asked.

"Um . . ."

"I've got a spot picked out by the lake. Lots of room and nothing to tangle your line on the back stroke."

"You're assuming that I'll get enough line out to tangle," Alana said, smiling wryly.

Rafe's soft laughter mixed perfectly with the sound of the stream flowing along the trail.

Though the sun hadn't yet cleared the ridges, predawn light sent a cool radiance over the land, illuminating the path and making boulders look as though they had been wrapped in silver velvet. In the deep pools where water didn't seethe over rocks, trout rose, leaving behind expanding, luminous rings.

Silently, letting the serenity of the land and the moment seep into Alana, Rafe led her to a narrow finger of glacier-polished granite that almost divided the lake into two unequal parts. As she stepped out onto the rock shelf, Rafe touched Alana's shoulder and pointed across the lake.

A doe and two half-grown fawns moved gracefully to the water. While the fawns drank, the doe stood guard. Beyond them the granite face of Broken Mountain flushed pink beneath the gentle onslaught of dawn. The sky was utterly clear, a magic crystal bell ready to ring with exquisite music at the first touch of sunlight.

The doe and fawns retreated, breaking the spell. Alana let out her breath in a long sigh.

Rafe watched her for an instant longer, then began assembling his fishing rod.

"Have you ever used a fly rod before?" he asked.

"No."

Alana watched intently as the long, flexible rod took shape before her eyes.

"I've always wondered how a fly rod works," she admitted. "With spinning rods, the weight of the lure is used to pull line off the reel. But there's no weight worth mentioning in a fly."

"With fly rods, the weight of the line itself is what counts," Rafe said. "The leader and the lure barely weigh anything. They can't. Otherwise they land with a plop and a splash and scare away any fish worth catching."

Using a smooth, complicated knot, he tied a nearly weightless fly onto the thin, transparent leader. Then he pulled a length of thick fly line off the reel, showing her the line's weight.

"Handled correctly, the fly line will carry the fly and set it down on the water as lightly as if the fly really had wings," Rafe said. "The point is to mimic reality as perfectly as possible. The leader is transparent and long enough that the fish doesn't associate the heavy fly line lying on the surface with the tasty insect floating fifteen feet away."

Alana looked at the opaque, thick fly line.

"If you say so," she said dubiously.

"See that fish rising at about two o'clock?" asked Rafe.

She looked beyond Rafe's hand to an expanding ring. It was at least fifty feet out in the lake.

"Yes, I see it."

"Watch."

With his right hand, Rafe held the butt of the fly rod near the point where the reel was clamped on. With his left hand, he stripped line off the reel. As he did so, his right hand began to move the rod forward and back in a smooth, powerful arc.

Kinetic energy traveled up the rod's supple length, bending it with easy, whiplike motions, pulling line from the reel up through the guides. With each coordinated movement of Rafe's arm, line leaped out from the tip of the rod, more line and then more, until it described fluid curves across the luminous sky.

Silently, smoothly, powerfully, Rafe balanced the forces of line and rod, strength and timing, gravity and flight, until an impossibly long curve of line hung suspended between sky and water. Then he allowed the curve to uncurl in front of him, becoming a straight line with the fly at its tip.

Gently, gently, the fly settled onto the water precisely in the center of the expanding ring left by the feeding trout. Not so much as a ripple disturbed the surface from the fly's descent. It was as though the fly had condensed out of air to float on the dawn-tinted mirror of the lake.

And then there was a silver swirl and water boiling as the trout rose to the fly.

The rod tip lashed down at the same instant that Rafe began pulling line in through the guides with his left hand. The supple rod danced and shivered as the trout tail-walked across the dawn like a flashing silver exclamation point.

Line slid through Rafe's fingers, drawn by the trout's power. But slowly, gently, the line returned, drawn by his sensitive fingers, until finally the trout swam in short curves just off the granite shelf, tethered to Rafe by an invisibly fine length of leader.

Just as the first rays of sunlight poured over the lake, the trout leaped again. Colors ran down its sleek side, forming the iridescent rainbow that gave the fish its name.

In reverent silence, Rafe and Alana admired the beauty swimming at their feet. It would have been a simple matter for Rafe to unhook the net at his belt, guide the fish into the green mesh, and lift it from the water. Instead, Rafe gave an expert flick of his wrist that removed the hook from the cartilage lining the trout's mouth.

There was a moment of startled stillness, then water swirled as the trout flashed away.

"See how easy it is?" murmured Rafe, watching Alana with eyes as luminous as dawn. "It's your turn now."

* * *

For what seemed like the hundredth time, Alana stripped line from the fat reel, positioned her hand to feed line from reel to rod, lifted her right arm, and began the forward and backward motion that was supposed to send line shooting up through the guides on the rod.

As she stroked the rod forward and back, line inched up through the guides and started to form the lovely, fluid curve that was the signature of fly-fishing.

And then the curve collapsed into an ungainly pile of line on the rock shelf behind Alana.

"I waited too long on the forward stroke, didn't I?" Alana muttered. "All the energy that was supposed to hold up the line went *ffft.*"

"But you got out nearly twice as much line," pointed out Rafe, his voice and smile encouraging her.

"And before that, I broke three hooks on the rock, hooked myself on the back stroke, hooked you on the back stroke, lashed the water to a froth on the forward stroke, tied ruinous knots in your beautiful leader, and in general did everything but strangle myself on the fly line."

Alana shook her head, torn between frustration and rueful laughter. Rafe had been incredibly patient. No matter how many times the line or the leader snarled hopelessly, he had neither laughed at her nor gotten angry. He had been gentle, reassuring, and encouraging. He had praised her and told funny stories about the monumental tangles he used to make when he was learning how to fly-fish.

"Alana," said Rafe softly, capturing her attention. "You're doing better than I did the first time I had eight feet of limber rod and fifty feet of fly line in my hands."

She grimaced. "I don't believe it. I feel so damn clumsy."

"You aren't. You're as graceful as that doe."

"Outrageous flattery," she said, smiling, "will get more knots tied in your line."

Alana positioned the rod again. "Here goes nothing."

Not quite nothing. A rather impressive snarl came next. Rafe untangled it with the same patience he had displayed for the last hour.

As he turned the rod over to Alana once more, he hesitated.

"If it wouldn't bother you," Rafe said quietly, "I could stand behind you, hold on to your wrist, and let you get the feeling of the timing. And that's all it is. Timing. There's no real strength involved. Fly-fishing is a matter of finesse, not biceps."

Alana nibbled on her lower lip as she eyed the deceptively simple appearance of fly rod and reel.

"All right," she said. "Let's give your way a try. Mine sure hasn't done much."

Rafe stepped into position behind Alana. Less than an inch separated them, for he had to be able to reach around her to guide the rod. He stood for several moments without touching her, letting her get used to his presence very close behind her.

"Okay so far?" he asked casually.

"Yes. . . . Just knowing that you understand how I feel makes it easier," Alana admitted in a low voice.

She took a deep breath. The mixed scents of high-country air and sunshine and Rafe swept over her. His warmth was a tingling sensation from her shoulders to her knees. She felt his breath stir against the nape of her neck, sensed the subtle movements of his chest as he breathed, the slight catch of his flannel shirt against hers.

"Ready?" asked Rafe.

Alana nodded, afraid to trust her voice. The breathlessness she felt had little to do with her fear of being touched.

"Take up the rod," he said.

She lifted the fly rod into position.

"I'm going to put my hand around your wrist and the rod at the same time," said Rafe. "Okay?"

She took a deep breath. "Okay."

He reached around Alana until his hand covered hers and wrapped around the rod.

The contrast of his tanned skin against her hand was arresting. It reminded Rafe of just how smooth Alana's skin was, how pale where the sun had never touched it, how incredibly soft when she had welcomed his most intimate caresses.

For an instant Rafe closed his eyes and thought of nothing at all.

"All right so far?" he asked.

His voice was too husky, but there was nothing he could do about that any more than he could wholly control the growing ache and swelling of his desire.

"Yes."

Alana's breath drew out the word until it was almost a sigh. The warmth and strength of Rafe's fingers curling around her hand fascinated her. She wanted to bend her head and brush her lips over his fingers. Just the thought of feeling his skin beneath her mouth made liquid fire twist through her.

Rafe took a quiet breath and hoped that Alana had no idea of how her closeness threatened his carefully imposed self-control.

"Now, remember," he said. "The rod is only supposed to move in the arc between ten and two on our imaginary clock. That's where the greatest power and balance are. You go above or below that and you'll get in trouble. Ready?"

Alana nodded.

Rafe guided her arm and the rod through the short arc between ten and two, counting softly as he did.

"*One*, two, three, four. Now *forward*, two, three, four. And *back*, two, three, four."

Smoothly, easily, the rhythm flowed from Rafe to Alana and then to the rod. She felt the energy curl up the length of the rod, pulling line through the guides, bending the rod tip at the end of the arc. Then came the soft hiss of line shooting up and back over her shoulder just before the rod came forward smoothly, energy pouring up its length on the forward stroke, fly line shooting out magically, Rafe's voice murmuring, counting, energy and line pulsing along the rod.

Alana felt the rhythm take her until she forgot everything but Rafe's voice and his warmth and the line suspended in curving beauty above the silver lake.

And still the rhythm continued, unvarying, serene and yet exciting, line pulsing out like a soundless song shimmering, lyrics sung in silence and written in liquid arcs curving across the dawn.

"Now," murmured Rafe, bringing the rod forward and stopping it precisely at ten o'clock. "Let it go."

Line hissed out in a long, ecstatic surge. Gracefully, delicately, the fly line, leader, and fly became a part of the lake. Not so much as a ripple marred the perfect surface of the water at the joining.

Alana let out a long breath, enthralled by the beauty of the line uncurling, the sweeping blend of energy and rhythm, the timeless consummation of line and lure and silver water.

"That was ... incredible," she said softly. "Thank you, Rafe."

"What for?"

"For your patience. For teaching and sharing this with me."

Rafe felt the shifting surface of Alana's body against his as she sighed. He wanted to close his arms around her, enfolding her. He wanted to feel her flow along his body as she fitted herself against him.

At the very least, he wanted to be able to trace the velvet edge of her hairline with the tip of his tongue, inhaling the sunlight and womanly scent of her, testing the resilience of her flesh with gentle pressures of his teeth.

Ruthlessly Rafe suppressed the hunger that pulsed through him, tightening his body with each heartbeat, drawing it upon a rack of passion.

"You're a joy to teach," Rafe said in a quiet voice. "You should take it easy for a while, though. You're using muscles you didn't know you had. Why don't we just sit in the sun and be lazy? There's a patch of grass and wildflowers farther up the lake."

"Sounds wonderful," said Alana.

As she spoke, she stretched the muscles in her shoulders by twisting them from side to side. She didn't hear the subtle intake of Rafe's breath as she accidentally rubbed against him when she straightened again.

"But aren't you supposed to be helping the dudes, too?" Alana asked.

"They know one end of a fishing rod from the other."

Rafe took the fly rod from Alana, removed the hook, and wound in the line. He began breaking the rod into its component parts with quick movements of his hands, working with an economy and expertise born of long familiarity.

Alana watched Rafe's skilled fingers and the

flex of tendons beneath the rolled-up sleeves of his navy flannel shirt.

"The dudes aren't what I expected," she said.

Rafe looked up suddenly. His whiskey glance pinned her.

"What do you mean?" he asked quietly.

The intensity of his voice belied the softness of his tone.

"Stan's looks, for one thing," Alana said, shrugging. "I'm having a hard time getting used to seeing Jack's ghost. Poor Stan. He must think I'm more than a little unwrapped."

"He'll survive," said Rafe unsympathetically.

"I know. It's just a bit awkward." Alana sighed. "He and Janice have been such easy guests. They don't complain. They don't expect to be waited on. They're funny and smart and surprisingly fit."

Rafe made a neutral sound.

"Not many people could have ridden the trail to Broken Mountain one day and popped out of bed the next morning ready to slay dragons—or even trout," Alana said dryly.

Rafe shrugged.

"And no matter how strange I act," Alana said, "the two of them take it in stride. Even Stan, when I literally ran screaming from him, acted as though it was his fault, not mine."

Rafe said something savage under his breath.

Abruptly Alana laughed. "I guess the dudes are as unusual as the dude ranch."

"Luck of the draw," he said tersely.

With quick motions Rafe slipped the rod into its carrying case.

"The fact that these good sports are your friends has more to do with it than luck," retorted Alana.

Rafe's eyes narrowed into topaz lines. "What are you hinting at?"

"I know what you're doing, Rafe."

"And what is that?" he asked softly.

"You're helping Bob get started."

Rafe said nothing.

"You know how much he needs cash to buy out Sam and Dave," Alana persisted, "and you know Bob doesn't want to destroy the land to make a quick cash killing. So you beat the bushes for friends who could help Bob launch a dude ranch."

Rafe grunted.

"Don't worry," added Alana quickly, resting her hand for an instant on Rafe's arm, "I won't say anything to Bob. I just wanted you to know that I appreciate what you're doing for him. He's got four left feet and he keeps them in his mouth most of the time, but he's a good man and I love him."

With a long, soundless sigh, Rafe let out the breath he had been holding. He smiled ruefully at Alana as he packed away the last of the fishing gear.

But Rafe said nothing about Bob, neither confirming nor denying her conclusions.

In companionable silence, Alana and Rafe walked along the margin of the lake, skirting boulders and gnarled spruces. Spring and summer had come late to the high country this year. Wildflowers still bloomed in the sheltered places, making windows of color against the pale outcroppings of granite. Delicate, tenacious, radiant with life, drifts of wildflowers softened the harsh edges of rock and stark blue sky.

At the head of the third lake, a broad cascade seethed over slick rocks into the shallows. The cascade drained the second, higher lake in the chain. That lake was invisible behind the rocky shoulder of Broken Mountain.

The cascade itself was a pale, shining ribbon of white that descended the granite slope in a breathtaking series of leaps. The sun was more than halfway to noon, pouring transparent warmth and light over the bowl where the third lake lay.

Rafe stopped in a small hollow that was a hundred feet from the cascade. Evergreens so dark they were almost black formed a natural windbreak. Topaz aspens burned in the sunlight and quivered at the least movement of air, as though the trees were alive and breathing with tiny, swift breaths.

Rafe pulled a waterproof tarp from his pack. Silver on one side, deepest indigo on the other, the tarp could gather or scatter heat, whichever was required. He put the dark, heat-absorbent side up, knowing that the ground was cool despite the sun. Spread out, the tarp made an inviting surface for two people to eat or sleep on comfortably.

"Hungry?" asked Rafe, lifting Alana's pack off her shoulders.

Alana was about to say no when her stomach growled its own answer.

With an almost soundless chuckle, Rafe went to his backpack. Quickly he pulled out a snack of apples, hard-boiled eggs, and chocolate raisins.

Alana's stomach made insistent noises. She looked chagrined.

"It's the air," said Rafe reassuringly, concealing a smile.

"If I do everything my stomach tells me to, I won't be able to fit into my clothes," she grumbled.

"Then buy new ones," he suggested, uncapping a canteen full of cold tea. "Ten more pounds would look good on you."

"You think so?" she asked dubiously.

"I know so."

"My costume designer is always telling me to lose more weight."

"Your costume designer is as full of crap as a Christmas goose."

Rafe divided the food between Alana and himself.

She smiled blissfully. "In that case, I'll have another handful of chocolate raisins."

"What about me?" asked Rafe, his voice plaintive and his eyes brilliant with amusement.

"You," she said with a sideways glance, "can have my hard-boiled egg."

Rafe laughed aloud and pushed his pile of

chocolate raisins over to Alana's side of the tarp. He left her egg in place. But when Alana reached for the new pile of sweets, he covered it swiftly.

"Nope," he said, smiling at her. "Not until you eat the egg and the apple."

"Slave driver."

"Count on it," said Rafe.

He bit into his own apple with a hearty crunching sound.

They ate slowly, enjoying flavors heightened by clean air and healthy appetites. When she had eaten the last chocolate raisin, Alana sighed and stretched luxuriously. The exuberant splash of the cascade formed a soothing layer of sound between her and the rest of the world. Nothing penetrated but Rafe's occasional low-voiced comments about fly-fishing and ranching, and the silky feel of high-country sunshine.

"Why don't you take a nap?" he suggested finally.

Alana caught herself in mid-yawn. "There's something sinful about taking a nap before noon."

"In that case, let's hear it for sin." Rafe smiled crookedly. "Go ahead, wildflower. You didn't get enough sleep last night, or a lot of nights before that."

He unbuttoned his flannel shirt, revealing a dark blue T-shirt beneath. With a few quick motions, he shaped the thick flannel shirt into a pillow.

"Here," Rafe said to Alana. "Use this. I don't need it."

Alana tried to object but couldn't get any words past the sudden dryness in her mouth.

Even in her dreams, Rafe had not looked so overwhelmingly male. The T-shirt defined rather than concealed the slide and coil of muscles. With every movement Rafe made, every breath he took, his tanned skin stretched over a body whose latent power both shocked and fascinated her.

Suddenly Alana wanted to touch Rafe, to trace every ridge and swell of flesh, to know again the compelling male textures of his body.

She closed her eyes but still she saw Rafe, sunlight sliding over his skin, sunlight caressing him, sunlight burning in his eyes and her blood.

"Alana?" Rafe's voice was sharp with concern.

"You're right," Alana said in a shaky voice. "I haven't been getting enough sleep."

Rafe watched as she stretched out on the tarp, her cheek against the shirt he had rolled up for her. He would rather she had used his lap as a pillow, but was afraid if he suggested it, the relaxed line of her lips would tighten with tension and fear.

Yet for a moment, when Alana had looked at him as though she had never seen him before, Rafe had hoped . . .

"Better?" he asked, watching Alana's body relax into deep, even breathing.

"Yes."

"Then sleep, wildflower. I'm here."

Alana sighed and felt herself spiraling down into a sleep where no nightmares waited.

10

WHEN ALANA WOKE UP, the sun was on the other side of noon. She rolled over sleepily and realized that she was alone.

"Rafe?"

No one answered.

She sat up and looked around. Through the screen of evergreens and aspens she saw Rafe outlined against blue water. He had found another rock shelf leading out into the lake. He was standing at the end of the granite finger. The fly rod was in his hands. Line was curling exquisitely across the sky.

For a few moments Alana watched, captured by the grace of the man and the moment when line drifted soundlessly down to lie upon still water.

Except Alana couldn't actually see the line touch the surface of the lake, because trees blocked her view.

She stood up and started toward the shoreline, then realized that once Rafe saw her, he would probably stop fishing and start teaching her once again. She wasn't ready for that. She felt too relaxed, too at peace—and too lazy—to attempt anything that required concentration.

What she really wanted to do was to sit quietly, watching Rafe and the lyric sweep of line against the high-country sky.

Alana looked back down the lakeshore to where she and Rafe had been earlier. She saw no place to sit and watch him that wouldn't immediately bring her into Rafe's view.

She looked left to the cascade dancing whitely down rocks turned black by water. Rafe was facing away from the cascade, looking down the lake toward the cabins. The position gave him a hundred feet in front of the fly rod and an equal amount in back without anything to obstruct the motion of the line.

And he was using every bit of that two hundred feet.

On tiptoe, Alana peered through the wind-twisted branches of a fir, holding her breath as the curve of the fly line grew and grew, expanding silently, magically. Rafe's left arm worked in perfect counterpoint to his right as he stripped line off the reel, almost throwing fly line up through the guides as his right arm pumped smoothly, sending energy coursing through the rod.

"How are you doing that?" muttered Alana, knowing Rafe couldn't hear her. "You aren't a magician, are you?"

She stepped farther to her left, but she still couldn't see exactly what Rafe was doing to make the line lengthen so effortlessly. With a small, exasperated sound, she worked her way along the increasingly rugged shoreline, trying to find a spot that would allow her to watch Rafe without being seen.

Alana leaped from stone to stone, avoiding the small boggy spots where coarse grass and tiny flowers grew, until she found herself confronted by the barrier of the cascade. She turned around and looked back at Rafe, who was about sixty yards away from her by now.

Unfortunately, she still couldn't see what he was doing with his hands. Nor could she go any farther forward without coming up against the cascade. She could either go back, or she could go up the boulder-tumbled slope.

With a muttered word, Alana looked at the jumble of stone rising on either side of the frothing water. She wouldn't have to go very far up the cascade to get the view she wanted. Just far enough to allow her to look over Rafe's shoulder, as it were. If she didn't get too close to the water, the climb wouldn't be too hard. Besides, she had been raised hiking and scrambling along mountain rivers and up steep slopes.

Alana turned and began climbing over the lichen-studded boulders. Twenty feet away, the cascade churned and boiled, making both mist and a cool rushing thunder. She avoided the slippery rocks, seeking the dry ones.

Within a few minutes she was breathless, gaining two feet in height for every foot forward. She persisted anyway, scrambling and balancing precariously, until she stood on a ledge of granite that was barely eighteen inches deep.

She stopped because there was no other choice. In front of her rose a slick outcropping of rock six feet high, and not a handhold in sight.

"Well, this had better be far enough."

When Alana turned to look, it felt like the earth was dropping away beneath her feet. Unexpected, overwhelming, a fear of heights froze her in place.

Twenty feet away, the cascade frothed down the steep mountainside, water seething and racing, white and thunder, and wind whipping drops of water across her face like icy rain. Thunder and ice and the world falling away, leaving her *helpless, spinning, darkness reaching up for her*.

Alana clung to the rough face of the granite and closed her eyes, struggling to separate nightmare and memory and reality.

The feeling of falling didn't stop. The boom of water over rock became remembered thunder. Drifting spray became ice-tipped winds

and her screams were lightning as memory
and nightmare and reality became one.

Cold.
God, it was cold, cold all the way to the center
of the earth. Jack with anger twisting his face. Jack
cursing her, grabbing her, hitting her, and the
storm breaking, trees bending and snapping like
glass beneath the wind.

Like her. She wasn't strong enough. She would
break and the pieces would be scattered over the
cold rocks.

Running.
Scrambling.
Breath like a knife in her side. Throat on fire with
screams and the storm chasing her, catching her,
yanking her backward while rocks like fists hit her,
bruising her, and she screamed, clawing and fight-
ing.

But she was swept up, lifted high, helpless, noth-
ing beneath her feet, and she was falling
*   screaming*
and Rafe was calling her name.

You're safe, wildflower. I've come to take you
home.

Distantly Alana realized that she had
heard the words before, over and over, Rafe's
voice reaching out to her, peeling away
layers of nightmare until only reality remained.

"You're safe, wildflower. I've come to take
you home."

Shaking like an aspen in a storm, Alana
clung to the rock face. She sensed Rafe behind

her, heard his voice, felt the warmth of his body along her back, Rafe standing between her and the drop-off at the end of the rocky ledge.

"R-Rafe," Alana said shakily.

It was the only word she could say.

"I'm here, wildflower. You're safe," he murmured, his words and the tone of his voice soothing her. "You're safe."

Alana let out a breath that was more a sob. "Rafe? I'm so s-scared."

She couldn't see the darkness of his eyes or his savage expression so at odds with the reassurance of his voice.

"I know," Rafe said. "You had a bad time up along the lakes, even if you don't remember it. Or," softly, "did you remember?"

Alana shook her head.

"Then why are you frightened?" he coaxed. "Is it because I'm close to you? Are you afraid of me?"

She shook her head again. "No."

Though weak, her voice was positive. It wasn't Rafe she feared.

For an instant, Rafe closed his eyes. A strange mixture of emotions crossed his face. Then his eyes opened. Relief eased the tightness of his mouth and brought light to his eyes again.

"What is it, then?" he asked. "Can you tell me?"

"Height," said Alana in a trembling voice. "I'm afraid of heights now and I never was before, not until Jack fell and I guess I fell, too."

The words tumbled over each other like water in the cascade. She made a ragged sound.

"Rafe, I felt so good when I woke up a few minutes ago. All morning I hadn't thought about Jack or Broken Mountain or the missing days. I hadn't thought about anything since breakfast but fly-fishing and sunshine and you being so patient and gentle with me."

"I'm glad you enjoyed the morning," Rafe said, his voice low and husky. "I know that I haven't enjoyed anything so much in years."

"Do you mean that? Even though I ruined your line and scared every fish away?"

Rafe's lips brushed against Alana's shoulder in a caress so light she didn't feel it.

"I'll buy a hundred miles of leader," he said, "and let you tie knots in every inch of it."

Alana let out her breath in a rush, then took another breath. She almost felt brave enough to open her eyes.

Almost.

"Don't make any rash promises," she said shakily, trying to make a joke even though her voice wouldn't cooperate. "I'll hold you to every one of them."

"Wildflower," whispered Rafe, brushing his cheek against her glossy hair, "brave and beautiful. I'd carry away Broken Mountain stone by stone if that would let you come to me again with a smile on your lips."

The words were a warmth unfolding in the center of Alana's icy fear. As fear melted away, some of her strength returned.

She opened her eyes. The rough granite textures of rock were only inches from her face. On either side of her shoulders, close but not touching her, were Rafe's arms. His hands were flattened on the rock as he stood behind her, his legs braced, his feet wide apart on the narrow ledge, his body between her and any danger of falling.

Slowly Alana put one of her hands over his. The warmth of him was almost shocking.

"But I'm not brave," she said, her voice tight with anger at herself.

Rafe's laughter was as harsh as it was unexpected.

"Bravery isn't a square jaw and a thick head," he said. "Bravery is standing toe-to-toe with fear every minute of every hour, never knowing if you're going to get through this second, and afraid the next second might be one too many."

Alana's breath stopped. It was as though Rafe were in her mind, reading her thoughts, putting into words what she had only sensed without understanding.

"And the worst of it is that you're strong," Rafe said, "so you survive when others would have broken and gone free, crazy free, but you survive day after day no matter how bad it gets. And it gets very bad, doesn't it?"

Alana nodded, unable to speak.

So Rafe spoke for her, and for himself.

"Some of those days are endless," he said,

"and the nights . . . the nights are . . . unspeakable."

Alana's grip on Rafe's hand was so tight that her nails left marks on his skin.

"How did you know?" she whispered.

"I've been there, Alana. Like you, I've served my time in hell."

She whispered Rafe's name as tears slid from her eyelashes down her cheeks, crying for him and for herself.

His lips brushed her neck very lightly. She wouldn't have felt it if she hadn't been so sensitized to him, his emotions, his physical presence, Rafe like a fire burning between her and the freezing blackness that came to her in nightmares.

Alana bent her head until her lips touched the back of Rafe's hand. She kissed him gently, not withdrawing even when his hand turned over and cradled her cheek in his palm.

Slowly Rafe leaned down, unable to resist the lure of Alana's tears. He murmured her name as his lips touched her eyelashes, catching the silver drops. He expected her to stiffen at the caress, at the knowledge that she was trapped between his strength and the granite face of the mountain.

She turned her cheek to his lips, leaning lightly against him, her eyes luminous with emotion. He kissed the corner of her mouth, delicately stealing the tears that gathered there, until finally there were no more tears.

"Are you ready to climb down now?" Rafe asked softly.

Alana took a ragged breath, then looked beneath Rafe's arm to the rocks tumbling away to the lake.

Everything spun for an instant. She closed her eyes and hung on to him, hard.

Rafe saw the color leave Alana's face even before he felt her nails digging into his arms and the shaking of her legs against his. Quickly he leaned inward, bracing Alana against the rock with his body so that she wouldn't fall if her legs gave way.

"Don't be afraid," said Rafe softly, urgently. "I'm not going to hold you or hurt you in any way."

There was an instant of stiffness before Alana sighed and nodded her head, unable to speak.

When Alana accepted his presence, his reassurance, relief came in a wave that for an instant left Rafe almost as weak as she was.

And with relief came hunger for Alana, the hunger that had haunted Rafe ever since he had come back to find the woman he loved married to another man . . . desire and rage burning Rafe like acid every time he saw a picture of Alana with Jack, Country's Perfect Couple, happiness condensed into two smiling faces on millions of album covers.

Ruthlessly Rafe suppressed both desire and the corrosive memories of rage. He ignored the sweet warmth of Alana's body pressed along his as he braced her against the cold granite.

"I'll support you until you aren't dizzy," he

said, his voice even, calm. "Tell me when you can stand again."

Eyes closed, Alana savored the sound of Rafe's deep voice, his warmth and reassurance, and his patience. If he didn't condemn her for being foolish, for being afraid, she wouldn't condemn herself, either.

"Alana?" asked Rafe, unable to see her face. Concern made his voice almost harsh.

"It's all right," Alana said.

And as she spoke, she realized that it really was all right. When she stopped being disgusted with herself, when she stopped being afraid of fear, she was able to react more rationally.

Rafe's strength and closeness made Alana feel as she should, protected rather than threatened. She sighed and felt the shaking in her legs diminish.

"You didn't frighten me, Rafael. I looked down the mountain, that's all."

He let out his breath with an explosive sigh.

"That wasn't a very bright thing to do, sweetheart."

Alana's mouth formed a smile that was gone as swiftly as it had come.

"I figured that out real fast," she said. "Now maybe you can figure out how I'm going to climb off this damned ledge with my eyes closed."

"Gracefully, smoothly, and quickly," murmured Rafe, brushing Alana's neck with his lips, not caring if she felt the caress, "like you do everything else."

"Including tie knots in your leader," retorted Alana.

Her voice was almost steady, but her eyes were still tightly closed.

"Most especially tying knots in my leader," he answered, laughing softly against her hair. "Ready?"

"To tie knots? I was born ready for that, obviously. No practice needed. Perfect tangle on the first try."

Then Alana took a deep breath.

"Rafe," she said softly, "I really don't want to open my eyes."

"How else can you admire the gorgeous tangles you make?"

"Braille," she said succinctly.

"Okay. Braille it is." Rafe hesitated. "For that to work, I'll have to be very close to you, Alana. Sometimes I'll have to take your foot and place it, or hold you, or even lift you."

"*No.*"

Then she spoke quickly, desperately, wanting to be sure Rafe understood how important it was.

"Don't lift me, Rafe. *Please.* That's my worst nightmare, my body being lifted high and then falling and falling and Jack— Oh, God," she said, horrified. "Jack. He fell. He fell into the darkness and rocks, and the water was like thunder everywhere and he died and—"

Alana's throat closed around screams and her eyes opened dark and wild, dilated with terror and memories that faded in and out like a nightmare.

Rafe ached to hold her, but he was nearly certain it would trigger the terror he sensed seething beneath her words, waiting to claim her.

"Hush, wildflower," Rafe murmured. "I won't lift you. You're safe with me."

Slowly Alana's eyes focused on the strong hands braced on either side of her. She made a despairing sound.

"Rafe, each time I come closer to remembering but never close enough. And each time I'm so afraid. Does it ever end?"

"It will end," Rafe said, his voice a curious mixture of reassurance and shared pain. "It will end. And you'll survive. Like the wildflowers survive ice and darkness, sure of the summer to come."

His lips brushed her nape.

"You're strong, Alana. So strong. I know you don't believe that now, but you are. If you didn't go under before, you won't go under now. Believe me. I know. I've been there, too. Remember?"

Alana put her forehead against Rafe's hand and fought to control her breathing. After a few minutes, she succeeded.

Only then did Rafe say quietly, "We're going to climb down, now. You'll have to help me, Alana."

"H-How?"

"You'll have to trust me," he said simply. "If you don't, you'll panic and then I'll have to knock you out and carry you down. I don't want to do that, Alana, even though I could do it and never leave a bruise on your body. Your mind, though . . .''

Alana shuddered, not noticing how intently Rafe was watching her.

"Being knocked out and carried down the mountain would be your worst nightmare come true, wouldn't it?" Rafe asked softly.

The words went through Alana's mind like a shock wave. Was that her nightmare? Being knocked out and carried?

Slowly, hardly even realizing it, Alana shook her head.

"No, that's not my nightmare. My nightmare is being lifted and then thrown, something throwing me away and then I'm falling, falling forever, ice and darkness and death."

Rafe's voice was calm, but his eyes were burning with the rage that came to him every time he thought of Alana hurt, frightened, screaming his name.

But none of his emotions showed in his voice.

"Then you won't panic if I have to hold you?" he asked matter-of-factly.

"I don't know," said Alana starkly. "I guess we'll just have to find out the hard way, won't we?"

"Yes, I guess we will."

When Alana felt Rafe move away, felt the cool wind on her back where his warmth had been, she wanted to cry out in protest. For a moment she simply stood, eyes closed, hands pressed against cold stone.

"About one foot below and slightly to your left is a flat stone," Rafe said.

He watched while Alana crouched slightly and felt around with the toe of her walking shoe, trying to find the surface he had described.

"Another inch down," he said. "That's it. Good."

Legs braced, arms outstretched but not touching her, Rafe followed Alana's progress.

"Now your right foot," he said. "Straight down, more, just another few inches. There. Feel it?"

Alana's answer was a drawn-out sound of relief when she felt the rock take her weight. She thought of opening her eyes again, but she didn't trust herself not to freeze.

Rafe described the next step, then the next, his hands always hovering just above Alana without touching her. He talked constantly, encouraging her.

Slowly Alana backed down the steepest part of the slope.

"Now, use your left foot," Rafe said. "This is a tricky one. There are two rocks close together. You want the one on the left. No, not that one, the—*Alana.*"

The rock turned beneath her foot, throwing her off balance. Rafe grabbed her and held her in a hard grip, but only for an instant. Carefully he put her back on her feet.

Other than a choked cry when the stone first slid out from beneath her foot, Alana had made no protest, even when Rafe's hands closed around her arms. Yet she was very pale, and her hands shook noticeably as she searched for support among the tall boulders. Shudders rippled through her body.

Rafe sensed that Alana had fallen into nightmare again. Gently he turned her until she was facing him. He kept his hands on her shoulders, more to give her contact with the world than to support her.

"Alana, open your eyes. Look at me, not at the lake or the rocks. Just at me."

Slowly Alana's black eyelashes parted.

Rafe was only inches from her, his amber eyes narrowed and intent. His mustache was a deep, rich brown shot through with metallic highlights of bronze and gold. The pulse in his neck beat strongly, hinting at the heat and life beneath his tanned skin.

"It's daylight, not night," Rafe said softly. "It's warm, not icy. Jack is dead. You're alive and safe with me."

Mutely Alana nodded. Then she sighed and leaned against him.

Rafe wanted very much to put his arms around her, to hold her against his body and rock her until both of them felt only the other, knew only the other, comfort replacing fear.

But, like Alana, Rafe was afraid if he held her, there would be only fear and no comfort at all.

"I'm sorry you were frightened," murmured Rafe, smoothing his cheek against her hair.

"I was—but I wasn't. Not really." Alana took another long breath. "I knew after I called your name that you wouldn't let me fall."

And Rafe knew that Alana hadn't called his name. Not *this* time.

If she thought she had, she was still caught between the past and the present, a hostage to fear. Yet she had trusted him not to let her fall.

That, at least, hadn't changed.

After a few moments, Alana straightened and stood on her own.

"Let's finish it," she said, her voice flat.

"Aren't you going to close your eyes?"

"I don't think so. It's not as steep here, is it?"

"No. If you're going to take a look, though, do it now, when I'm close enough to catch you if you get dizzy."

Alana's mouth relaxed into a tiny smile. "I can't see through you, Rafe."

He turned partially, just enough to give her a brief view of the tumbled slope behind him. As he turned, he watched her face, ready to grab her if vertigo struck again.

Other than a flattening of her mouth, Alana showed no reaction. Even so, Rafe stayed very close for the first few steps. She glanced at him and tried to smile.

"I'm all right now," she said.

Rafe nodded, but he remained within reach of her. Together they worked their way down the last of the slope. When there was only lake in front of them, they stopped.

With a sense of triumph, Alana turned and looked back. She shook her head as she realized that the slope, which had seemed so steep and deadly from above, didn't look like much at all from the bottom.

"Fear always looks like that from the other side," Rafe said quietly.

Alana looked from the mountainside to the man beside her. Rafe's understanding of what she had been through, and his acceptance of her fear, untied knots deep inside her as surely as he had untied the snarls of fly line she had created. She put her palm against his cheek, savoring his warmth and the masculine texture of his skin.

"Rafael," she murmured, making music of his name. "You make me believe that someday I may even sing again."

Rafe turned his head until he could kiss the slender palm that rested against his cheek. He whispered Alana's name against her hand and smiled as her fingers curled up to caress his lips. Slowly Alana's other hand crept up to Rafe's head, hungry for his warmth and the smooth thickness of his hair between her fingers.

Moving as slowly as Alana did, Rafe tilted his head down until his lips could slant across hers. The kiss was so gentle that it was impossible to tell the exact instant when it began.

Alana neither hesitated nor pulled back when she felt Rafe's mouth caress hers. Instead, she whispered his name again and again, lost in the sensations that came as his lips brushed slowly against hers. His mouth moved from side to side with gentle pressures that made her fingers tighten in his hair, pulling his head closer in silent demand.

The tip of Rafe's tongue slid lightly over

Alana's lower lip, then traced the curves of her mouth until she sighed and her fingers kneaded down his neck to his shoulders, seeking the long, powerful muscles of his back. Her mouth softened, fitting itself to his.

When Alana's tongue touched first his lips, then his teeth, Rafe made a sound deep in his chest. His hands clenched at his sides as he fought not to give in to his hunger to hold her, to feel her body soften and flow over his as surely as her mouth had.

Hesitantly Rafe touched the warmth and sweetness of her tongue with his own. Even then she didn't retreat. The kiss deepened until the sound of his own blood beating inside his veins drowned out the cascade's rushing thunder.

Rafe heard Alana call his name with hunger and need, a sound out of his dreams. As gently as a sigh, his fingers dared to touch her face, the smooth curve of her neck, the slenderness and feminine strength of her arms. When she showed no fear, he rubbed his palms lightly from her shoulders to her hands and back again.

She murmured and moved closer to him, letting his heat radiate through her. He shifted his stance, fitting her against him, touching her very gently with his hands while the sweet heaviness of desire swelled between them.

Alana forgot the past, forgot the nightmare, forgot everything but the taste of Rafe and the rough velvet of his tongue sliding over hers. Fire shimmered through her, called by his hunger and her own, fire melting her until she sagged against him, giving herself to his strength.

Rafe's arms circled Alana, holding her as she held him, molding her against the heat and hunger of his body. She responded with a movement that brought her even closer, standing on tiptoe, trying to become a part of him.

And then she moved sinuously, caressingly, stroking his body with her own.

With a ragged sound, Rafe let his arms close around Alana. As his arms tightened, they tilted Alana's hips against his thighs. The movement lifted her just enough that for an instant her toes lost contact with the ground.

In that instant, Alana went from passion to panic.

11

EVEN AS ALANA TRIED TO
wrench free of his embrace, Rafe realized what
had happened. Cursing himself, he released
her completely.

"I'm sorry."

They both spoke quickly, as one, identical
words and emotions.

"It's not your fault."

Again their words tangled, each hurrying to
reassure the other.

When Alana would have spoken again, Rafe
gently put his fingers across her mouth.

"No," he said in a husky voice. "It's not
your fault. I should have known better than to
hold you. I thought I could trust myself. But

I'd forgotten how sweet and wild you are. Even in my deepest dreams, I'd forgotten."

Alana's black lashes closed. She tilted her face down so that Rafe couldn't see her expression until she was more certain of her self-control. When she looked at him again, there was no fear in the dark clarity of her eyes, only apology and the luminous residue of passion.

"Did you really dream of me, Rafael?" Alana asked, music and emotion making her voice as beautiful as her eyes.

"Yes," he said quietly. "It was all that kept me sane in hell."

Alana's breath caught at the honesty and pain in Rafe's voice. Her eyes searched his expression.

"What happened?" she asked.

Rafe hesitated. "It's not a pretty story. I'm not sure it's something you want to know."

"If you can stand to tell me, I can stand to hear it."

When Rafe still hesitated, Alana took his hand and started back along the lakeshore, leading him with a gentle pressure of her fingers.

"Never mind," she said. "We'll eat lunch and then we'll lie in the sun and count aspen leaves. Remember?"

The darkness left Rafe's eyes. His lips curved into an off-center smile.

"I remember," he said. "The first one who blinks has to start all over again."

"After paying a forfeit."

"Of course," Rafe said in a husky voice. "I remember that part very well."

A sideways look into his brilliant whiskey eyes told Alana that Rafe indeed hadn't forgotten. Her fingers tightened in his as he brought her hand up to his lips. He rubbed his mustache teasingly over her sensitive fingertips. Then he nibbled on the soft pad of flesh at the base of her thumb.

"What's that for?" asked Alana breathlessly.

"I blinked," admitted Rafe. "Didn't you see me?"

"No. I must have blinked, too."

"That's one you owe me."

"But we haven't started counting aspen leaves yet," Alana pointed out.

"Well, if you're going to get all technical on me, I guess I won't start keeping score until after lunch."

Smiling, Alana led Rafe to the hollow where they had left their backpacks. While he retrieved the fishing gear he had abandoned when he heard her scream, Alana set out a lunch of sandwiches and fruit.

They ate slowly, letting the sun and silence dissolve away the last residue of fear and nightmare. When Rafe was finished, he stretched out on his back with his hands linked behind his head.

After a few moments he said lazily, "Twenty-three."

"What?"

"I counted twenty-three aspen leaves before I blinked."

"You can't even see any aspens from where you are."

"Sure I can," Rafe said, his voice deep. "Just off over your shoulder."

Alana turned and looked. Sure enough, a golden crown of aspen leaves rose above a thick screen of dark evergreen needles.

"You blinked," Rafe said. "How many?"

"Eleven."

"That's two you owe me."

Saying nothing more, Rafe resumed staring over her shoulder.

"Aren't you ever going to blink?" asked Alana finally.

"Nope." Then, "Damn. Got me. Thirty-seven."

Alana shifted until she could look at the aspen without twisting around. She counted swiftly, then groaned when she blinked.

"It's coming back to me now," she said. "I used to lose this game all the time."

Rafe smiled. "Yeah. I remember that best of all. That's three you owe me."

He settled into counting again.

After a long pause he said, "It's coming back to me now. The trick is not to stare too hard—and be sure the wind isn't in your face. Then—damn. Forty."

Alana got as far as thirty-five before she blinked. She groaned again.

"That's four," Rafe said.

"Aren't you worried about collecting?" Alana asked, for he had made no move to kiss her.

Rafe's glance shifted.

"Are you?" he countered in a soft voice, watching her.

Alana's breath shortened, then sighed out.

"I don't know," she admitted, remembering both the pleasure and the panic she had felt by the lakeshore.

"Then I'll wait until you know," he said simply.

Alana propped herself on her elbow and rolled over to face Rafe. He ignored her, counting quickly, aspen leaves reflected in his amber eyes.

She looked at the grace and strength of him as he lay at ease, legs crossed at the ankles, jeans snug over his muscular thighs and lean hips. The dark blue T-shirt had pulled free of his pants, revealing a narrow band of skin the color of dark honey. A line of hair so deeply brown that it was almost black showed above the low-riding jeans. Where the shirt still covered him, it fit like a shadow, smooth, sliding, moving when he did, a cotton so soft that it had felt better than velvet against her palms when she had touched him by the lake.

"Seven thousand six hundred and ninety-two," Rafe said.

"What?"

"Seven thousand six hundred and ninety-two."

"You can't have counted that many leaves without blinking," she protested.

Rafe smiled. For the last few minutes, he had been watching Alana rather than aspen leaves, but she hadn't noticed because she had been watching every part of him except his eyes.

And her smile told him that she very much approved of what she saw.

"Would you believe two thousand?" Rafe asked innocently.

Alana shook her head so hard that the motion sent her silky cap of hair flying.

"Two hundred?" asked Rafe.

"Nope."

"Fifty?"

"Well . . ."

"Sold," Rafe said smoothly. "That's five you owe me."

"But I haven't had my turn yet."

"Think it will do any good?"

Alana sighed and stared very hard at an aspen, but all she saw was the image of Rafe burned into her mind, into her very soul. She blinked to drive away his image, then groaned when she realized that single blink had cost her the contest.

"Fifteen," she said in disgust.

Rafe smiled and turned his attention back to aspen leaves quivering in the breeze. When Alana's fingers touched his cheek, his counting paused, then resumed. When her hand slid up the arm that was pillowing his head, his counting slowed. When her fingertip traced the supple veins showing beneath his skin, her touch sliding slowly up and down the sensitive inner side of his arm, Rafe stopped counting altogether.

"You're cheating, wildflower," he said in a husky voice.

"I finally remembered."

"What did you remember?"

"How I used to win this game."

"Funny," he said, "I remember us both winning. Every time."

"I wish—" Alana's voice broke. "I wish that it could be like that again. I wish you had never gone away that last time."

She took a ragged breath and then asked the question that she had asked herself a thousand times since she had learned that Rafe was alive.

"What happened, Rafe? What did I do to deserve your silence?"

He didn't answer for so long that Alana was afraid he would refuse to answer at all.

"Do you mean the letter I returned to you?" he asked finally.

"Yes, but even before that. Why did you let me believe you were dead? Other people knew you were alive, but not me. I didn't find out until a year ago."

"I thought you were happily married."

Alana searched Rafe's expression with eyes that were too dark, remembering too much of pain and not enough of happiness.

"How could you believe that?" she asked. "I loved you. I thought you loved me."

"I did."

"Then how could you believe I loved Jack?"

Rafe's lips flattened into a grim line. "It happens all the time to soldiers. The Dear John syndrome. One man goes off to war and another man stays to comfort the girl who was left behind."

"It wasn't like that," whispered Alana. "I married Jack because singing was all I had left after they told me you were dead. It was a business marriage."

"Alana—"

"He never touched me," she said, talking over Rafe. "I wouldn't let him. I couldn't bear to be touched by any man but you."

Rafe closed his eyes. When they opened again, they were hard, focused on the past, a past that had nearly destroyed him.

"I didn't know," he said. "All I knew was that six weeks after I 'died,' the woman who once said she loved me became half of Country's Perfect Couple. Everywhere I turned I saw Jack 'n' Jilly, America's favorite lovers, singing songs to each other, love songs that were beautiful enough to make Broken Mountain weep."

"Rafael . . ." Alana's voice frayed.

"Let me finish," Rafe said tightly. "I may never talk about it again. God knows I'd just as soon forget it, every second of it."

"The way I did?" she asked, her voice flat, all music gone. "That wouldn't make it better. Believe me, Rafe. Forgetting the way I did just makes it worse in the long run. I can't imagine anything more awful than my nightmares."

Rafe closed his eyes and let out a long, harsh breath.

"I know," he said. "I learned the hard way

that forgetting or ignoring doesn't make anything go away. So I'm going to tell you something that's buried in filing cabinets in the Pentagon and in the minds of the very few men who survived. Something that never happened at all, officially."

Alana said nothing, afraid to move, straining to hear Rafe's low voice.

"I told you I was in the army," he said. "Well, I was, but in a very special branch of it. I was trained in counterinsurgency, with special attention to rural areas." He smiled grimly. "Really rural. God, but I learned to hate jungles."

After the silence had stretched for several moments, Alana touched Rafe's arm with gentle fingers.

"What happened?" she asked, her voice soft.

"Four years ago, I'd just about decided that I'd rather fight lost causes with my thick-skulled father in Wyoming than fight lost causes in the jungles of Central America. I owed the army some more time, though."

Alana waited, remembering. When Rafe had asked her to marry him, he had also told her that they would be separated a lot of the time for two more years. Then he would quit the army and come back and marry her.

"Just before I left Wyoming the last time, some of our men were taken prisoner along with a native guerrilla leader," Rafe said. "There was no chance of getting our men back through regular diplomatic means, because the men weren't officially there in the first place. The records had them posted to Chile or West Germany or Indochina, anywhere but Central America."

Motionless, Alana listened.

"We couldn't just write off the men," Rafe said, "even though word was that nobody survived prison there for long. And we needed that guerrilla leader. My group was asked to volunteer for a rescue attempt."

Alana's eyes closed, knowing what was coming next.

"You volunteered," she said, her voice barely a thread of sound.

"I knew the men who had been caught. One of them was a very good friend. Besides," Rafe said matter-of-factly, "I was good at what I did. With me leading the raid, it had a better chance of succeeding."

She took a deep breath and nodded. For the first time, some of the agony she had gone through four years ago began to make sense.

"I understand," she said quietly.

"Do you?" Rafe asked.

He looked directly at Alana for the first time since he had begun to speak of the past.

"Do you really understand why I left you?" he asked. "Why I *volunteered* to leave you?"

"You couldn't have lived with yourself if you had stayed safe and the other men had died," Alana said simply, stroking the hard line of Rafe's jaw with a gentle fingertip. "That's the kind of man you are. You'd never buy your own comfort with another person's life."

Rafe kissed the finger that had moved to caress his mustache.

"Most women wouldn't understand."

"Most women never know a man like you."

"Don't kid yourself," Rafe said harshly. "I'm no hero. I scream just as loud as the next guy when the rubber-hose brigade goes to work."

Alana's eyes widened darkly as the meaning of Rafe's words sank in. She touched his face with gentle fingers, smoothing away the lines of rage that had come when he remembered the past.

"You're a man of honor, Rafael. That's all anyone can ask."

For long moments Rafe said nothing, responding to her with neither look nor words. Then he let out his breath.

"I'm glad you think so, Alana. There were times I didn't think much of myself. Men died. I was their leader. I was responsible for their lives."

"They were soldiers. Volunteers. Like you."

"And I led them right into hell."

Alana's fingers smoothed the grim lines bracketing Rafe's mouth.

"Was there another way you could have done it?" she asked softly.

"No." His voice was bitter. "That's how I knew I'd led them into hell. The road there is paved with the best intentions. The better the intentions, the deeper you go.

"And all the way down you know that there was nothing you could have done differently, that if you were put in the same position again you'd do the same thing again, the honorable thing . . . and you'd take the same good people down with you.

"And that," he said savagely, "is my definition of hell on earth."

Words crowded Alana's throat, all but choking her. She spoke none of them, sensing that the only words that could help Rafe right now were his own. She caressed him gently, her fingers smoothing his skin in undemanding touches that told him she was there, listening, sharing his pain as much as she could.

"I've thought about that mission a lot," Rafe said after a time. "But I've never said anything to anyone since I was debriefed."

"You couldn't."

"It wasn't so much the security regulations that kept me quiet. I just never found anyone who I thought would understand what it was like to be scared every second of every day, to be scared and fight not to show it, to face each dawn knowing that it probably wouldn't be better than yesterday and often it would be worse."

Alana touched Rafe's wrist, felt the life beating beneath his supple skin.

"Not many people know what it is like to serve an indeterminate sentence in hell," Rafe said. "Waiting and listening to the screams while the damned are tortured, waiting and listening and knowing that soon you would be screaming, too."

Alana made a stifled sound and turned very pale. Yet after a brief hesitation, her hand never stopped touching Rafe, giving him what comfort she could while he relived a nightmare she could barely imagine, but could understand all too well.

The man she loved had been imprisoned and tortured until he screamed.

Whatever memories I have hidden in my nightmares, Alana told herself silently, Rafe's must be worse, memory and nightmare alike. Yet he survived. He is here, strong despite the cruel violence of the past, patient with me despite my weakness, gentle with me despite the brutality that he has known.

As Rafe continued talking, low-voiced and intense, Alana took his hand and pressed it against her cheek, as though simple touch could take the agony and bitterness from his past. And her own.

"I went into the jungle alone," he said, "about three days ahead of the others. They needed someone to get inside the prison for a fast recon so we'd know how many of the men were alive and able to walk on their own. It was too dangerous a job to ask anyone to volunteer for."

Rafe stared past Alana, his eyes unfocused, remembering. Yet even then his fingers moved lightly against Alana's cheek, telling her that her presence helped him as much as anything could.

"I got into the prison without any problem," Rafe said. "Wire fences and a few perimeter guards. They were counting on the jungle and the prison's reputation as a hellhole to keep people away."

Rafe's fingers tensed on Alana's cheek.

"It was a hellhole, all right," he said. "What I saw there made me want to execute every guard, every government officer, everyone I could get my hands on. And then I wanted to burn that prison with a fire so hot it would melt through to the center of the earth."

Rafe closed his eyes, afraid that if they were open, Alana would see what he saw. Men chained and tortured, maimed and slowly murdered for no better reason than the entertainment of guards who were too brutal to be called men and too inventive in their savagery to be called animals. Grinning devils ruling over a green hell.

"I got the information and I got out," Rafe said. "The next day I led my men back in."

His eyes opened. They were clear and hard as topaz, the eyes of a stranger.

"As soon as we pulled out the men we came for, I went back to that prison. Three of my men came with me, against my orders. They were the three who had seen the wing where prisoners were tortured. The four of us freed every prisoner and then we blew that building straight back to the hell that had spawned it."

Alana held Rafe's hand against her lips, trying to comfort him and herself, rocking slowly.

"One of the men who came back with me

was injured. The other two carried him to the rendezvous while I stayed behind to cover the retreat.

"Some of the guards survived the blast. I held them off until my gun jammed. They caught me, shot me, and left me for dead in the clearing. The helicopter got away, though. I heard it lift off just after I was shot."

Alana made a low sound.

"I survived. I don't remember much about it. Some of the peasants hid me, did what they could for my wounds. Then the government soldiers came back. I was too weak to escape."

Alana bit her lips against the useless protests aching in her throat.

Rafe kept talking quietly, relentlessly, getting rid of the savage memories from the past.

"They took me to another prison just like the one I'd blown to hell. I knew there was no hope of rescue. My men had seen me shot. They would assume I was dead. Besides, you don't risk twenty men to save one, unless that one is damned important. I wasn't."

Wanting to speak, afraid to stop the flow of Rafe's words, Alana murmured softly against his palm and tried not to cry aloud. Her hands smoothed his arm and shoulder again and again, as though to convince herself that he really was alive and she was with him, touching him.

"I spent a long time in that prison," Rafe said. "I don't know why I didn't die. A lot of men did and were happy to."

Then Rafe turned and looked at Alana.

"That's not quite true," he said. "I know why I survived. I had something to live for. You. I dreamed of you, of playing the harmonica while you sang, of touching you, making love to you, hearing you laugh, feeling and seeing your love for me in every touch, every smile."

"Rafael," she whispered, and could say no more.

"The dreams kept me sane. Knowing that you were waiting for me, loving me as much as I loved you, gave me the strength to escape and to live like an animal in the jungle until I crossed into a country where I wouldn't be shot on sight."

Alana bent over to kiss Rafe, no longer caring if he saw her tears.

"And then," Rafe said, his voice flat, "I came home to find that the woman I'd loved enough to live for didn't love me enough to wait for me."

"That's not true!" Alana said, her voice a low cry of pain.

"I know. Now. I didn't know then. All I knew was what the papers told me. Jack 'n' Jilly. Perfect marriage. Perfect love. No one told me any different."

"No one knew," Alana said raggedly. "Not even my family. Jack and I worked very hard to keep the truth of our marriage a secret."

"You succeeded."

Rafe looked at Alana for a long moment, seeing his pain and unhappiness reflected in her dark eyes and pale face. He touched her lips with his fingertip, loosening the tight line of her mouth.

"I left the army as soon as my time was up," Rafe said. "My father was dead by then. I came back to the ranch as bitter a man as has ever watched the sun rise over Broken Mountain. Until a year ago, I ran the ranch through my lawyers and lived out of the Broken Mountain fishing camp. Alone."

Alana closed her eyes against the tears she couldn't control.

"If only I had known you were alive . . ." she whispered.

"But I wasn't sure that I was alive," Rafe said. "Not really. Most of my time was still spent in hell. No one on this side of the mountain even knew that I hadn't died. Except Sam, and he wouldn't tell anyone."

"Sam?" Alana asked, startled.

"He took some training in Panama. Different outfit. Civilian, not military. We worked together once, just before I left the army. He's a good man, if a bit hardheaded. And that's all I have to say on the subject of Sam Burdette."

Alana started to object, then realized that it would do no good. Rafe might share his own secrets with her, but her brother's secrets were not Rafe's to share. She looked at Rafe with eyes that understood, eyes as dark as midnight, as dark as her nightmares.

"When did you decide to tell people that you were alive?" she asked.

"I didn't. It just happened."

Rafe shook his head slowly, remembering his rage and bitterness at life and the woman who had married another man just six weeks after her fiancé had been declared dead.

"I ran into Bob one day in the high country," Rafe said. "He was fishing that crazy fly he favors. And he went straight down the mountain to you."

Without realizing it, Alana's fingers tightened on Rafe's arm as she remembered the moment that Bob had burst into the house talking about Rafe Winter, a man come back from the dead—and looking like it. Hard and bitter, eyes as cold as a February dawn.

Rafe. *Alive.*

And Alana was married to a man she didn't love.

"A day later," Rafe said, watching her, "Bob brought me a letter. I recognized your handwriting on the envelope. I looked at it for a long, long time."

"Why didn't you—" she began.

"I knew I couldn't open my own Dear John letter," Rafe interrupted savagely. "I couldn't force myself to read the words describing your perfect marriage, perfect career, perfect man, perfect lover. I couldn't read the death of my dream written in your own hand, the dream that had kept me alive when most of me hurt so much that death looked like heaven itself."

Alana shook her head. Tears fell from her tightly closed eyes. With a ragged sound, she put her head on Rafe's chest and held him until her arms ached. She couldn't bear the thought of Rafe being tortured, dreaming of her, surviving because he loved her.

And then coming home to find her married.

"What was in the letter?" Rafe asked.

His voice was so soft that it barely penetrated the sound of Alana's tears.

"The truth," Alana said hoarsely. "I was going to leave Jack. When I was free, I was going to write to you again, if you wanted me to."

"But you didn't leave Jack."

"No." She drew a ragged breath. "When I lost you a second time, I thought nothing mattered. I went back to Jack."

Rafe's eyelids flinched. It was the only sign he gave of the pain within him at the thought that he had sent her back to Jack Reeves.

"But when I knew you were alive," Alana said, "I couldn't stay with Jack. Not even to save our singing career. So we lived separately, but very discreetly."

Slowly she shook her head, remembering the past.

"Separation wasn't enough," she whispered. "You didn't want me, hadn't even cared for me enough to tell me you were alive, but I had to be free of the sham marriage. I had lived with lies for too long. When you were dead, the lies hadn't mattered to me. Nothing had mattered except singing.

"That's how I survived, Rafe. I sang to the memory of the man I loved, not to Jack. Never to him."

"And then," Rafe said bitterly, "I wrote

your death sentence on an envelope and sent
it back to you."

"What?"

Rafe swore savagely.

Alana trembled, not knowing why he was
so angry with himself.

"What did you mean?" asked Alana, her
voice shaking as she looked at Rafe's narrowed eyes. "Why was that envelope my
death sentence?"

"It sent you back to Jack Reeves."

"What—"

"The answer is in your nightmares," Rafe
said, cutting off Alana's question.

Her eyes searched Rafe's, looking for answers but seeing only herself reflected in the
clear amber.

"How do you know?" she asked.

"That, too, is in your nightmares."

Rafe's hands came up to frame Alana's face.

"There's something else in those lost days,
wildflower," he murmured, kissing her lips
gently. "There's the moment you saw me,
knew me, turned to me."

He kissed her again, more deeply.

"Rafe—"

"No," he said softly. "I've told you more
than the good doctor wanted me to. But I
thought it might help you to know that something other than horror is buried with those
six missing days."

$\approx$ ✆ **12**

FOR A LONG TIME THERE WAS
only silence and the rushing sound of the distant cascade.

Rafe's expression told Alana that questioning him would be futile. He had the same closed look that he had worn when he talked about leading his men into hell.

But it angered her that Rafe knew something about her six lost days and wouldn't tell her.

"Why?" Alana asked finally, her voice harsh. "Why won't you help me?"

"You didn't know Jack was dead. People told you he was. How much help was that?"

Alana searched Rafe's topaz eyes.

"But—" she began.

"But nothing," he interrupted in a flat voice. "Did knowing Jack was dead help you remember anything?"

Alana clenched her hands.

"No," she said.

"Did waking up in that hospital beaten and bloody tell you how you got hurt?"

Silence. Then, tightly, "No."

"Did reading about Jack's death in every newspaper help?"

"How did you know?" she whispered.

"In some ways you're a lot like me," Rafe said simply.

"But if you'd tell me what you know, it would help me sort out reality from nightmare."

"The doctors don't think so. They're afraid I might tell you something you don't want to know."

"What?"

"I might tell you that your nightmares are pieces of the truth."

Rock and ice and wind, something lifting her, throwing her out into the darkness
falling
she was falling and rocks waited below, waited to break her, hatred breaking her.

Alana made a small sound and went pale. She wrapped her arms around herself as she felt the cold of nightmares congeal inside her, fear and truth freezing her. She closed her eyes as though it would shut out the fragments of nightmare.

Then she wondered if it was memory that she was shutting out, reality chasing her through her nightmares, truth saying to her, *remember me.*

Rafe reached for Alana, wanting to gather her into his arms and comfort her.

When his hands touched her, she gasped and flinched away.

Rafe withdrew instantly, but the cost of controlling himself made muscles stand out rigidly along his jaw. He looked at Alana's pale skin and black lashes, her mouth shaped for smiling but drawn by fear into a thin line, the pulse beating too quickly in her throat.

With a soundless curse, Rafe closed his eyes. The doctors were right. Telling her wouldn't help.

Even worse, it could hurt her.

At first Rafe had been afraid that Alana would remember too soon, before he had a chance to win her love again. Now he was afraid that she wouldn't remember soon enough, that she would lose faith in herself and then tear herself apart.

Yet Rafe couldn't bring back Alana's memory for her, no matter how much he wanted to. The bitterness of that knowledge made the brackets around his mouth deeper, harder.

"If telling you everything I know about those six days would stop you from freezing when I touch you, I'd shout the truth from the top of Broken Mountain," Rafe said, his voice rough with suppressed emotion.

Alana said nothing.

"My God, don't you know that I'd do anything to have you in my arms again?" Rafe whispered. "I want you so badly. I want to hold you, comfort you, love you . . . *and I can't.* All I can do is hurt you again and again."

Rafe's hands became fists. With a quick movement, he rolled over until his back was turned toward Alana.

"It's like Central America all over again," he said harshly, "only it's worse because this time it's you I'm leading into hell, knowing with every step that there's no other way, knowing and hating myself just the same."

His laugh was a short, savage sound.

"Christ," Rafe said harshly, "I don't blame you for shrinking away every time I touch you."

The raw emotion in Rafe's voice called Alana out of the depths of the nightmare as nothing else could have. She knew what it was like to feel snarled and helpless, hating yourself, feeling as though everything you did made the tangle worse, not better.

The thought of Rafe feeling that way because of her made Alana ache with tears she couldn't shed. In just the past day, Rafe had given so much to her, laughter and protection, patience and companionship, subtle passion, and, above all, acceptance.

She might rail at herself for being weak, she

might be angry and disgusted with herself . . .
but Rafe was not.

When she was close to hating herself, he had
told her about strength and weakness and survival, torture and the breaking point every human being has. He had told her about his own
time in hell, and in doing so he had coaxed
her out of the depths of her own self-disgust.

Rafe had given her hope when all she had
was nightmare.

And for that she flinched when he touched
her.

"Rafael," murmured Alana, touching his
arm.

He made no response.

She shifted her position until she was on her
knees. She leaned over Rafe, stroking him
from the thick silk of his hair down to the
corded tension of his neck. She repeated his
name again and again, a slow litany that was
nearly a song.

Her hand moved down, trying to loosen the
rigid muscles of his shoulders and back. The
dark cotton of his T-shirt felt like warm velvet
to her. Her fingers kneaded the hard flesh beneath. He felt so good to her, heat and smooth-
ness and strength.

With a sigh, Alana bent over until she could
put her lips just below the dark brown of his
hairline. Rafe's neck was warm and firm,
tanned skin stretched tautly over tendons,
tempting her tongue to taste and trace each
subtle change in texture.

She kissed him lightly, lingeringly, before

she gave in to temptation and touched his skin with the tip of her tongue. He tasted of salt and heat and man, slightly rough where his beard began and amazingly smooth on the back of his neck.

Delicately Alana's teeth closed on Rafe's neck, testing the resilience of the muscle beneath. He moved his head and shoulders slowly, increasing the pressure of her teeth on his flesh, making her hand slide over the muscles of his back.

Rafe tasted good, felt good. Alana wanted to touch and savor more of him. Her fingers dug into the bunched muscles beneath her hand as her teeth tested the male power of his shoulders.

Rafe arched against her touch like a hungry cat.

The honesty of his response made an equal hunger sweep through Alana, a hunger that only Rafe had ever called from her. She wanted to lie down next to him, to fit her body along his, to feel his passion surround her as she surrounded him.

Yet even as fire licked through her, melting her, Alana knew that if Rafe's arms closed around her, she would freeze. And in freezing, she would hurt him cruelly. Then she would hate herself all over again.

"Oh, Rafe," she said, her voice breaking on his name, "what are we going to do?"

"What we're doing right now feels wonderful."

"But I'm afraid I'll freeze."

Alana's words trembled with fear and the beginning of anger at herself.

"Does touching me frighten you?" Rafe asked.

Alana made an odd sound that could have been laughter.

"Touching you is like singing, Rafael. Only better."

She heard his breath come in sharply and felt the fine tremor that went through his body.

"Then touch me as much as you want," he said simply.

"That isn't fair to you."

Rafe's back shifted beneath Alana's hand, urging her to explore him, telling her more clearly than words that he wanted to be touched by her.

"Remember when you were nineteen?" he asked.

Alana's hand hesitated, then slid up Rafe's back to his hair. Eagerly her fingers sought the warmth of him beneath the thick pelt.

"Yes," she whispered. "I remember."

"You didn't object then."

"I didn't know what I was doing to you. Not really. Virgins can be very cruel."

"Did I complain?" asked Rafe, laughter and memories curling just beneath his words.

"No," she said softly.

"Did I ask for more than you wanted to give?"

"No. Never, Rafael."

"I never will."

With a smooth motion, Rafe rolled onto his back and looked at her with eyes that were clear amber, brilliant with emotion and desire.

"Do you believe me?" he asked.

"Yes."

"Then touch me."

"Even though I can't . . ." Alana's voice faltered.

"Yes," said Rafe swiftly, almost fiercely. "However much or little you want. Everything. Anything. I've dreamed of you for so long. Touch me, wildflower."

Hesitantly Alana's hands came up to frame Rafe's face. Her lips brushed across his while her fingers again sought the silky brown depths of his hair. With a sigh, her breath mingled with his and she knew again the heat and textures of his mouth. She made a throaty sound of pleasure as his taste spread across her tongue.

Forgotten sensations stirred, awakening. The kiss deepened into a timeless sensual joining as they gave themselves to each other, knowing only one another.

Finally, Alana lifted her mouth and looked at Rafe with eyes that remembered passion.

"The first time you kissed me like that," whispered Alana, "I thought I would faint. I think I could faint now. You take the world out from under me."

"Are you frightened?" Rafe asked quietly, watching Alana with smoky amber eyes.

She smiled slowly and shook her head.

"With you, there's no danger of falling,"

Alana said. "With you, I'm as weightless as heat balanced on fire."

She bent her head and kissed Rafe again, savoring every instant, every changing pressure of tongue on tongue, the heat and pleasure of his mouth joined with hers.

Her hands slid from his hair, caressing him with each tiny movement of her fingers. One hand curved around his neck just beneath his ear, her palm fitting perfectly against the slide and play of muscle as he moved his mouth across hers. Her other hand slid down his arm, only to return as her fingers sought the warmth of his skin beneath the short sleeve of his T-shirt.

She stroked Rafe, murmuring her pleasure as she felt him flex against her touch. Her hand slid higher until her palm rubbed his shoulder under the soft T-shirt. Catlike, Rafe arched into her caress, telling her how much he liked having her hand on his bare skin.

When Alana's mouth left his and she began to nibble on his mustache and his neck and finally, delicately, his ear, Rafe made a deep sound in his throat. She responded by tracing the outline of his ear with her mouth, then caressing him with slow, probing touches of her tongue that made his breath quicken.

"I remember how I shivered the first time you did that to me," whispered Alana, her breath warm against Rafe. "Do you remember?"

"Yes," he said huskily. "You had goose bumps all the way up and down your arms."

"Like you, now."

"Like me, now."

Alana's tongue touched Rafe's neck just as her teeth closed on his skin. Rafe moved his head, urging her to touch more deeply, to bite harder. Her teeth pressed into his flesh and she felt the male power in the tendon sliding beneath her mouth.

He had caressed her like that when the storm had chased them to the Broken Mountain cabin. His bite had been just short of pain and had brought a pleasure that had left her weak.

With a small sound, Alana caressed Rafe's neck down to his shoulder until her teeth closed on the T-shirt. Her hands kneaded down his chest to the warm band of skin where his shirt had pulled free of his jeans.

When her fingers touched his naked skin, Rafe's breath came in sharply. His weight shifted as his arms moved.

Alana waited, frozen, anticipating his embrace.

"It's all right," Rafe said softly. "See? No hands."

And it was true. Rafe had moved, but only to put his hands behind his head, fingers tightly laced against the nearly overwhelming temptation to touch Alana as she was touching him.

Alana smiled and relaxed against Rafe's side.

"Does that mean I can still touch you?" she asked.

He smiled just enough to show the tip of his tongue between the serrations of his teeth.

"What do you think?" he asked in a deep voice.

Alana's approving glance went from the rich pelt of Rafe's hair down the hard, masculine length of him.

"I think," said Alana, "that it's a miracle I kept my hands off you until I was twenty."

"And here I thought I was the one who deserved a medal."

"That's probably true," Alana admitted, her eyes brilliant with memories of a storm and a cabin loft. "I didn't know what I was missing. You did."

"Not really," Rafe said softly. "You were unique, sweet and wild, as generous as summer. You gave yourself to me so completely that you made me realize that I'd never made love to a woman until you. Not completely. And I've never made love since. Not completely."

"Rafael," Alana said softly, pleasure and pain and regret in a single word.

"I'm not asking you for anything," he said. "I know you're not ready to give yourself again. That doesn't mean I've forgotten how it was between us once—and how it will be again.

"But not now, this instant," Rafe added, regret and certainty evenly balanced in his deep voice. "I don't expect that now. It's enough that you're touching me, that you're here with me, that you're alive."

Alana felt the heat of Rafe's skin beneath her fingers, the tempting, silky line of hair curling down below his navel, and the sharp, involuntary movement of his body as her fingers slid beneath the soft T-shirt. She traced the long muscles of his torso from his waist to his ribs.

Eyes closed, smiling, Alana let her hands savor Rafe's strength and stillness and the changing, compelling textures of his body beneath her palm. Her fingers searched among the crisp hairs on his chest, alive to the feel of him, the silk and the hardness and the heat of him.

And Rafe watched her, wanting her.

Without stopping to think, Alana tugged at his T-shirt, impatient with even the soft cotton restricting the freedom of her touch. She had the T-shirt bunched up beneath his arms before she realized what she was doing.

"I'm sorry," Alana said raggedly, her eyes still closed. "I wasn't thinking."

"I was."

Rafe's voice was deep, caressing.

"What were you thinking?" she whispered. "That I'm a tease?"

"Open your eyes and I'll tell you."

His voice was gentle, coaxing, an intangible caress that made Alana shiver.

Her eyes opened slowly. She saw her hands against Rafe's chest, his nearly black hair curling up over her slender fingers. Her hands flexed sensuously, pressing her nails against his skin.

"What are you thinking?" she asked, watching his eyes as her nails bit gently into his flesh with tiny, sensual rhythms.

"I was thinking of the first time we made love. When I unbuttoned my shirt, you looked at me as though you'd never seen a man before, but I knew damn well that you lived with three brothers. And now," added Rafe softly, "you're looking at me like that again."

"Am I?" asked Alana, her voice barely a breath of sound.

"Do you want to take off my shirt?" Rafe asked, his eyes watching her with hungry intensity.

"Yes."

Alana bent to brush her lips across Rafe's mouth, loving the feel of him, firm and sweet, answering his heat with her own. She felt his lips smile beneath her caress; then his tongue moved teasingly over her mouth until she smiled in return.

"Then what are you waiting for?" asked Rafe. "Take off my shirt."

As he spoke, he unlocked his hands and stretched his arms above his head.

Alana's hands moved up Rafe's body, pushing the soft folds of T-shirt over his chest, his head, his arms, until the shirt fell aside, forgotten. Her breath came in, then went out in a long sigh as she ran her hands freely from Rafe's fingertips to his waist. His breath sounded more like a groan as he laced his hands behind his head once more.

For an instant, Alana hesitated. Then Rafe's

body twisted sinuously beneath her hands, asking to be touched. She whispered his name as she bent down and kissed him, hungry for the feel of his tongue against hers. Her palms rubbed slowly over his chest, stroking him, enjoying him. When her nails scraped gently over his nipples, she felt him shiver. Her fingertips circled him caressingly, then tugged at the small, hard nubs. His tongue moved sensually in her mouth, stealing her breath until she was dizzy.

With a ragged sound, Alana shifted her position and sought the powerful contours of Rafe's shoulders, tasting and biting and kissing him until her mouth slid down and found the hard male nipples her fingers had teased. Her teeth closed lightly over him. She felt the tension in him, felt his body flexing, felt the powerful muscles of his arms harden beneath her palms.

Memories raced through her, burning her.

"Funny," Alana murmured, rubbing her cheek over Rafe's chest, "I never thought of you as really strong, until the storm and the cabin loft."

Rafe smiled, though his fingers were so tightly laced around each other that his hands ached.

"Thought I was a weakling, did you?" he said, his voice soft but almost rough, hungry and laughing at the same time.

"Weakling?"

Alana laughed against Rafe's ribs before she turned her head and began caressing the long

muscles of his torso with slow movements of
her cheek and hand.

"No," she said. "But Dad was six foot five,
and my brothers were all over six feet tall
when they were twelve. Bob was six foot six
and weighed two hundred and twenty pounds
when he was fourteen."

"Whatever attracted you to a shrimp like
me?" asked Rafe.

The question ended in a groan when the
hard tip of Alana's tongue teased his navel.

"First it was your eyes," she said, her voice
blurred as she caressed the taut skin of Rafe's
stomach. "Like a cougar, clear amber and
more than a little untamed."

"And that made you want to tame me?"

"No. It made me want to be wild with you."

Rafe's hands clenched until the fingers went
numb. He tried to speak, but Alana's fingers
had gone from his waist down to the hard
muscles of his thighs. He could think of nothing except her touch and the fierce ache of
hunger swelling so close to her hand.

"But I didn't know it then," continued
Alana, kneading the long muscles that flexed
and shifted beneath her fingers, "not in so
many words. I just knew I got a funny, quivering feeling deep inside whenever you
looked at me in a certain way."

"What way?"

Rafe fought to keep his voice even despite
the waves of hunger that hammered through
his blood. His fingers twisted against each
other until bone ground over bone.

"The way you looked at me when you took off my wet blouse and hung it by the fire," Alana said.

Her breath was a warm flow across the naked skin above Rafe's waist.

"The way you looked at me when you peeled off that soaking, lacy bra," she whispered. "And then you touched me until I couldn't stand by myself. Do you remember?"

"God, yes." Rafe closed his eyes, remembering. "You were barefoot. Your jeans were black with rain and outlined you perfectly, those beautiful legs and hips. . . . Did you know that my hands were shaking when I took off your blouse?"

"Yes," she whispered, her fingers clenching for an instant on Rafe's leg. "I was trembling, too."

"You were cold."

"Was I?" she asked.

Her voice was almost breathless as she caressed Rafe's navel again, biting him gently.

"I burned when you touched me," Alana whispered. "Your hands were so warm on my skin."

"I didn't mean to undress you, not at first. But once I started, I couldn't stop. You were so beautiful, wearing only firelight. I couldn't stop looking at you, touching you."

"I didn't want you to stop. I felt like the most exquisite woman ever born when you looked at me, when you kissed me, touched me. And your body fascinated me."

Alana traced the line of skin just above

Rafe's jeans with her tongue. Her hand smoothed his thigh, enjoying the feel of his strength, remembering.

"When I finally touched you," she said, "every bit of you tightened until each muscle on your body stood out. You felt like warm steel. You feel like that now."

"*Alana.*"

The word was involuntary, a response torn from his control when he felt her hand settling over him.

"I found out how strong you were then," Alana whispered. "You lifted me high, then let me slide slowly, slowly down your body. So strong, yet so gentle. The eyes of a mountain cat and the hands of a poet."

Alana's mouth caressed Rafe's skin as her fingers unfastened his jeans, seeking him beneath layers of cloth, finding him. Her breath came out raggedly.

"And the rest of you so very male," Alana said huskily.

She rubbed her cheek across Rafe's stomach, then she turned her mouth to his skin and kissed him quickly, fiercely.

"Alana," Rafe said, his voice hoarse as he moved reflexively, sensually against her hand. "I can't take much more of this."

"Then don't," she said simply.

She traced the rigid muscles of his arm with one hand, feeling the mist of passion and restraint that covered his body.

"You've given me so much," she said. "Let me give you something in return. It's not as much as either of us wants, but it's all I have right now."

Rafe closed his eyes for a moment, knowing if he looked at Alana, he wouldn't be able to keep his fingers locked behind his head.

Her hand moved again in a devastating, sensual glide of flesh over flesh. Fire thickened in Rafe's veins, fire pooling heavily beneath Alana's hand until he could only twist against the sweet agony of her touch. He groaned aloud, his breath hissing between clenched teeth.

"Oh, God . . . don't," he said hoarsely.

"Rafael," said Alana. "I can't give myself to you now, but you can give yourself to me. Please, give yourself to me. Let me know that I've been able to bring you some pleasure. I need to know that."

Her voice was husky and urgent as she rubbed her cheek against his hot chest.

Rafe's eyes opened, an amber hot enough to burn.

"Look at me," he said.

Alana lifted her head. He saw the silent plea in her dark eyes, saw the fire and fierce pleasure when he moved against her hand, and he knew that she had been utterly honest with him.

Slowly he unlocked his fingers, but he moved only one hand, and then only to hold it out to her. When her lips pressed against his palm, his hand shifted, gently bringing her mouth up to his. What began as a simple brush of lips deepened with each heartbeat until it became a kiss of shattering hunger and sensuality.

And then he gave himself to her as freely and generously as she had given herself to him four years ago, in a cabin warmed by firelight and love.

13

ALANA PULLED THE BUB-bling, spicy apple pie out of the oven, using oversize pot holders that felt as soft to her touch as Rafe's T-shirt had. She smiled to herself as she set the second pie on the wooden counter to cool, feeling more at peace than she had in a long time. Notes of music kept gliding through her mind, chased by lyrics that hadn't yet condensed into songs.

"What is that marvelous smell?" asked Janice from the doorway.

"Pie," said Alana, turning and smiling over her shoulder at the tall, slender woman.

"A miracle," Janice said.

Alana smiled. "Actually, it's just dried apples, sugar, and spices."

"In this wilderness, on that stove, those pies are a miracle," said Janice firmly. She looked at Alana with blue eyes that missed nothing. "Anything I can do to help?"

"I've got everything under control, but thanks anyway."

Janice smiled. "Must be a wonderful feeling."

"What?"

"Having everything under control."

Alana looked startled for an instant. Then she nodded slowly.

It was true. Since she had awakened in the hospital, she had felt as though her life was out of her control, as though she was a victim instead of a person. Fear had eroded her self-respect and confidence.

But today she had been able to talk and laugh with Rafe. Today she had taken the first steps toward overcoming her fear of heights. Today she had realized that Rafe respected and cared for her despite her amnesia and irrational fears.

Rafe had accepted her as she was, imperfect, and then he had given himself to her instead of demanding that she give herself to him.

"Yes," Alana said quietly. "It's an incredibly good feeling."

Janice's eyes narrowed in an instant of intelligent scrutiny that Alana didn't notice.

"I'm glad," said Janice, unmistakable satisfaction in her voice.

Alana looked up quickly, seeing for the first time the compassion in the other woman.

"Rafe told you about my husband, didn't he?" Alana asked.

Janice hesitated while her shrewd blue eyes measured the emotions apparent on Alana's face.

"Don't be angry with him," Janice said finally. "Rafe just wanted to be sure that Stan and I wouldn't accidentally hurt you."

Frowning, Alana wiped her hands on the enormous white apron that she wore.

"It's not fair to ask you to walk on eggs so I won't be upset," Alana said. "This trip is for your pleasure, not mine."

Janice smiled. "Don't worry. We're having a ball."

Alana looked at her with skeptical dark eyes.

"Uh-huh," Alana muttered. "Sure you are—when I'm not screaming at Stan or stealing your fishing guide."

"Stan's a big boy," said Janice dryly. "And as for Rafe, he showed us the water and we caught our limit. Besides, he cleans the trout for us and you whip up hot apple pies. What more could we ask?"

Laughing and shaking her head, Alana gave in.

"You two are very special dudes," Alana said. "If other clients are half as easy to be around, Bob will think he's died and gone to heaven. Most dudes can't find their way downhill without directions and a hard push."

From the next room came the sound of cupboard doors being opened and closed briskly.

"Hey. sis," called Bob from the dining room, "where did I put the dishes last night after I washed them?"

Janice and Alana exchanged a look and burst out laughing. Bob stuck his head in the kitchen.

"What's so funny?" he asked.

"You wouldn't understand," said Alana. "But that's all right. I love you anyway."

She stood on tiptoe and kissed Bob's cheek quickly.

He looked surprised, then very pleased. He started to hug Alana in return, then stopped, remembering. He patted her shoulder with unexpected gentleness and put his blunt index finger on the tip of her nose.

"You look better, sis. Rafe was right. You needed to be home."

Then Bob shook his head and smiled, giving Alana a somewhat baffled look. He still wasn't used to seeing his sister as a contemporary rather than as a substitute mother.

"What?" Alana asked.

"How did you get to be so small, anyway?" Bob said in a rueful voice.

"You grew up."

He smiled. "Yeah, guess so. Why don't you go get dressed? I'll whip up the potatoes and get everything on the table."

Alana blinked, startled by the offer. Then she blinked again, several times, fighting back sudden tears. Bob was being as protective of her as he was of Merry.

"Thanks," Alana said, her voice husky. "I'd like that."

She showered quickly, then climbed into the loft wrapped in Bob's oversize terry cloth robe, which she had found hanging from a peg in the downstairs bathroom. She stood in front of the closet and tried to choose from the array of clothes that Bob had packed for her.

After an unusual amount of time, she decided on a pair of heavy silk slacks that were a rich chocolate color. The blouse she chose was long sleeved and the color of fire, its sensuous texture and folds in stark contrast to its businesslike cut.

Automatically Alana began to button up the blouse so the chain she always wore was concealed. Then she stopped, realizing that she no longer had to hide Rafe's engagement gift. It no longer mattered if people asked her about the unusual design of the necklace.

Jack was dead.

She no longer had to conceal the fact that half of Country's Perfect Couple wore another man's gift in the vulnerable hollow of her throat.

Alana smoothed the collar open. The elegant symbol of infinity shifted and gleamed with each movement of her head. She touched the symbol with her fingertip and felt another tiny bit of peace settling inside her, another step on the way to rebuilding her strength.

For the first time since she had awakened in

the hospital, she began to believe that she not only would survive, but would be able to love again.

Even if her nightmares were true.

"Alana?" Rafe's voice came from the bottom of the steep stairway. "Are you ready?"

"Almost," she whispered, too softly for Rafe to hear. "Almost."

She hurried downstairs, truly hungry for food for the first time since the six missing days. High-country air had a magical effect on her appetite.

It was the same for everyone else. Even after a dinner of trout, potatoes, green beans, and biscuits, everyone found room for a piece of pie.

Rafe sliced and served the warm apple pie to the accompaniment of good-natured complaints as to which person was or wasn't getting the biggest piece. Bob and Stan swapped pieces with each other several times before Rafe gave in and put the last piece of pie between them.

Smiling, Rafe watched Alana as she ate the last bite of the generous slice of pie he had cut for her. When she threw back her head and sighed that she was too full to move, he saw the gleam of gold in the hollow of her throat.

With a callused fingertip, he traced the length of the chain and its elegant symbol.

"You still wear this," he said softly.

"I've never taken it off since you gave it to me."

Rafe's eyes were tawny in the late-afternoon

light that was streaming through the window, tawny and very intent.

"Not even after I sent back your letter?" he asked, searching her eyes.

"Never. It was all I had left of you."

The back of Rafe's finger caressed Alana's throat.

"I wish we were alone," he whispered. "I would like very much to kiss you. Many times. Many places. Would you like that, wild-flower?"

A suggestion of color bloomed beneath Alana's skin. She smiled and smoothed her cheek against Rafe's finger.

"Yes," she murmured. "I'd like that."

Then Alana looked across the table and saw Stan watching her closely, his eyes so blue they were almost black, his fair hair shimmering in a shaft of sunlight that came through the cabin window and fell across his thick shoulders. Quickly she looked away, still unable to accept Stan's unnerving physical resemblance to Jack Reeves.

When Stan asked Rafe about a particular kind of dry fly, Alana turned to Janice and asked the first question that came to mind.

"Somehow you aren't what I'd expect a travel agent to be. How did you choose that career?"

There was a sudden silence, then a determined resumption of the casual conversation taking place around the women.

Alana looked at Rafe suddenly, wondering if she had done something wrong.

Rafe ignored her, apparently caught up in his talk with Stan.

"I'm sorry," Alana said to Janice. "Did I ask the wrong question?"

Janice's smile had a wry twist as she glanced sideways at Rafe.

"I'd say you asked just the right one," Janice said.

Rafe looked up sharply but said nothing.

"I used to be a psychiatrist," Janice explained. "After ten years, I burned out. So many problems. So few solutions."

Her voice was light but her eyes were narrowed against memories that still had the power to hurt her.

Alana thought of what had happened to Rafe, to her, to Jack. *So many problems. So few solutions.*

"So I became a special kind of travel agent," Janice said. "I match people with the kind of vacation that will do the most for them."

"Solutions," said Alana.

"Yes."

Alana wanted to ask more. Suddenly she was very curious about Janice's past, about the pressures that had driven her to change careers.

And about Rafe, who had known Janice before.

"Would you like to hear about what happened?" asked Janice.

"If you don't mind," Alana said.

Janice and Rafe exchanged a quick look. He

raised his dark eyebrows slightly, then shrugged.

Janice turned back to Alana.

"I used to work for the government, like Rafe," said Janice.

Though she spoke quietly, at her first words Stan and Rafe's conversation died.

Stan gave Janice a hard look, then looked questioningly at Rafe. Rafe ignored him. Stan seemed about to speak when a gesture from Rafe cut him off.

"Men and women who work under impossible conditions," Janice said calmly, "often have trouble living with themselves. If something goes wrong and people die, or if nothing goes wrong and people die anyway, the person in charge has to live with it."

Alana looked at Rafe. His eyes were hooded, unreadable.

"The key words are *in charge*," Janice said. "These are intelligent people who care about the world. They are the actors, not the audience. They are in control of themselves and of life."

Janice smiled wryly and took a sip of her coffee.

"At least," she added softly, "they *think* they're in control. Then it all goes from sugar to shit and they're left wondering what hit them. My job was to explain that it was reality that ran over them and left them flat."

Stan made a sound halfway between protest and laughter. When Janice looked at him, he winked. The smile she gave him was both gentle and sensual.

Alana sensed the nearly intangible currents of affection and respect that flowed between the two people.

"People come in all kinds," Janice said, turning back to Alana, "but the ones I dealt with usually fell into three categories. The first was people who couldn't cope with an unpredictable, unforgiving reality and simply fell apart."

Alana looked down at the bit of pie left on her plate and wondered if she was one of the ones who couldn't cope.

"In the second category were the people who survived by stuffing down their feelings of inadequacy, bewilderment, and fear. These people did exactly what they had been trained to do and they did it magnificently."

Alana looked at Rafe. He was watching her. For an instant he put his fingertip on the golden symbol she wore around her neck.

"The third category," Janice said, "was made up of people who had so little imagination or such great faith in 'going by the book' that they had the same untouchable serenity that religion gives to some people."

"It must be nice," Alana said.

"I wouldn't know," Rafe answered.

Janice picked up her coffee cup, sighed, and put it down again without tasting the dark brew.

"People in the first category, the ones who couldn't cope, didn't last long as operatives,"

Janice said bluntly. "The third type, the ones who went by the book, did very poorly in the fluid world of fieldwork. We tended to put them in office positions as soon as they were discovered."

"And the second category?" Alana asked Janice, but it was Rafe whom she watched.

"Those in the second category did most of the work," Janice said. "They were the survivors, the people who got the job done no matter what it cost them."

The brackets around Rafe's mouth deepened.

"Unfortunately," Janice said, glancing quickly at Rafe, "sooner or later the survivors paid a high psychic price when they were confronted by the randomness of reality and the fact that Superman exists only in cartoons."

Alana touched the corner of Rafe's mouth as lightly as he had touched her necklace. He turned and brushed a kiss over her fingertip.

"Real men bleed and make mistakes," Janice said softly. "If, once the crisis is past, the survivors can't deal with their feelings of weakness, can't accept that all any person can do is his or her best . . . well, then they begin to hate themselves. If they can't accept the fact that they can be afraid, be hurt, even be broken and *still* be damned fine, brave, effective human beings, then they tear themselves apart."

Alana's hand trembled. Rafe caught it between his own, kissed her palm, and released her.

"My job was to help the survivors accept their own limitations, their humanity. I was supposed to help them accept themselves." Janice stared out over the table, seeing something from the past. "Because if they couldn't accept their humanity, I lost them. I—lost—them."

Janice's hand clenched into a fist, softly pounding the table with each word.

Impulsively Alana put her hand over the other woman's.

"It wasn't your fault," Alana said quickly. "You couldn't open up their hearts and make them believe in their own worth. All you could do was care, and you did."

Janice looked at Alana for a long moment. Then Janice's lips shaped a sad smile.

"But when you love them, and you lose them," Janice said, "it hurts like hell. After awhile there was one too many, and I quit."

Alana looked quickly at Rafe, wondering if he had been the "one too many" for Janice.

"You did all anyone could," Rafe said quietly, "and that was a lot more than most."

"So did you." Janice's blue eyes measured Rafe. "Did you think that was enough?"

"No," he said, meeting her eyes without flinching, "but I'm learning to live with it. Finally."

Janice looked at Rafe for a long moment, then smiled gently.

"Good for you, Rafe Winter," she said. "Very good. It was a near thing, wasn't it?"

Janice turned and looked at Alana.

"The strongest ones," Janice said quietly, "have the hardest time. They go the longest before they come up against human limitations. And then they blame themselves. They reach a state where they are, in effect, at war with themselves. Some survive even that. A lot don't."

Alana looked at Rafe with dark, haunted eyes. The thought of how close she had come to losing him forever was like a knife turning in her soul.

"For the strong ones," Janice said, "it's a case of the sooner they accept their own limitations, the better. There are very few ways to win a war with yourself, and a whole lot of ugly ways to lose."

There was silence. Then Janice set down her coffee cup and said briskly, "Enough of my past. Who's going to catch the biggest fish tonight?"

"I am," Bob and Stan said at the same moment.

The two big men looked at each other, grinned, and began placing bets on the outcome.

Rafe and Janice exchanged knowing glances and shook their heads.

After Bob and the guests left, Alana stood and began to clear the table. Rafe immediately took the plates out of her hands.

"You look too elegant to handle dirty dishes," he said. "Come sit in the kitchen and talk to me."

Alana looked at Rafe in disbelief. He was

wearing black wool slacks and a tailored black shirt made of a wool so fine it felt like silk. The supple fabric fit him like a shadow, outlining the power of his arms and shoulders.

"You look too elegant, too," Alana said.

She touched the black fabric where it pulled lightly across Rafe's chest. The warmth of him radiated through the shirt to her hand, making her want to rub her palm against him, to curl up next to him like a cat by a fire. And then she wanted simply to hold him, to comfort him, to take away whatever hurt she could from his past.

Alana had no doubt that Rafe was one of the very strong ones whom Janice had talked about, the ones who had the hardest time accepting their own limitations.

"What are you thinking?" Rafe asked, his voice deep, velvety.

"That you're one of the strong ones."

"So are you."

The thought startled Alana. She didn't feel strong. She felt weak, useless, foolish, hiding from herself and reality behind a wall of amnesia and irrational fears.

Before she could protest, Rafe spoke, his voice quick and sure.

"You are strong, Alana. You were only a child, yet you held your family together after your mother died. When you thought I was dead, you saw your best chance of emotional survival in a singing career, and you took it.

"And when another crisis came, you fought

for life. You fought as bravely and fiercely as anyone ever has."

"Then why am I afraid?" whispered Alana.

"Because it wasn't enough," Rafe said grimly. "You came flat up against the fact that Wonder Woman, like Superman, doesn't exist in the real world."

"I didn't think that I was Wonder Woman."

"Didn't you? Who was the strongest Burdette, the one everyone came to when dreams and favorite puppies died? Your dad? No way. It was years before he was worth a damn after your mother's death. As for Jack—"

Alana's mouth turned down in a sad, bitter smile.

"Jack was a user," Rafe said, his voice clipped. "If it hadn't been for your discipline, your intelligence, your sheer ability to take apart a song and put it back together in a new, vivid way, Jack would have been just another beer hall tenor."

"He had a fine voice."

"Only with you, Alana. He knew it better than you did. He used you to make the world more comfortable for himself. And he acted as though using you was his God-given right."

Alana closed her eyes, hearing her own unwanted thoughts coming from Rafe's lips.

"I used him, too," she whispered. "I used him to survive after they told me you were dead."

"Were you the one who demanded marriage?"

Alana shook her head. "I just wanted to sing."

"That's what Bob said. He remembered Jack hounding you and then finally telling you that if you wouldn't marry him, he wouldn't sing with you."

"Yes," Alana whispered, her voice shaking.

"Jack knew exactly what he wanted, and he knew how to get it. When it came to his own comforts, he was as selfish as any man I've ever known."

"But he didn't want me, not as a wife, not as a woman."

Rafe laughed harshly.

"Wrong, Alana. You didn't want *him*. He could have your singing talent, but he couldn't have you. Easy street was more important to Jack than sex, so he accepted your conditions."

"I didn't want him to want me," Alana said.

Her voice was strained, her eyes tightly closed, memories and nightmares turning. She shivered despite the warmth of the cabin, for she was feeling again the cold afternoon before the storm, hearing fragments of words, *Jack cursing, reaching for her.*

"I think—" Alana's voice broke, then came back so harshly that it sounded like a stranger's. "I think Jack wanted me on Broken Mountain. I think we fought about it."

From the front porch came the sound of Stan's laughter as he and Bob shouldered each other to see who would be first through the door.

Alana swayed alarmingly. Her eyes opened, black with memories and nightmare combined.

"No," she whispered. "Oh, God, *no*."

14

ALANA DIDN'T HEAR THE
clatter of plates as Rafe put them on the table
and stood close to her, not touching her, prepared to catch her if she fainted.

Rafe was afraid she was going to do just
that. Her skin was as pale and translucent as
fine china..Her pupils were dilated to the point
that only a small rim of brown remained.

"Jack was laughing," Alana whispered.

Rafe's eyelids flinched. He bit back the
words he wanted to say, the futile cry that she
shouldn't remember. Not yet. Reality was brutal.

And Alana looked so fragile.

"The lake was ice cold and Jack was laughing at me," she said. "All my clothes, my sleeping bag, me—soaked and so cold. He said I could sleep in his sleeping bag. For a price. He said he'd be glad to warm me up."

Rafe's breath came in swiftly.

Alana didn't notice. She heard nothing but the past that haunted her.

"At first, I didn't believe him," she said numbly. "Then I tried to ride out. He grabbed my braids and yanked me out of the saddle and kicked Sid until she bolted down the trail. He—he hit me. I couldn't get away. He wrapped my braids around his hand, holding me, and he hit me again and again."

Rafe's expression changed, pulled by hatred into savage lines of rage, the face of a man who had once gone through a jungle hell like an avenging angel.

Alana didn't see. Her wide eyes were blinded by the past that she had hidden from herself, but not well enough.

Not quite.

"Then Stan tied me and dumped me on a rock ledge by the lake," Alana said. "He said we wouldn't go down the mountain until I changed my mind. 'When we come down off this damned mountain, you're going to heel for me like a bird dog.' And then he laughed and laughed."

Rafe reached for Alana with hands that trembled, rage and love and helplessness combined.

He couldn't touch her.

"But Jack didn't want me," Alana said in a

raw voice. "He just wanted to—to break me. I think he must have hated me."

Alana's eyes closed slowly. She made an odd sound and covered her mouth with her hand.

"It was so cold. The lake and the rock and the night. Cold."

The words were muffled, but Rafe heard them, felt them like blows.

Helpless.

In the silence of his mind, Rafe cursed the fact that Jack Reeves had died quickly, painlessly, a hundred feet of darkness and then the deadly impact of granite.

Alana drew a deep, shuddering breath. When her eyes opened, they were focused on the present. She ran shaking fingers through her hair. Short hair. Hair that couldn't be used as a weapon against her, chaining her.

"That's why I cut off my braids," Alana said, relief and pain mixed in her voice. "I'm not crazy after all."

"No." Rafe's voice was soft and yet harsh with the effort of holding his emotions in check. "You're not crazy."

"Are you sure?" she asked, trying to smile. "Because I have a really crazy thing to ask you."

"Anything. Anything at all."

"Run your fingers through my hair. Take away the feel of Jack's hands."

Rafe brought his hands up to Alana's head, ready to retreat at the first sign of returning fear. Gently he eased his fingers through her soft, short hair.

Slowly closing her eyes, Alana concentrated on the sensation of Rafe's strong fingers moving through her hair. She tilted her head against his palms, increasing the pressure of his caresses.

Chills of pleasure chased through her.

"More," she murmured.

Rafe's fingers slid deeper into the midnight silk of Alana's hair, rubbing lightly over her scalp, caressing her.

"Yes," she sighed.

Alana moved against his hands, increasing the contact, deepening the intimacy, until the heat of Rafe's hands surrounded her, taking away memories, warming her.

When Alana opened her eyes, Rafe's face was very close. His concentration on the intimate moment was as great as hers. So was his pleasure. By quarter inches he lowered his mouth to hers, waiting for the least sign of the fear that might come when she realized she was caught between his hands and his lips.

Alana's answer was a smile and a sigh as her lips parted, welcoming Rafe. He kissed her very gently, not wanting to frighten her. Her arms stole around his waist, held him.

"You feel so good," Alana whispered against Rafe's lips. "So warm, so alive. And you want me. Not to break, but to cherish."

She kissed him slowly, savoring the heat of him, shaping herself to him, absorbing him like a flower absorbing sunlight.

"So warm," she murmured.

Rafe felt Alana's breasts press against him as her arms tightened around him. Hunger swept through him, a fierce surge of fire.

"Very warm," he agreed, smiling, nibbling on the corner of her mouth.

One of Rafe's hands slid from Alana's hair to her shoulder, then to her ribs. Instead of retreating, she moved closer. Her scent and sweetness made the breath stop in Rafe's throat.

Slowly he moved his hand away from the soft temptation of Alana's breast. With light touches he ran his right hand over her back, enjoying the resilience of her body. His left hand rubbed through her hair, then stroked her neck.

Finally, slowly, he moved his left hand to her back until he held her loosely in his arms.

"I'm not frightening you, am I?" Rafe asked huskily.

Alana shook her head and burrowed closer to him.

"I love your warmth, Rafael. When I'm close to you like this, I can't even imagine ever being cold again."

The front door slammed open.

"Hey, sis, where did I put the—oops, sorry!"

Rafe glanced up over Alana's black cap of hair.

Stan, who had followed Bob inside, gave Rafe a long, enigmatic look.

"Lose something?" asked Rafe mildly, keeping his arms around Alana.

"My net," admitted Bob. "I had it when I came in for dinner, but I can't find it."

"Last time I saw your net," Rafe said, "it was leaning against the back door of the lodge."

"Thanks."

Bob walked quickly around the dining room table and out the back door. When he realized Stan wasn't following, Bob called back over his shoulder to the other man.

"Come on, Stan. Don't you know a losing cause when you see one?"

The instant Alana realized that Bob wasn't alone, she stiffened and turned to face the living room.

Stan was walking toward her.

Quickly Alana spun around, holding on to Rafe's arms as though he were all that stood between her and a long, deadly fall.

"Stan," Rafe said.

Rafe's voice was quiet, yet commanding.

Stan paused, waiting.

"The trout are rising," Rafe said. "Why don't you try that dark moth I tied for you? *The one we both agreed on.*"

"You sure it will get the job done?" Stan asked sardonically. "You have to be real careful with trout. If they get away, they're even harder to lure the next time."

"What I've made matches the environment almost perfectly," Rafe said, choosing each word with care. "That, and patience, will get the job done. Ask Janice."

Stan paused, then nodded.

"I'll do that, Winter. I'll do just that."

Without another word, Stan brushed past Rafe and Alana. In a few seconds, the back door banged shut.

"Two bulls in a china shop," Rafe muttered, resting his cheek against Alana's hair.

Alana shifted in Rafe's embrace. Immediately he loosened his arms. She moved closer, kissed him, and stepped back.

"I'm going to change clothes and then do the dishes," she said. "You should get into fishing clothes and help Stan win his bet with Bob."

"I'd rather stay here. With you."

"I'm all right, Rafe. Really. Stan startled me. He looks so damn much like Jack."

"Are you afraid that Stan is going to pick you up and throw you in the lake?" asked Rafe, his voice easy, casual.

Alana stood very still for an instant before she slowly shook her head.

"No. I don't think . . ."

Her voice died and her eyes were very dark. She said nothing more.

"What is it?" asked Rafe softly, coaxingly.

"I don't think that was the worst of it," she said starkly.

"Alana," he whispered.

She stepped away from Rafe.

"I need to think," Alana said, "but when you're near, all I can think about is how good you feel, how patient you are with me, how much I want to reach back four years and touch love again. Touch *you*."

She took a breath and let it out slowly. "I'll catch up with you at sunset, when it's too dark to fish."

"That's two hours from now," protested Rafe. "You won't even know where Stan and I will be."

"Sound carries in this country. And Stan has the kind of voice that carries, period. I'll find you."

"We'll be fishing just below the cascade," Rafe said. "If you don't show up before sunset, I'm going to stuff Stan into his own net and come looking for you." Then, softly, he said, "I wanted to fish with you tonight."

"Oh, no," Alana said, shaking her head. "I can hear your fly line whimpering for mercy right now."

Rafe's smile flashed, softening the hard lines of his face.

"But," Alana added, running her fingertips across his mustache, "I'd love to watch you fish. You please me, Rafael Winter. You please me all the way to my soul."

Then Alana turned and slipped from Rafe's arms. Hungrily he watched her walk across the living room to the loft stairs. His skin tingled where she had touched him, her scent was still sweet in his nostrils, and he wanted her so much that he hurt.

Abruptly Rafe turned away and went to the downstairs bedroom. With quick motions he changed into his fishing clothes. Then he let himself out of the cabin quietly, knowing if he saw Alana again, he wouldn't leave her.

Alana changed into jeans and a sweater and had the kitchen cleaned long before sunset. Her mind was working as swiftly as her hands. She reviewed what she remembered about the six missing days, and what she didn't.

She remembered parts of the ride up the trail with Jack. Then the first night . . .

Was it the first night when Jack and I fought? Alana asked herself silently.

Frowning, she stacked wood in the stove for the morning fire.

Three days in the hospital, of which she remembered only one. That left three days unaccounted for.

No, two.

We must have spent one day traveling to Wyoming and one night at the ranch house, Alana thought. So it must have been the first night on Broken Mountain, up by the lake, when Jack threw me and my clothes and my sleeping bag into the lake.

Alana's body tightened as she remembered what had followed. Jack had slapped her all but senseless when she had tried to run from him. That was the night she had spent curled over herself on a piece of granite, shivering.

That's why I'm so cold in my nightmares, Alana realized. Memory and nightmare combined.

She let out a long breath, feeling better

about herself. Not all of her fears were irrational.

But then, why does the sound of a storm terrify me? Alana asked herself.

The wind hadn't been blowing that night. It hadn't been storming. No lightning. No ground-shaking thunder. Alana was certain of it. If that night had been the ice-tipped storm of her nightmare, she would have died of exposure before morning.

Yet wind and thunder and ice were a vivid, terrifying part of Alana's nightmares.

"The storm must have come the second night on Broken Mountain," Alana whispered, needing more than the cabin's silence to comfort her. "The night I fell."

The night Jack died.

"Why did Jack untie me? Did I give in, go to him?"

The sound of her own questions made Alana shudder. She wasn't certain she wanted to know if she had traded her self-respect for a dry sleeping bag and cold sex with Jack. Prostitution, in a word.

Alana waited, listening to her own silences, sensing her body's response to her thoughts.

Nothing changed. No nightmare closing around. No fear. No sense of connection with hidden reality.

"All right," Alana said tightly. "It's probably not that. Did Jack get too drunk to be patient? Did he untie me, rape me, beat me?"

Once more, Alana waited, forgetting to breathe, anticipating the return of nightmare as her waking thoughts closed in on the truth.

Once more, nothing came.

When Alana remembered Jack hitting her, her stomach turned over and her breath came shallowly.

When she thought of submitting to him, there was . . . nothing. When she thought of being raped, there was . . . nothing. No fear, no desire to scream, no sickness rising in her throat, no chill, no hammering heart or cold sweat. None of the physiological signals that had warned her in the past when she was approaching the truth.

If the truth could even be approached.

Abruptly Alana pulled off her apron and went to find Rafe, unable to bear any more questions, any more answers, any more fear and silence.

The path to the lake was overgrown, clearly showing the bruised grass that marked the passage of at least two people. Alana walked quickly, barely noticing the crimson cloud streamers stretched across the sky. Nor did she see the deep amethyst mountain slopes crowned by luminous ramparts of stone, nor the fragrant shadows flowing out of the forest around her.

The path approached the lake at an angle in order to avoid an area that was a bog in the early summer and an uneven, rough meadow in the fall. Winding through the trees, yielding only occasional glimpses of the water, the path kept to the forest until the last possible moment.

Alana heard Rafe and Stan before she could see them. At least, she heard Stan, his voice pitched to carry above the exuberant thunder of the cascade. She could only assume he was talking to Rafe.

Then Stan's voice came clearly and Alana was certain. He was talking to Rafe.

"No, you listen to me for a change, Captain Winter, *sir*," Stan said sardonically. "I've got a nasty mind for situations like this. I was trained to have a nasty mind."

There was a pause, but whatever Rafe replied was lost in the sound of the cascade. Alana hesitated, then continued toward the lake, screened by spruce and aspen.

"Try this scenario on for size," Stan said. "There's a woman you've wanted for years. Another man's woman. It grinds on you real hard. So the woman you want and the man you hate come up here for a little camping trip."

Alana froze in place, suddenly cold.

She didn't want to hear any more, but she couldn't move.

"You wait around, see your chance, and chuck good old Jack over the nearest cliff," continued Stan. "Then you go to collect the spoils."

"... half-assed pop psychol ..." Rafe's voice wove in and out of the cascade's throaty rumble.

Stan's voice was as clear as thunder.

"But she's not used to that kind of violence," Stan said. "She runs away. She spends a night in the open, cold and exposed. And then she just shuts it all out, forgets."

". . . leave the thinking to people with . . ."

"Her amnesia leaves you with a real problem," Stan said, ignoring the interruption. "If she remembers, it doesn't matter whose friend the sheriff is. Your ass is in a sling."

Alana took a ragged breath and continued down the trail. She stumbled like a sleepwalker, using her hands to push herself away from the rough trunks of the trees that seemed to grow perversely in front of her feet, as though to hold her back.

". . . crock of . . ." Rafe's voice faded in and out of the cascade's thunder.

"I'm not finished," cut in Stan, his voice very clear, carrying like a brass bell across the evening. "You can save yourself by marrying her. She won't go telling tales on her own husband."

"Jesus, you've been reading too many tabloids."

"Maybe. From what Bob tells me, good old Jack wasn't much of a loss to this world, so it's not like Alana is going to spend a year mourning the son of a bitch. Besides, it's plain enough that she likes you."

"You noticed," Rafe said sarcastically.

"You've got a little problem, though. If she remembers before you marry her, you're up shit creek without a paddle."

"Then why am I helping . . ."

Alana leaned forward, straining to hear all of Rafe's words. She couldn't. Unlike Stan,

Rafe's voice became softer, not louder with anger.

Rafe was furious.

"Are you really helping her to remember?" retorted Stan. "Then why in hell won't you let me off the leash?"

". . . Janice."

"Janice would do a marine crawl through hot coals for you, Winter, and you damn well know it!"

"I'd . . . same for . . ."

Alana left the trees behind and began walking over the rocks and logs that were between her and the lake. Each step brought her closer to the men.

Closer to their words.

"And I'm supposed to just shut up and go along with the program," shot back Stan.

"Hell of an idea, hotshot!"

"Maybe, and maybe not. That's a damned good woman you're hunting, Winter. I'm not real sure she wants to be caught. I think she should remember first. That's the only way her choice will have any meaning. That's the best chance she has of surviving."

"Is that what Janice thinks?" Rafe asked.

Alana was less than fifty feet away, close enough to hear Rafe clearly. He and Stan were facing one another. If the men noticed her slow progress toward them, they made no sign.

"I'm not sure Janice is able to think straight where you're involved," said Stan.

Alana stopped, held by the stark pain in Stan's voice.

"There's nothing between me and Janice," Rafe said. "There never was."

Stan hesitated, then made an odd gesture, turning his hands palms up as though to accept or hold something.

"I'd like to believe that. I really would."

"Believe it," Rafe said.

"Hell, it doesn't matter right now. It wouldn't matter at all, except that I don't want Alana trapped because Janice allowed emotion to louse up her judgment."

"She hasn't."

"If it all goes to hell," Stan said, "I don't want Janice blaming herself. She's been through enough of that on your account. But that doesn't matter, either. Not up here. It's just like the bad old days. All that matters is the mission."

"Then quit screwing it up."

"You've got two more days," Stan said flatly. "If your way doesn't work by then, I'll try mine."

When Rafe spoke, the suppressed violence in his voice curled and cracked like a whip, making Stan flinch.

"If you do anything that hurts Alana," Rafe said, "you'll go back down Broken Mountain the same way Jack Reeves did—in a green plastic bag. Do you read me, corporal?"

"I'm not a corporal anymore. And you're not a captain."

Stan turned slightly.

For a moment Alana thought he had spotted her, for she was directly in his line of sight.

Suddenly Stan made a swift feint toward Rafe. At the first hint of movement, Rafe swiftly assumed a fighting stance. Legs slightly bent, hands held slightly apart at chest level, he waited for Stan to move again.

"You're as fast as ever," Stan said, something close to admiration in his voice.

Stan moved again very quickly, his big hands reaching for the other man. Rafe stepped into the attack, pivoted smoothly, and let Stan slide by, not touching him except for the hand that closed around Stan's wrist.

With fluid grace, Rafe twisted Stan's arm and brought it up behind his back, applying pressure until Stan was on his knees. Stan's blond hair shimmered palely in the twilight as Rafe bent down, his face a mask of cold rage.

"No!"

Rafe's head snapped around at Alana's scream. When he saw the frightened, hunted look on her face, he released Stan and started toward her.

"Alana!" Rafe said.

Alana spun away from him and ran back into the forest.

Rafe started after her, then realized that chasing her would only increase her fear. With a soundless snarl, he turned on Stan, who had made no move to get to his feet.

"You knew she was there, didn't you?" Rafe demanded.

Stan nodded and smiled grimly.

"I saw her out of the corner of my eye," he agreed. "That's why I jumped you. Think it reminded her of something, old buddy?"

"Get up."

Rafe's voice was soft and deadly.

"So you can take me apart?" Stan asked, smiling oddly. "No way, Winter. I've seen what you can do when you're mad. I think I'll just sit out this dance."

"And I think," Rafe said, spacing each word carefully, showing how much his control cost, "that if you don't get out of my sight, I'll take you apart anyway."

15

WIND FLEXED AND FLOWED around the lodge, bringing with it the sound of laughter. After the laughter came words without meaning, wind, more laughter.

Alana rolled over in bed, tangling in the covers for the tenth time and wishing that everyone would enjoy the poker game with a little less enthusiasm.

She wondered if Rafe was with the happy card players. Then she remembered his fury at Stan. She doubted that Rafe was in the last cabin, laughing and drawing cards.

Stan's accusations turned and prowled inside Alana's mind like the wind. She wanted to reject them out of hand, completely, yet they kept finding weaknesses in her resolve, cracks in her wall of refusal, little doubts clinging like tentacles.

From the moment Alana saw Rafe at the airport, she had been certain that he still loved her. It wasn't a thoughtful conclusion; it was instinct, pure and simple and very, very deep. Yet assuming that Rafe loved her was groundless, even ridiculous.

He had believed she was happily married six weeks after his "death" had been reported. A year ago he had returned her letter unopened. Before yesterday, nothing had happened to make him believe any differently.

Before yesterday, Rafe must have hated her.

Then why did he pressure Bob to get me home? Alana asked silently. Why has Rafe been so very gentle, so understanding, from the moment he met me at the airport?

No answer came but that of the wind blowing over mountains and forest and cabin alike.

Did something happen on Broken Mountain? Alana wondered. Something that I can't remember, something that made Rafe believe my marriage to Jack was a desperate sham from the beginning?

The wind curled and shook the cabin like a powerful, transparent cat.

A chill condensed in Alana. She pulled the covers closer and rolled over again, seeking the comfort that had never come to her since Broken Mountain.

Yet no matter where she turned, she kept

hearing Stan's voice, Stan's accusations.

They horrified her.

Is the truth that brutal? Alana cried silently. Did Rafe pursue me to save himself?

Was Jack's death less than accidental?

Is that why Rafe refused to tell me what happened on Broken Mountain?

Waves of coldness swept over Alana, roughening her skin. She lay very still, curled around herself, shivering despite the blankets heaped on top of her.

Alana knew that Rafe was capable of deadly violence. He had been trained for it, was skilled in it, had lived with it for most of his adult life. But she couldn't believe that he was capable of such sly deception, that he would coolly plan to murder Jack and then seduce and marry her in order to ensure her silence.

That didn't sound like the Rafe she had known, the Rafe she had loved.

The Rafe she still loved.

If Stan had accused Jack of such vicious lies, Alana would have been sickened—*but she would have believed.*

Jack had been a totally selfish man. Jack had been capable of smiling lies and chilling cruelties, whatever it took to bend the world to his comfort.

Jack had been capable of cold-blooded murder.

Alana's stomach moved uneasily. Cold sweat broke out over her body. Suddenly she couldn't bear the clammy sheets and slack, heavy blankets any longer. She needed the lively warmth and flickering companionship of a fire.

She sat up in bed and groped for her housecoat. All she found was the thick robe she had borrowed from the downstairs bathroom. Impatiently she pulled on the indigo robe, letting the sleeves trail down over her knuckles. The hem was long enough to brush the tops of her toes.

Groping along the wall, Alana worked her way down the inky darkness of the stairway. The living room was empty, without light. The fireplace ashes were as cold and pale as the moon.

Rafe hadn't been in the lodge at all tonight. He hadn't seen or spoken to Alana since she had run from him through the forest. After her irrational panic had passed, she had waited for Rafe by the trail.

He hadn't come.

Finally, when the moon had risen in pale brilliance over Broken Mountain, Alana had given up and gone inside, shivering with cold and loneliness.

She struck a wooden match on the fireplace stone. Using its flickering light, she peered into the wood box. There was a handful of kindling and a few small chunks of stove wood. Not enough to warm the hearth, much less her.

With a dispirited curse, Alana let the top of the wood box fall back into place. She turned to go back to bed, then froze.

A subtle sound drifted through the cabin, a

distant keening that floated on the shifting mountain wind.

The strange, bittersweet music held Alana motionless, aching to hear more. She held her breath, listening with an intensity that made her tremble.

Music curled around her lightly, tantalizing her at a threshold just below memory, music curving across the night like a fly line, lengthening in grace and beauty with each surge of energy, each magic, rhythmic pulse.

Blindly Alana felt her way through the lodge to the front door, lured by the elusive music. She opened the door, shut it silently behind her, and held her breath, listening and looking.

There was laughter tumbled by wind, bright squares of light glowing from the cabin at the end of the row. Silhouettes dark against one curtained window, wordless movements of hands and arms, more laughter.

But no music.

It wasn't somebody's transistor radio or tape player that had slid through Alana's defenses, calling to her in a language older and more potent than words.

Yet there was nowhere else the music could be coming from. Of the three cabins that stretched out east of the lodge, only one was glowing with light, only one was brimming with laughter when people won or lost small bets. The two other cabins were empty, as black as night itself. Blacker, for the cabins had neither moon nor stars to light their interior darkness.

The wind stirred, blowing across the back of Alana's neck, teasing her ears with half-remembered, half-imagined music. Slowly she turned, facing west.

The fourth cabin was several hundred feet away, wrapped in forest and darkness, not really part of the fishing camp. No light gleamed from the cabin in welcome, no laughter swirled, no sense of brimming life came to her.

And then the music called to Alana, an irresistible lure drawing her closer with each note.

She stood and listened for a moment more, her heart beating hard, her blood rushing so quickly that it overwhelmed the mixed murmur of music and wind.

Without stopping to think, she stepped off the porch onto the overgrown path to the fourth cabin. Pine needles and sharp stones smarted against her bare feet, but she noticed them only at a distance. The small hurts meant nothing, for she had recognized the source of the music.

Rafe.

Rafe and his harmonica, mournful chords lamenting love and loss.

It was Alana's own song curling toward her across the night, drifting down on the seamless black surface of her despair, music shimmering with emotion. Once she had sung this song with Rafe. Once they had looked into each other's eyes and shared sad songs of death and broken dreams.

And they had smiled, certain of the power and endurance of their own love.

I heard a lark this morning
Singing in the field.
I heard a lark this morning
Singing wild.

I didn't know
You had gone away.
I didn't know
Love had gone to yesterday.

I heard a lark this morning
Singing wild.
I heard a lark this morning
Singing free.

Maybe tomorrow I'll know.
Maybe tomorrow you'll tell me
Why the lark sang.
And maybe yesterday
Never came.

I heard a lark this morning
Singing in the field.
I heard a lark this morning
Singing free.
It did not sing for me.

The music Alana had once picked out on her guitar now came back to her in haunting chords sung by Rafe's harmonica. The words she had written ached in her throat and burned behind her eyes.

Thick terry cloth folds wrapped around her legs, slowing her. She picked up the hem of the robe and began to run toward the cabin, not feeling the rough path or the tears running down her face, drawn by her music.

By Rafe.

The cabin stood alone in a small clearing. There was no flicker of candlelight, no yellow shine of kerosene lamps, nothing but moonlight pouring through the cabin windows in a soundless fall of silver radiance. Sad harmonies shivered through the clearing, shadows of despair braiding through the pale brilliance of moonlight.

Slowly, like a sigh, the song changed into silence. The last transparent notes of music were carried away on a cold swirl of wind.

Alana stood at the edge of the clearing, transfixed by music, aching with silence. Only her face was visible, a ghostly oval above the textured darkness of her robe and the sliding black shadows of evergreens flexing beneath the wind.

She hesitated, feeling the wind and tears cold on her cheeks. Then the mournful chords began all over, sorrow coming back again, unchanged.

I heard a lark this morning . . .

Alana couldn't bear to stand alone in the haunted, wind-filled forest and listen to her yearning song played by the only man she had ever loved.

Slowly she walked across the clearing, seeing only tears and moonlight, hearing only song and sorrow. She went up the cabin steps like a ghost, soundless, wrapped in darkness. The front door stood open, for there was neither warmth nor light to keep inside.

The cabin had only one room. Rafe was stretched out on the bed that doubled as a couch during the day. Only his face and hands were visible, lighter shades of darkness against the overwhelming night inside the cabin.

Silently, without hesitation, Alana crossed the room. She didn't know if Rafe sensed her presence. He made no move toward her, neither gesture nor words nor silence. He simply poured himself into the harmonica, music twisting through her, chords of desolation shaking her.

Alana knelt by the bed, trying to see Rafe's face, his eyes. She could see only the pale shimmer of moonlight, for the sad strains of music had blinded her with tears.

> *I heard a lark this morning*
> *Singing wild.*

With each familiar chord, each aching harmony of note with note, Alana felt the past sliding away, nightmare draining into song until she knew only music and no fear at all.

Swaying slightly, her body lost to the music,

Alana's mind slowly succumbed to emotions that were as wary and elusive as trout shimmering deep within a river pool. She didn't know how many times the song ended and began, notes curling and curving across her inner darkness, music drifting down, floating, calling her, luring her up from the dark depths of her own mind.

Alana knew only that at some point she began to sing. At first her song was wordless, a supple blending of her voice with the harmonica's smooth chords, clear harmonies woven between instrument and singer. The melody line passed between them, changed by one and then the other, renewed and renewing each other by turns.

And then, like a wild lark, Alana's voice flew free.

It soared and turned on invisible currents, swept up emotions and transmuted them into pouring song, a beauty so transparent, so flawless, that a shiver of awe rippled through Rafe. For an instant the harmonica hesitated. Then he gave himself to the music as completely as Alana had, pursuing the brilliant clarity of her voice, soaring with it, sharing her ecstatic flight out of darkness, touching the sun.

Finally there was nothing left of the song but the last note shimmering in the darkness, sliding into moonlight and the soft whisper of the wind.

Alana put her head in her hands and wept soundlessly. Rafe stroked her hair slowly, gently, until her lips turned into his palm and he felt her tears slide between his fingers. With careful hands, he eased Alana onto the bed beside him, murmuring her name, feeling her shiver as she came close to him. Her hands were cool when she touched his face, and she shivered again.

Rafe shifted until he could free the sleeping bag he had been lying on. He unzipped it and spread smooth folds of warmth over her. When he started to get out of bed, she made a sound of protest and sat up. He kissed her cold hands.

"Lie still," he said. "I'll start a fire."

But first Rafe closed the cabin door, shutting out the wind. He moved swiftly in the darkness, not bothered by the lack of light.

There was a muted rustle of paper and kindling, then the muffled thump of cured wood being stacked in the fireplace. A match flared in the darkness.

Alana blinked and held her breath, shivering again. Rafe's face looked like a primitive mask cast in pure gold, and his eyes were incandescent topaz beneath the dense midnight of his hair. For long moments he and the fire watched one another, two entities made of heat and potent light.

With the silence and grace of a flame, Rafe turned toward Alana, sensing her eyes watching him. He stood and came toward her, his expression concealed by shadow.

The bed shifted beneath his weight as he sat and looked at her face illuminated by the gliding dance of flames. Her eyes were both dark and brilliant, her skin was flushed, and her lips were curved around a smile. Reflected fire turned and ran through her hair in liquid ribbons of light.

"You are even more beautiful than your song," whispered Rafe.

His fingertip traced Alana's mouth and then the slender hand that rested on top of the sleeping bag. He took her hand and rubbed it gently between his palms.

"You're cold," Rafe said. "How long were you outside?"

Alana tried to remember how long she had stood in the clearing, but all that seemed real to her now was Rafe's heat flowing into her as he touched her.

"I don't know," she said.

Silently Rafe rubbed Alana's hand until it no longer felt cool to his touch. When his fingers went up her arm, he encountered the heavy cloth of the robe she wore. He made a startled sound, then laughed softly.

"So that's where it went," said Rafe.

"What?"

"My bathrobe."

"Yours?" asked Alana, surprised. "I thought it was Bob's. The sleeves come down over my knuckles and the hem drags on my toes and—"

"—I'm such a shrimp," finished Rafe, smiling.

"Rafael Winter," Alana said, exasperation and laughter competing in her voice, "you're more than six feet tall and must weigh at least a hundred and seventy pounds."

"Closer to one-ninety."

In startled reappraisal, Alana looked at the width of Rafe's shoulders, outlined by fire-light.

"Those are hardly the dimensions of a shrimp," she pointed out.

"I know. You're the one who keeps thinking that my clothes belong to Bob."

Rafe's weight shifted, sending a quiver through the bed. Alana's breath caught as she sensed him coming closer.

"You're such a tiny thing," he said. "I'll bet you got the hem all muddy. Unless you're wearing high-heeled slippers?"

"No. Twice."

Rafe looked at Alana. A smile made firelight glide and gleam over his mustache.

"Twice?" he asked.

"I'm five feet five. Not a tiny thing at all. And I'm barefoot."

"Barefoot?"

All amusement was gone from Rafe's voice. He moved to the end of the bed and pulled aside the sleeping bag until he could see Alana's feet.

"There's glass on the path from here to the main cabin," Rafe said. "Not to mention sharp rocks and roots."

He hissed a curse as he saw thin, dark lines of blood on Alana's feet.

"You cut yourself," he said flatly.

Alana wiggled her toes. She tucked her feet

up beneath the warm sleeping bag.

"Little scratches, that's all," she said.

Rafe got up, went to the stove, and tested the water in the kettle. He had intended to make coffee, but when he found the harmonica on the kitchen shelf, he had forgotten about everything else.

Although the fire in the stove had long since died, the water was still warm. He poured some into a basin, took a bar of soap from the sink, and searched for a clean cloth. When he found one, he returned to Alana.

"Give me your feet," he said.

"They're fine."

Rafe flipped back a corner of the sleeping bag, captured one of her feet, and began washing the abrasions with warm water. He sat sideways on the end of the bed, resting her ankle on his thigh.

"Rafe," Alana protested, squirming slightly.

"Rafe what? Am I hurting you?"

"No," she said softly.

"Tickling you?"

Alana shook her head, watching Rafe as he washed her feet and rinsed them carefully. Then he examined the cuts with very gentle touches, making sure that all the dirt was out.

"Hurt?" he asked.

"No."

"I don't have any antiseptic in this cabin."

"I don't need it."

"Yes, you do," countered Rafe in a firm voice. "Dr. Gene made a big point about how run-down you were, fair game for any bug that came along."

"Dr. Gene is wrong."

Rafe grunted, then smiled crookedly.

"I take it back," he said. "I do have some antiseptic here, after a fashion."

Alana watched while Rafe took rag, soap, and basin back to the tiny corner kitchen. He opened a cupboard and pulled out a fifth of Scotch. He knelt by the end of the bed, one of her feet in his hand.

"I'll bet it stings," she said.

"Bet you're right. Bet that next time you go walking you'll remember to wear shoes, tenderfoot."

Using the tip of his finger, Rafe applied whiskey to the first cut. Alana's breath came in sharply. He blew across the cut, taking away some of the sting. Then he went to work on the next scrape, applying Scotch, blowing quickly, his eyes and the whiskey glowing gold in the firelight.

When Alana's breath hissed out over the last cut, Rafe's fingers tightened on her foot.

"Why am I always hurting you?" he asked.

Pain turned in his voice, tightening it into a groan. He bent his head until he could kiss the delicate arch of Alana's foot. His lips lingered on her skin in silent apology for having caused her pain, no matter how necessary it might have been.

One hand cradled the arch of her foot, warming her, while the other hand stroked from the smooth skin at the top of her foot to the graceful curve of her ankle. He caressed her warmly, hands and mouth moving over her, savoring the heady mixture of Scotch and her sweet skin.

"Rafael," cried Alana softly.

Her toes flexed and curled against his palm with an involuntary sensual response.

Rafe's whole body tightened as he fought a short, savage battle with himself for control. With an invisible shiver of rebellion, his hands obeyed the commands of his mind.

Swiftly he put Alana's feet under the sleeping bag and tucked it around her.

"Rafe . . . ?"

Without answering, he stood and went to the fire. Using swift, abrupt motions, he added wood to the fireplace until the flames rushed upward into the night with a sound like wind. Only then did he turn from the savage leap of flames to face Alana.

"Warm enough?" he asked neutrally.

"No."

She shivered slightly, watching Rafe with dark eyes, wondering why he looked so hard, so angry.

He crossed the room in three strides, grabbed the daybed, and pulled it closer to the fire with an ease that shocked Alana. Because he was so gentle with her, she kept on forgetting how powerful he really was.

Rafe turned away from Alana and watched the fire with eyes that also burned.

"How's that?" he asked. "Better?"

"Not as warm as your hands felt," Alana

said softly. "Not nearly so warm as your mouth."

Rafe spun toward her as though she had struck him.

"Don't," he said, his voice harsh.

Alana's eyes widened. Then her eyelashes swept down, concealing her confusion and pain. But nothing concealed the change in her mouth from smiling softness to thin line, happiness flattened by a single word.

Rafe saw and knew that he had hurt Alana once again. He swore silently with a savagery that would have shaken her if she had been able to hear him.

"I'm sorry," Alana whispered. "I thought—"

Her voice broke. She made a helpless gesture, then slid out from beneath the sleeping bag and stood up, pulling the robe tightly around her. His robe.

"I thought you wanted me," she said.

"That's the problem. I want you so much I get hard just looking at you. I want you so much that I don't trust myself to be petted and then to let you go. I want you—*too much*."

The gesture Rafe made was as curt as his voice.

"A thousand times I've dreamed of having you in my arms," he said, "of loving you, touching you, tasting you, and then burying myself in your softness, feeling you loving me deep inside your body until nothing is real but the two of us and then there is only one reality. *Us*."

Alana made a breathless sound that could have been Rafe's name. His words had washed over her in a torrent of desire so consuming that she could barely breathe.

Rafe looked away from her to the fire raging in the hearth.

"I've dreamed too often, too much," he said bluntly. "You'd better go, wildflower. Go now."

Instead, Alana sank back onto the bed, for her legs felt too weak to support her. She thought of Rafe holding her, her body helpless beneath his strength as he became a part of her, and then she waited for the fear to come, freezing her.

Fire came instead, freeing her.

Slowly Alana stood. She walked soundlessly across the short distance separating her from Rafe. He stood with his back to her, his neck corded with tension.

When her arms slid around his waist, his whole body stiffened.

"I'm yours, Rafael," she said softly.

16

ALANA FELT THE TREMOR that went through Rafe at her words. Then she felt the slide and flex of powerful muscles as he turned in her arms and looked down into her eyes. Watching her, waiting for the least sign of withdrawal, of fear, he closed his arms gently around her.

Rafe's arms tightened slowly, inevitably, drawing her against his body. He gathered her close and held her with the power and hunger that he had fought so long to conceal from her.

Alana tilted back her head and watched Rafe through half-closed eyes. Her lips parted, hungry for his kiss.

With a muffled groan, Rafe bent his head

and took what she offered, searching the softness of her mouth with hard, hungry movements of his tongue. The force of his kiss bent her back over his arm, but she didn't protest.

Instead, she clung to him with fierce joy, giving herself to his strength. She sensed that he was testing her, trying to discover if she would freeze, trying to find out while he could still stop himself and let her go.

Rafe shifted Alana in his embrace, holding her head in the crook of one arm and bringing her hips against him with the other. She answered with a soft moan and a supple movement of her body that sent whips of fire flicking over him.

Despite the passion and power of Rafe's embrace, he was careful not to lift Alana off her feet. He didn't want to test either of them to that extent, for he suddenly knew that he couldn't let her go.

He had dreamed of Alana too long, and this was too much like his dreams, cabin and firelight and her sweet, passionate abandon in his arms.

"You aren't afraid," Rafe murmured against Alana's lips, pleading and urging and asking at the same time.

"I'm not afraid of you."

Slowly Alana turned her head from side to side, rubbing her moist lips over Rafe's, savoring the heat and life of him.

"You were never the one I feared," she whispered.

Alana felt one of Rafe's strong hands slide

up to her neck, felt gentle fingers trace the gold chain he had given to her, felt the slight roughness of his fingertip resting on the rapid pulse beating beneath her soft skin. She sighed and softened against him even more.

His head moved and his lips slid down Alana's neck until his tongue touched her pulse so delicately that he could count her rapid heartbeats. Then his hand shifted, sliding inside her robe until the firm curve of her breast fit into his hand and her heartbeat accelerated wildly.

"Yes," Rafe said hoarsely. "This is my dream. Your response, your hunger, the way your nipple rises against my palm, wanting my touch."

Alana's body curved against Rafe, enjoying the hard muscles of his thighs, the heat of him as he moved against her, the texture of his flannel shirt beneath her palms. With a small sound, she slid her hands up to his head and buried her fingers in his hair.

"Winter mink," she said, sighing. "Thick and soft and silky."

She flexed her fingers sensually, shivering as Rafe arched against the caress, his whole body tightening against her, stroking her.

"I'd like to feel you all over me," Alana said. "All of you. All of me."

"You're going to," Rafe promised.

He bit her neck in a caress that was neither wholly gentle nor wholly wild.

"Every bit of you," he said deeply. "Every bit of me."

Yet even as Rafe spoke, his embrace gentled. The certainty that Alana wasn't going to run away brought a greater measure of control back to him. He no longer felt driven to steal what he could before she became afraid.

Alana wasn't retreating from his strength. She was coming closer to him with every breath, every heartbeat, every touch.

Rafe untied the heavy robe with slow motions. Then he took it from Alana with hands that cherished the pleasure of the moment and the woman who turned to him, smiling.

When Rafe dropped the robe onto the bed, the indigo cloth shimmered invitingly in the firelight. He didn't notice. He saw only Alana and the soft, floor-length nightgown that was the color of a forest at dusk.

Tiny, flat, silver buttons flickered, reflecting the dance of flames. The silver flashes tempted Rafe's finger to trace the shining circles from Alana's throat to her thighs. His hand lingered on the buttons, gently kneading the slight, resilient curve of her stomach before continuing down.

When he stroked the soft mound at the apex of her thighs, her breath rushed out. He stroked more deeply, shaping the thin gown to Alana's hidden curves, cupping her in his palm. She moaned and her fingernails dug into his shoulders.

Rafe laughed softly, triumph and hunger combined. And then he groaned as Alana's satin heat reached out to him, spilling over him like sunrise.

"You tempt me without mercy," he said, his voice deep.

"Look who's talking," Alana said shakily.

Slowly Rafe retreated, tracing once again the line of tiny buttons until it stopped just below the hollow of Alana's throat. His fingers moved over the first button, trying to open it.

But the button was very small, very stubborn, and his hand was less than steady, for every breath he took was infused with the elemental perfume of Alana's desire.

"This nightgown would try the patience of a saint," Rafe muttered, amusement and passion mixed equally in his voice.

Alana bent her head to brush her lips across Rafe's fingers. Her teeth closed delicately on his knuckle. Her tongue slid between his fingers, caressing the sensitive skin.

"You're not helping," he said.

"The neckline is wide enough that I don't bother with the buttons."

"But I've dreamed so many times of undressing you slowly, so slowly . . ."

When Alana looked up, Rafe was smiling and very serious. The heat of his eyes made her feel deliciously weak.

"I'm going to enjoy each button, Alana. Each new bit of you revealed. And when I'm done, I'm going to look at you wearing nothing but firelight."

The shimmering promise in Rafe's eyes sent an answering fire through Alana.

"I won't even touch you at first," he said, brushing the back of his fingers lightly across

Alana's soft lips. "I'll just look at you and remember all the times I could see you only in
my dreams. I've dreamed of that, too, a dream
within a dream."

Alana trembled, caressed as much by Rafe's
words as she was by his hands.

Rafe saw her shiver, felt the warm rush of
her breath against his fingers. He moved both
hands to the line of buttons, but he became
distracted when Alana's breasts brushed
against the sensitive skin of his inner wrist.

It felt so good that Rafe couldn't resist moving his wrists lightly against her soft, firm
curves. Alana's breasts changed as he stroked
her, until her nipples stood boldly against the
tantalizing softness of her nightgown.

Rafe bent his head and caressed the tip of
one breast with his teeth. The response that
shivered through Alana made him want to
groan with pleasure and raw need combined.
He wanted to part her soft thighs and feel the
silky heat of her welcome washing over him.
He wanted that until he was shaking with his
hunger.

But he wanted the dream, too. He wanted
that even more.

Reluctantly Rafe's hands returned to the
tiny buttons. One by one he unfastened them
until Alana's skin glowed between dark green
folds of cloth. She watched with eyes that also
glowed, and her breath made soft, tearing
sounds in the hushed darkness.

Rafe kissed the satin warmth of Alana's
skin, following the yielding line of buttons

with his mouth. Slowly, sensuously, his tongue slid down her body, following the buttons that melted away, unveiling her for his caresses. In a silence that shivered with possibilities, he tasted the heat and sweetness of his dream.

He paused to cherish one breast, then the other, caressing her with teeth and tongue until Alana moaned and her fingers tangled helplessly in his hair. Only then did he continue down, his hands less steady, his breathing quicker, the taste and feel of her consuming him while passion pooled heavily, urgently, between his thighs.

With a swift, supple motion Rafe knelt in front of Alana, his fingers moving over the remaining buttons until they were all undone. Gently he tugged at the cloth. Soft folds clung to each feminine curve for breathtaking moments. Finally, reluctantly, the gown slid to the floor, yielding the secrets of Alana's body.

For the space of several breaths, Rafe simply looked at Alana. Her skin was flushed by firelight and passion. Her breasts rose smoothly and their tips glistened from the caresses of his mouth. The rich contrast of her dark nipples against her glowing skin held his eyes for a long moment, and then he looked at the tempting midnight gleam of hair below her narrow waist.

When the tip of Rafe's tongue teased Alana's navel and his hands found the taut swell of her hips, she swayed even closer to him, calling his name. He closed his eyes, letting the sound and scent and feel of Alana sink into him, healing and inflaming him at the same instant.

He had dreamed of this so many times, of touching her until she was too weak to stand and then carrying her to the bed, caressing her softness intimately until she cried aloud her need for him.

But now Rafe was afraid to lift Alana, to carry her. He was afraid he would shatter both dream and reality with a single incautious act.

Rafe brushed his mouth across Alana's stomach, savored again the sweetness of her breasts, taut and flushed with heat, beneath his hands. Dream and reality fused into a passion that raged at the restraint he imposed on himself.

Quickly he came to his feet, ignoring the hammer blows of desire in his blood, the talons of need raking him until he could count his heartbeat in the hardened flesh between his legs. With impatient hands he pulled off his own clothing and threw it aside.

At the sound of Alana's swiftly drawn breath, Rafe turned toward her, suddenly afraid that she would flinch from the blunt, heavy reality of his desire.

And then Rafe stood motionless but for the tremors of hunger ripping through him, a hunger that increased with each instant. Alana was looking at him the same way he had looked at her, raw yearning and hunger and tenderness combined. Her eyes reflected fire as she touched him with hands that shook, want-

ing him with a force that made her whole
body tremble like an aspen in the wind.

Alana's fingers went from Rafe's shoulders
to his thighs in a single, shivering caress that
almost destroyed his control. For an instant he
let her fingertips trace the hard outline of his
desire and count the heavy beats of his blood.
Then he caught her hands between his own.

"No," said Rafe hoarsely.

"But—"

"If you touch me again, I'll lose control. This
time, let me touch you. Next time you can
tease me until I go crazy, but not this time.
This time is too much like my dreams. This
time it's all I can do not to pull you down and
take you right here on the cabin floor."

Alana closed her eyes, knowing if she
looked at Rafe right now she would have to
touch him. With a graceful motion she turned
away and stretched out on the daybed. Only
then did she open her eyes and look at the
man standing beside the bed, Rafe with firelight licking over his powerful body, molten
gold pooling in his eyes, the most beautiful
thing she had ever seen. When she spoke, her
voice was a soft, husky song.

"Then come dream with me, Rafael."

He came down onto the bed and gathered
Alana into his arms in one continuous movement. He held her as though he expected
something to wrench her from his embrace,
ending the dream, leaving him to awaken
hungry and despairing, the past repeating it-

self endlessly, dream sliding into waking nightmare.

Alana felt Rafe's mouth demand hers, felt his arms close powerfully around her, felt the bruising male strength of his body, the hardness and the hunger of him; and she returned the embrace, holding on to him with every bit of her strength.

After a long time, Rafe drew a deep, shuddering breath and released her.

"I'm sorry. I didn't mean to hurt you," he said, kissing Alana gently, repeatedly, tasting her with each word, unable to stay away from her for more than a second at a time.

"You didn't hurt me."

Rafe touched Alana gently. His hand trembled as it moved from her temple to her lips. Eyes closed, she twisted blindly beneath him, seeking to hold him again, to feel the heat and power of his body against hers, sliding within her, moving with her.

With a throttled groan, Rafe trapped Alana's restless hands. He kissed her palms, bit her fingertips and the flesh at the base of her thumb, sucked lightly on her wrist and the inside of her arm. She moved against his loving restraint, wanting more than his inciting, teasing caresses.

Rafe laughed softly and watched Alana with smoky golden eyes. He stroked her body almost soothingly, and when he spoke his voice was deep, husky with memory and desire.

"At first," he said, "after they tortured me, I dreamed only of revenge. Blood and death and the devil's laughter. But later . . .''

Rafe's head bent until he could touch the tip of Alana's breast with his tongue.

"Later, hatred wasn't enough to keep me alive," he said. "It was for some men, but not for me. That's when I began to dream of you, deep dreams, dreaming all the way to the bottom of my mind, dreaming with everything in me.''

Rafe's teeth closed lightly, tugged, then he took Alana's nipple into his mouth and cherished her with changing pressures of his tongue until she cried his name and her love again and again.

"Yes," he whispered, smoothing his mustache across her taut nipple until she shivered, "I heard you calling for me when I wanted to die, calling for me and crying . . . and so I lived, and I dreamed.''

The words came to Alana like another kind of caress sinking into her soul, Rafe's voice dreaming of her while his hands and mouth moved slowly over her, memorizing her as she burned beneath his touch.

Strong fingers stroked down her stomach, her thighs, sensitizing her skin until her breath came in raggedly. When his cheek slid up from her thigh and ruffled the blackness of her hair, she moaned his name. His hands smoothed the curve of her legs, pressing gently, asking silently. Her legs shifted beneath his touch, giving him another measure of his dream.

When Rafe felt the waiting heat and need of

Alana, his hand shook. She was even softer than his dreams, hotter, more welcoming. His fingers slid over her, cherishing and parting her in the same loving caress.

Alana tried to say Rafe's name, but she could only moan while he caressed her deeply, telling her of his dream and her beauty as she moved sinuously, helplessly, clinging to his touch.

When his mouth brushed over her, tasting and teasing her, she gave up trying to speak, to think. She cried for him with each ragged breath, each melting instant, fire spreading in rhythmic waves through her body.

Rafe moved over Alana slowly, covering her body with his own, sliding into her, filling her, and she came apart beneath him. Motionless, rigid, he listened to the song of her ecstasy, better than his dreams, wilder, hotter, sweeter.

And then Rafe could hold back no longer. He moved within Alana's melting heat, sliding slowly, fiercely, then more quickly. She called his name huskily, tightened around him, holding him with all her strength.

They moved together, wound tightly around one another, sharing each heartbeat, each rhythmic melting of pleasure, until neither one could bear any more. Rafe cried out and gave himself to Alana even as she gave herself to him and to the incandescent ecstasy they had created.

Finally they knew the shimmering silence and peace that followed such a complete sharing.

It was a long time before Alana stirred languidly and looked up at Rafe. He was watching her with smoky amber eyes that remembered every touch, every cry, every moment, everything.

She smiled and smoothed his mustache with fingers that still trembled.

"I love you, Rafael Winter."

Rafe gathered Alana against his body a little fiercely, like a man hardly able to believe that he wasn't dreaming.

"And I love you, Alana. You're a part of me, all the way to my soul."

He kissed her eyelids and her cheeks and the corners of her smiling lips, and he felt the kisses returned as quickly as they were given.

"As soon as we get off the mountain," Rafe said, "we'll be married. On second thought, the hell with waiting. I'll get on the radio and have Mitch fly in a justice of the peace."

Rafe felt the change in Alana, tension replacing the relaxed pressure of her body against his. He lifted his head and looked into her dark, troubled eyes.

"What is it, wildflower? Your singing career? You can live with me and write songs, can't you? And if you want to do concert tours, we'll do concert tours."

Alana opened her mouth. Words didn't come. But tears did, closing her throat.

"I'd like to have kids, though," Rafe added, smiling. "Boys as clumsy as me and girls as graceful as you. But there's no rush. You can do whatever you want, so long as you marry me. I can't let you go again."

"Rafael, my love." Alana's voice broke and tears spilled over her long eyelashes. "I can't marry you yet."

"Why?"

Rafe looked at Alana's dark eyes. Where passion had recently burned, there were only shadows now.

"Because Jack has been dead only a month?" Rafe asked bluntly. "The marriage was a mistake. A pretend mourning period would be a farce."

"Jack has nothing to do with it."

"Then—"

Alana touched Rafe's lips with gentle fingertips, silencing him.

"I want to be the woman who gives you children," she said softly. "I want to live with you and love you all the way to death and beyond, because I can't imagine ever being without you again."

Rafe took Alana's hand and kissed her palm with lips that clung and lingered over her skin. He began to gather her gently into his arms, then stopped.

She was still speaking softly, relentlessly.

"But I can't marry you until I can trust myself not to shatter into a thousand pieces with every thunderstorm," Alana said. "I can't marry you until the sight of a big, blond stranger doesn't send me into a panic. I can't marry you until I can come to you whole, confident of myself, of my sanity."

Alana felt Rafe's retreat in the withdrawal of his hand, saw it in the narrowing of his eyes and the expressionless mask that replaced a face that had been alive with love for her.

"Until you remember what happened on Broken Mountain?" asked Rafe, his voice neutral.

"Yes. Before I marry you, I have to be able to trust myself," she said, pleading with him to understand.

"Trust yourself—or me?" retorted Rafe.

The amber eyes that measured Alana were remote, as cool as his voice, showing nothing of the pain that his words cost him.

"I trust you more than I trust myself," Alana said.

Her voice was urgent, almost ragged, and her eyes searched Rafe's face anxiously.

"Then trust me to know what's best for us," he said. "Marry me."

Alana shook her head helplessly, wondering how she could make Rafe understand.

"So much for trust," said Rafe, his voice clipped.

"I trust you!"

"Yeah. Sure." He said something savage beneath his breath. "Well, at least I know how long you were standing by the cascade today. Long enough to hear Stan. Long enough to believe him. Long enough to kill a dream."

"No!" Alana said quickly. "I don't believe Stan. You aren't like that. You couldn't kill Jack like that!"

Rafe's laugh was a harsh, nearly brutal

sound that tore at Alana almost as much as it tore at him. With a vicious curse, he rolled off the bed and began pulling on his clothes.

When Rafe snatched up his shirt, the harmonica fell out of the pocket onto the floor. Firelight ran over the instrument's polished silver surface, making it shine.

He scooped up the harmonica, looked at it for a long moment, then tossed it casually onto the bed.

"Rafe?"

"Take it. Souvenir of a dream," Rafe said roughly, kicking into his boots. "I won't need it anymore. Any of it."

Alana picked up the harmonica, not understanding, not knowing what to say, afraid to say anything at all.

But when Rafe pulled open the cabin door and started to walk into the night, Alana came off the bed in a rush and threw her arms around him, preventing him from leaving.

"Rafe, *I love you*," she said against the coiled muscles of his back, holding on to him with all her strength.

"Maybe you do. Maybe that's why you forgot."

Rafe started to move away, but Alana's arms tightened, refusing to let him go.

The pain that had come with her refusal to marry him raged against Rafe's control, demanding release. He jerked free of Alana's arms and spun around to face her, his pain naked in his expression—and his anger. Yet when he spoke, his voice was so controlled, it lacked all inflection.

"I tried to be what you wanted, wildflower. I tried everything I could think of to lure you out of your isolation. I reassured you in every way I could. And it wasn't enough."

Rafe's voice roughened with each word, sliding out from his control. To see Alana in front of him right now, so lovely, so unattainable, to lose her all over again . . .

Rafe made a harsh sound and closed his eyes so that he wouldn't touch her, hold her, stir desperately among the ashes of impossible dreams.

"No matter how carefully I constructed my lures, you didn't want them enough to trust me," he said. "Finally, I even tried music. I hadn't played the harmonica since the day I found out you were married. I had played it too often for you, loving you with music the way I never could with words. After you married Jack, even the thought of touching that harmonica made me blind with rage."

"Rafael," Alana began, but he talked over her.

"Music had always been irresistible to you. So I picked up that beautiful, cruel harmonica and I called to you with it."

Tears trembled in Alana's eyelashes. "Yes."

"And you came to me."

"Yes."

"You sang with me."

"It was the first—"

But Rafe was still talking, and his eyes were as haunted by pain as his voice.

"You made love with me more incredibly than in my dreams," he said. "But it wasn't enough to make you trust me. Nothing will be enough for you."

"That's not true!"

"What's true is that you may never remember what happened on Broken Mountain. And even if you do—"

Rafe shrugged and said nothing more.

Tears and firelight washed gold down Alana's cheeks. Her hands reached for him.

"No," Rafe said gently.

He stepped away, out of reach of her slender hands.

"I once said my hooks were barbless, Alana. I meant it. I can't bear hurting you anymore. You're free."

Frozen in disbelief, Alana watched as Rafe turned and walked away from her, Rafe passing from silver moonlight into dense ebony shadows, Rafe moving as powerfully as the wind, leaving her alone with the echoes of her pain.

And his.

"Rafael . . . !"

Nothing answered, not even an echo riding on the wind.

17

For a long time Alana stood in the cabin doorway, staring into moonlight and darkness, unaware of the cold wind blowing over her naked skin. Finally, the convulsive shivering of her body brought Alana out of her daze.

She closed the door and stumbled back into the cabin. With shaking hands she pulled on her nightgown, but her fingers were too numb to cope with all the tiny, mocking buttons. She kept remembering Rafe's long fingers unfastening the buttons one by one as his mouth caressed her body with fire and love.

With a choked sound, Alana grabbed Rafe's heavy robe. The harmonica tumbled free of the indigo folds and fell gleaming to the floor. She hesitated, looking at the firelight caressing the harmonica's chased silver surface.

Then she bent and picked up the instrument and put it deep in the robe's soft pocket. She pulled the robe tightly around her and sat at the edge of the broad granite hearth, staring into the hypnotic dance of flames.

But all her eyes saw was the darkness that came after fire was lost.

Eventually dawn came. Alana realized she was cold. The rock hearth she sat on was cold. She ached from the chill of unforgiving stone.

Cold.

Stone.

Darkness.

Heart hammering, Alana tried to move but could not. She was chained by stiffness and memories summoned by the icy touch of granite.

"Rafe—"

Alana's voice was hoarse, as though she had spent the night calling futilely for help that never came.

But not last night.

She had called all through the darkness nearly four weeks ago, when she had spent the night on the rock ledge by the lake. She hadn't called to Jack that night. She remembered now.

She had called to Rafe, crying his name again and again, cries that had come from deep inside her, from the love for him that was as much a part of her as her own soul.

Jack had laughed.

Cold. Helpless. A prisoner tied to stone.

It was devastating to be so helpless, to know that beyond the tiny, icy circle constricting her, there was a world of heat and sunlight and laughter and love.

And none of those things could reach her.

Cold.
Ice raining down. Darkness and wind lifting her, tearing her from . . .

"No!" said Alana fiercely, denying her nightmare. "There's no ice here. I'm in a cabin. I'm not tied by that lake. I'm not waiting helplessly for Jack to come and either free me or maul me. I'm not a tiny, shivering aspen leaf at the mercy of cold winds. I'm Alana. I'm a human being."

Her body shivered convulsively, repeatedly.

"Get up," Alana whispered hoarsely to herself. "*Get up!*"

Slowly, stiffly, she pulled herself to her feet. She moved awkwardly toward the cabin door. When she finally managed to open it, she saw that a new day was pouring down the stone ramparts in a thick tide of crimson light.

Alana stared up at Broken Mountain's ruined peak, rocks shattered and tumbled, cliffs and miniature cirques sculpted by winters without end.

She climbed down the cabin's steps to the clearing. Her feet were too cold to feel the impact of sharp stones. She hurried to the main lodge, wanting only to get dressed before Bob got up and saw her and asked questions that she had no way to answer and no desire to hear.

Stumbling in her haste, Alana went up the lodge's steps. For an instant she was paralyzed by the thought that Rafe might be inside, that she would run to him and he would turn away from her again, leaving her freezing and alone.

A nightmare.

No, worse than that, for in Alana's nightmares Rafe didn't turn away from her, he came to her and—

Alana froze in the act of opening the door.

Rafe. In her nightmares. Like Jack.

Shaking, suddenly clammy, dizzy, Alana leaned against the closed door, wondering if it was memory or nightmare or a terrible combination of both that was breaking over her, drenching her in cold sweat.

Rafe had been on Broken Mountain.

He had told her as much. He had told her that with the horror she had buried beneath a black pool of amnesia, there was an instant of beauty when she had turned to him.

Did Rafe tell me that only to help me remember? Alana asked silently. *Did he use the promise of beauty like a single, perfect lure drifting down onto the blank surface of my amnesia, luring me beyond its dark, safe depths?*

Alana waited for memory or nightmare to come and answer her questions, freeing her.

Nothing came but the too-fast beating of her heart, blood rushing in her ears like a waterfall . . .

Ice and darkness and falling, she was falling to the death that waited below!

With a hoarse cry, Alana wrenched herself out of nightmare. She opened the lodge door and hurried up the loft's narrow stairway. She pulled on clothes at random, caring only for warmth.

The fiery orange of Alana's sweater heightened the translucent pallor of her face and the darkness below her eyes. She rubbed her cheeks fiercely, trying to bring color to her face.

It didn't help. Her eyes were still too dark, too wide, almost feverish in their intensity. She looked brittle and more than a little wild, as though she would fly apart at a word or a touch.

Abruptly Alana decided that she would find Rafe. She would find him and then she would demand that he tell her what he knew.

"To hell with what Dr. Gene said about what would or would not help me remember," Alana whispered savagely. "To hell with what everyone else thinks is good for me. *I have to know.*"

No matter how horrible the truth, it could be no worse than what Alana was enduring now . . . Rafe turning away from her, sliding into night, nothing answering her cry, not even an echo.

Alana heard someone in the kitchen. She went down the stairs quickly, determination in every line of her body. She would confront Rafe now. She was through running, hiding, feeling screams and memories clawing at her throat.

But Rafe wasn't in the kitchen.

"Morning, sis," Bob said as she walked in.

His back was to her as he finished filling the coffeepot with water, but he had recognized her step.

"You're late, but so are the rest of us," Bob said. "Poker game didn't break up until after three."

Still talking, he turned toward her as he set the coffeepot on the hot stove.

"Janice is the luckiest—my God, Alana! What's wrong?"

"Nothing that coffee won't cure," she said, controlling her voice carefully.

Bob crossed the room in two long strides. He reached for Alana before he remembered Rafe's very explicit instructions about touching her.

"I'm going to see if you're running a fever," said Bob, slowly raising his hand to her forehead.

"I'm not."

Alana didn't step away from her brother's touch. Nor did she flinch. Finally she could see him clearly, no nightmare to cloud her eyes.

Bob's big palm pressed against Alana's fore-head with surprising gentleness.

"You're cold," he said, startled by the cool-ness of her skin.

"Right. Not a bit of fever." Alana's voice was as clipped as the smile she gave her brother. "Have you seen Rafe?"

Bob's dark eyes narrowed. "He left."

"Left?"

"He told me he'd gotten a holler on the ra-dio from the ranch. Something needed his at-tention right away. Said he'd radio us as soon as he got home."

"How long?"

"It's a long ride to his ranch house, even on that spotted mountain horse of his. Tonight, probably."

"When did he leave?"

"About an hour ago. Why?"

"No reason," Alana said, her voice as dry and tight as her throat. "Just curious."

"Did something happen between you two? Rafe looked as rocky as you do."

Alana laughed strangely.

"Did you know that Rafe was on the moun-tain four weeks ago?" she asked.

Bob gave her an odd look.

"Rafe was on Broken Mountain when Jack died," Alana said fiercely.

"Of course he was. How did you think you got off the mountain after you were hurt?"

"What?" whispered Alana.

"C'mon, sis." Bob smiled despite his worry. "Even you can't walk down three miles of icy mountain switchbacks on a badly wrenched ankle. The storm spooked all the horses, so Rafe carried you out on his back. If he hadn't, you'd have died up there, same as Jack did."

"I don't remember," Alana said.

"Of course not. You were out of your head with shock. Hell, I'll bet you don't even remember Sheriff Mitchell landing on the lake and flying you out of here in the middle of a storm. Mitch told me it was the fanciest piece of flying he'd ever done, too."

"I don't remember!"

Bob smiled and patted Alana's shoulder gently.

"Don't fret about it, sis. Nobody expects you to remember anything about the rescue. When I got to the hospital, you didn't even recognize me."

"I—don't—"

"Remember," Bob finished dryly. "Hypothermia does that to you. Turns your brain to suet every time. Remember when we went after that crazy rock climber way up on the mountain? By the time we found him, he had less sense than a chicken. He did fine after we thawed him out, though."

Alana looked at Bob's very dark eyes, eyes like the night, only brighter, warmer.

Eyes like her own before she had forgotten.

But Bob remembered and she didn't. Even when he told her, she could hardly believe what she was hearing. It was like reading about something in the newspaper. Distant. Not quite real.

Rafe had carried her down Broken Mountain.

She didn't remember.

No wonder Rafe hadn't told her what had happened. Telling her would do no good. Being told wasn't the same as remembering, as *knowing*.

Rafe had saved Alana's life, and she didn't even know it. He had carried her down a treacherous trail, ice and darkness all around, risked his own life for her.

And to her it was as though it had never happened.

"Rafe waited for you to remember after you ran out of the hospital," Bob said.

"I didn't. Remember."

She hadn't remembered, hadn't called Rafe, hadn't even known that he was waiting back on Broken Mountain.

Waiting for her.

"Yeah," Bob said. "Rafe figured that out for himself. So he gnawed on me to get you back here."

Numbly Alana nodded. She had come home, and Rafe had treated her with gentleness and understanding, asking nothing of her, giving everything. When being in the mountains frightened her, he apologized as though he were responsible.

Rafe had shared her pain to a degree that she hardly believed even now. He had given her all the reassurance he could. And never once had he shown how much she was hurting him.

He had loved her, cherished her, done everything possible for her, except remember. No one could remember for her.

That she must do for herself.

"Sis?" asked Bob, his voice worried. "You better sit down. You look like death warmed over."

"Thanks a lot, baby brother."

Alana's voice was as thin as the smile she gave Bob. She forced her throat to relax, using the discipline she had learned as a singer.

It was important that Bob not worry about her.

It was important that he not hover or watch over her, preventing her from doing what must be done.

It was important that she act as though there was nothing wrong with her that breakfast and a day lazing around the lake wouldn't cure.

Nothing wrong.

Absolutely normal.

"Check the wood box in the kitchen, okay? I don't want to run out of fire halfway through the eggs."

Alana's voice sounded calm, if a little flat. The smile she gave Bob echoed her voice precisely.

"Why don't you let me do breakfast?" asked Bob, a worried frown creasing his forehead. "You go sit and—"

"I'll sit later," she interrupted, "while you and the dudes are out fishing. I have a place all picked out. Grass and sunshine and a perfect view of aspen leaves."

Alana's throat constricted as she remembered counting aspen leaves with Rafe while he lay quietly with his hands locked behind his head, smiling and aching as she touched him.

Rafe.

She closed her eyes and forced herself to take a breath.

"Get cracking on the wood box, baby brother. I don't want to spend all day in the kitchen."

Bob hesitated, then went out the back door of the cabin. A few minutes later the clear, sharp sound of a ten-pound maul splitting cured wood rang through the dawn.

Carefully thinking of nothing at all, Alana moved through the kitchen, letting the routine of cooking and setting the table focus her mind. Whenever her thoughts veered to Rafe, she dragged them back ruthlessly.

First she had to get through breakfast. When everyone was safely caught up in fishing, when she was alone with only her erratic memory, then she would think of Rafe.

Thinking of him would give her the courage to do what had to be done.

A moment of panic rippled through Alana. A piece of silverware slipped from her hands and landed with a clatter on the table. With fingers that trembled, she retrieved the fork and put it in its proper place. She finished setting the table just as Janice came in.

"Good morning," Janice said cheerfully.

"Morning. Coffee's ready."

"Sounds like heaven. Is Rafe up yet?"

"Yes. I'll get you some coffee."

Quickly Alana turned away, avoiding the scrutiny of the other woman's eyes. The former psychiatrist was entirely too perceptive for Alana's comfort right now.

"Is that Rafe chopping wood?" asked Janice, falling into step beside Alana.

In an instant of memory that almost destroyed her control, Alana's mind gave her a picture of Rafe working by the woodpile four years ago. His long legs had been braced, his shirt off, the powerful muscles of his back coiling and relaxing rhythmically as he worked with the ax beneath the July sun, chopping stove wood. She could see him so clearly, the heat and life of him so vivid, she could almost touch him.

Yearning went through Alana like lightning, hunger and love and loss turning in her, cutting her until she could feel her life bleeding away.

"No," whispered Alana.

Desperately she pushed away the memory. If she thought of Rafe right now, she would go crazy.

Or crazier.

Before Janice could ask any more, Alana said, "Bob drew the short straw this morning."

Despite Alana's efforts to keep her voice normal, Janice looked at her sharply.

"You look a bit feverish," Janice said. "Are you feeling all right?"

"Fine. Just fine."

Alana poured coffee. Her hand shook, but not enough to spill the coffee.

"Tired, that's all," Alana said. "Altitude, you know. I'm not used to it. That and the cold nights. God, but the nights are cold on Broken Mountain."

And I'm babbling, added Alana silently, reining in her thoughts. And her tongue.

She handed Janice her coffee.

"Breakfast will be ready in about twenty minutes," Alana said.

Janice took the cup and sipped thoughtfully, watching Alana's too-quick, almost erratic movements around the kitchen.

"I thought I heard a horse ride by earlier this morning," Janice said. "Before dawn."

"That must have been Rafe," said Alana very casually.

She concentrated on laying thick strips of bacon across the old stove's huge griddle. Fat hissed as it met the searing iron surface.

"Rafe left?" asked Janice, startled.

"He has to check on something at the ranch. He'll be back later."

And pigs will fly, thought Alana, remembering Rafe's pain and anger. He won't come back until I'm gone. I've used up my chances with him. Rafael, I never meant to hurt you. Never . . .

Alana's hand shook, brushing against the griddle. She took a steadying breath and thought only about getting through breakfast.

One thing at a time. Now, this moment, that meant frying bacon without blistering herself through sheer stupidity.

Later she would think about Rafe leaving her, about his pain, about what she must do, about remembering.

Later. Not now.

"I hope everyone likes scrambled eggs," Alana said.

She went to the refrigerator and opened the door. No light came on. Rafe had forgotten to start up the generator. She pulled out a bowl of fresh eggs, then went to the back door and called to Bob.

"Do you know how to start up the generator?"

"Sure thing." Bob gestured toward a pile of split wood with the maul he was holding. "How much do you need?"

Alana remembered the night before, when she had found the living room wood box all but empty.

"Enough for the fireplace, too," she said. "You'll want a nice fire tonight."

"What about you?" asked Bob dryly, looking over his shoulder at Alana. "Don't you want a nice fire tonight, too?"

I won't be here tonight.

But the words were silent, existing only in Alana's mind.

"Does that mean I have to chop it myself?" she retorted, her voice sounding rough.

"Just teasing, sis," answered Bob. "You

never could split wood worth a damn."

He swung the maul again, burying its edge deep in the wood, splitting it easily into two smaller pieces.

Alana turned back to the stove. She was relieved to see that Janice had gone. The woman's eyes were just too intent, too knowing.

Breakfast was an ordeal Alana hoped never to have to repeat. The toast was impossible to chew, much less swallow. She forced herself to eat anyway. If she didn't, Bob would stick to her like a mother hen for the rest of the day, worrying over her.

Alana couldn't allow that to happen. So she ate grimly, washing down eggs and bacon with coffee, eating as little as she thought she could get away with.

As soon as Bob finished, he looked at Alana, then at Stan and Janice.

"I'm going to stay behind and help Alana with the dishes," Bob said. "Rafe thought you should try the water on the north side of the lake, where that little creek comes in. Some real big trout hang around there, feeding on whatever washes down."

"Sounds good to me," Stan said.

"Rafe suggested using dark flies," Bob added, "or the grasshopper imitation he tied for each of you. Me, I'm going to use the Lively Lady."

Alana got up, her plate and silverware in her hands.

"I'll take care of the dishes," she said, grateful that her voice sounded casual rather than desperate, the way she felt. "If you're doing dishes while Stan is fishing, he'll get the prize for the biggest fish."

"What prize?" asked Bob.

"Apple pie," Alana said succinctly. "Winner takes all."

A friendly argument began over big fish and winner taking all of the pie. In the end, everyone stayed and helped Alana with the dishes. When the last lunch had been packed and the last dish was draining on the counter, she turned and smiled rather fiercely at everyone.

"Thank you and good-bye," she said. "The trout are rising. The best fishing time of the day is slipping away. Have fun. I'll see you for dinner."

Stan and Janice exchanged glances, then left the kitchen. Alana looked expectantly at Bob.

"I'll leave in a while," Bob said, smiling genially and reaching for an apron. "Stan needs a handicap in the trout sweepstakes. I'll help you with the pie."

Alana looked at Bob in disbelief. Determination showed in every line of his face. He didn't know what was wrong, but he plainly wasn't going to leave until he did.

"You'll have a long wait," she said finally. "I'm going to take a bath. A very long, very hot bath. And no, baby brother, I don't need you to scrub my back."

Bob had the grace to laugh. But the laugh faded quickly into concern.

"You sure?" he asked softly.

"I've never been more sure of anything in my life." Alana's eyes held her brother's. "It's all right, Bob. Go fishing. Please."

Bob expelled a harsh breath and ran his hand through his black hair.

"I'm worried," he said bluntly. "Rafe looked like hell. You look worse. I feel like the guy who grabbed for the brass ring and came up with a handful of garbage. I want to help you, but I'm damned if I know what to do."

"Go fishing," Alana said.

Her voice was soft and very certain.

"Hell," Bob muttered. Then, "I'll be at the north side of the lake if you need me. Why don't you come over for lunch?"

"I'll probably be asleep."

"Most sensible thing you've said today," retorted Bob.

He looked pointedly at the dark circles beneath his sister's eyes. Then he threw up his hands and walked out of the kitchen.

"We'll be back for dinner about five," he called over his shoulder.

"Good luck," said Alana.

A grunt was Bob's only reply.

She held her breath until she heard the front door of the cabin close. Then she ran to the window and looked out. Bob had picked up his rod, net, and fishing vest. He was stalking over the lake trail with long, powerful strides.

"Take care," whispered Alana. "Don't be too mad at me. You did everything you could. Like Rafe. It's not your fault that it wasn't enough. It's mine."

Alana pulled off her apron with shaking hands and hung it on a nail by the back door. Then she raced upstairs and began stuffing warm clothes into the backpack she had found in her closet.

Broken Mountain could be cold, brutally cold. She of all people knew that.

Alana went back down the stairs, listening to her racing heart and the harsh thump of her hiking boots on the wooden stairs. She ran to the kitchen and began throwing food into the backpack. Cheese, raisins, granola, chocolate. She closed the flap and secured it tightly.

For a moment Alana stood and looked around the kitchen, wondering what she had forgotten.

"A note," she said. "I have to leave a note."

Alana scrambled through kitchen drawers, looking for paper and a pencil. But when she found them, she couldn't think of anything to say.

"How can I explain in words something that I barely understand myself?" Alana asked, staring helplessly at the paper.

Yet she had to write something.

She owed Bob that much. If he came back early and found her gone, he would be frantic.

Alana bent over and wrote quickly:

If Rafe calls, tell him I've gone to find the lark.
This time it will sing for me.

18

ALANA WALKED ALONG THE trail, grateful for the trees screening her from the lake. Through the breaks in the forest, she could see three people spaced out along the north side of the water. Bob looked no bigger than her palm. Bits of sound floated across the lake to her, fragments without meaning.

When she came to a fork in the trail, she hesitated for a moment. The right-hand path wound back to the lake, coming out just in front of the cascade where she had overheard Stan and Rafe arguing. The left-hand path skirted the worst of the rock jumble that caused the cascade.

Alana adjusted the backpack and turned

onto the left fork of the trail. Once past the fork, the trail began the long climb to the top of Broken Mountain.

The first part of the climb consisted of long switchbacks looping through the forest. Before Alana had gone half a mile, she wished she had Sid to do the work for her. But taking the horse would have been too great a risk. Sid would have spent the first mile neighing to the horses hobbled in the meadow behind the main cabin. Short of a siren, nothing carried better in the high mountains than the neigh of a lonely horse.

Sunlight quivered among aspen leaves and fell silently through evergreen boughs. The air was crisp, fragrant with resin, motionless but for the occasional stirring of wind off the lake. The cascade's distant mutter filtered through the forest, telling Alana that she was approaching one of the open, rocky sections of the trail. She would have to be careful not to be spotted by the fishermen below.

The forest dwindled, then vanished as the trail crawled over a steep talus slope. Broken stone of all sizes littered the ridge. The thunder of the cascade came clearly across the rocks. To the right of the trail the land fell away abruptly, ending in the sapphire depths of the lake.

Alana took one look, then did not look again. Fixing her eyes on the rugged ground just in front of her feet, she picked her way across the talus. For the first hundred yards her breath came shallowly, erratically. Then she regained control of her breathing. Slowly her fear of heights diminished, giving strength back to her legs.

Just before Alana dropped out of sight over a fold of Broken Mountain, she turned and looked down at the lake. Wisps of brilliant white cloud trailed iridescent shadows over the water, emphasizing the clarity and depth of both lake and air.

Alana's heart beat faster and her palms felt clammy, but she forced herself to look at the north shore. There were three specks, dark against the gray granite of the shoreline.

Three fishermen.

No one had spotted Alana and run after her to bring her back. With luck, no one would even notice that she was gone until dinnertime. And then it would be too late to come after her.

No one rode or walked high mountain trails at night unless a life was at risk.

Besides, even when Bob discovered that Alana wasn't at the lodge, he wouldn't know where she was. The last place he would expect to find her was farther up Broken Mountain, all the way up to the first and highest lake, up to the lip of the cliff where water leaped into darkness, standing in the exact spot where Jack had died and she had lost her mind.

Surely there, if anywhere, I'll remember, Alana told herself. Surely there, where conditions most exactly match the environment of my nightmare. . . .

There she would rise from the bleak, safe

pool of amnesia into the transparent light of reality. There, if anywhere on earth.

If Alana didn't remember right away, she would simply stay until she did, sleeping on a rock by the lake if she had to. She would do whatever she must to remember. Then she would accept whatever came.

In truth, now there was little at stake. That was why she finally had come to Broken Mountain.

She had nothing left to lose.

Alana climbed steadily through the morning. Though the second lake was less than two miles from the cabins, it took Alana three hours to make the climb. Part of the problem was the altitude. Another part was the roughness of the trail.

The hardest part was her own fear. Every step closer to the first lake was like a pebble added to her backpack, weighing her down.

By the time she scrambled up the saddle of land that concealed the second lake, Alana was sweating freely and felt almost dizzy. She stood and looked down on the tiny, marshy stretch of water. More pond than true lake, during the driest years the second lake existed only on maps. This year, though, the winter had been thick with snow and the summer ripe with storms. The water was a rich wealth of silver against the dense green of meadow and marsh plants.

The lake had been full the last time Alana was there. Clouds seething and wind bending the aspens, wind shaking the elegant spruce trees, storm winds moaning down the slopes.

It hadn't rained, though. Not then. Just clouds and a few huge water drops hurled from the heights by the wind.

Thunder had been distant, erratic. The peak next to Broken Mountain had been mantled in blue-black mist and lightning. But not Broken Mountain. Not then. Thunder hadn't come to Broken Mountain until the next night.

Seeing nothing but the past, Alana stared blindly at the ribbon of water nestled in a green hollow between folds of granite.

Remembering.

They had rested the horses there. She had gone to the edge of the small meadow and leaned against a tree, listening to the distant song of water over rock.

Jack had come up behind her, and she had wanted to put her hands over her ears, shutting him out. But she hadn't been able to then.

She was remembering now, Jack and the argument and the mountain rising cold and hard . . .

"Jilly, don't be stupid about this. We won't be famous forever. A few more years, that's all I ask."

She wanted to scream with frustration. Jack simply wouldn't accept that she couldn't go on with the farce of Country's Perfect Couple.

She had to be free.

"Jilly, you better listen."

"I'm listening," she said flatly. "I'm just not agreeing."

"Then you don't understand," he said confidently. *"As soon as you understand, you'll agree."*

"You're the one who doesn't understand. You're not getting your way this time, Jack. You shouldn't have demanded that I marry you in the first place. I shouldn't have given in."

Not looking at Jack, she ran her hand down the long black braids that fell between her breasts.

"It was a mistake," she said finally. *"A very bad mistake. It's time we faced it."*

"You're wrong. Think about it, Jilly. You're wrong."

"I've thought of nothing else for several years. I've made up my mind."

"Then you'll just have to change it."

She had turned suddenly, catching the black look he gave her. Then Jack had shrugged and smiled charmingly.

"Aw, c'mon, Jilly. Let's stop arguing and enjoy ourselves for a change. That's why we're here, remember?"

Yes, Alana was remembering.

Too late. Rafe was gone. She was remembering.

And she was afraid.

Alana shuddered and shifted the weight of her backpack, letting echoes and memories of the past gather around her as she climbed.

At first she remembered small things, a little bit at a time, minutes slowly building into whole memories. The closer she came, the higher she climbed on Broken Mountain, the thinner the veil of amnesia became—and the greater her mind's rebellion at what she was demanding of herself.

Alana no longer told herself that her rapid heartbeat and dragging breaths came from altitude or exertion. She was struggling against fear just as she had struggled against Jack's stubborn refusal to face the reality of her decision to leave him.

Suddenly Alana realized that she had stopped walking. She was braced against a rock, shaking, her eyes fixed on the last, steep ascent to the highest lake.

Broken Mountain rose behind the lake, granite thrusting into the sky. It waited for her, the cliff and the talus where wind howled and water fell into blackness and exploded far below on unyielding stone.

It waited for her, and she was terrified.

"Pull up your socks and get going, Alana Jillian," she said between gritted teeth. "Like Dad always said, you can't keep the mountain waiting. Besides, what do you have to lose that you haven't already lost?"

Nothing.

Not one damned thing.

Alana fastened her eyes on the trail just in front of her feet and began walking. She didn't look up, didn't stop, didn't think.

One by one, memories came, wisps of cloud gathering over the blank pool of amnesia, clouds and memories condensing into columns of white seething over the mountaintops, over her.

She stood at the edge of the tiny, hanging

valley where the first lake lay beneath the sullen sky. Thunder rumbled distantly, forerunner of the storm to come.

But not yet. The clouds hadn't met and wrapped around each other and the peaks. Only then would the storm begin, bringing darkness in the midst of day, black rain and white ice and thunder like mountains torn apart.

But not yet. She had a breathing space in the shelter of the stunted trees that grew in the lee of the mountain looming raggedly against the sky.

Broken Mountain.

At the base of the shattered gray peak lay the lake, mercury-colored water lapping at the very lip of the valley. Alana looked away from the white water leaping over the valley's edge, water falling and bouncing from rock to boulder, water exploding like thunder.

Jack flying out, turning and falling, white water and screams.

Alana slipped out of her backpack and went like a sleepwalker to the end of the trail.

Was it here Jack fell? she asked herself.

She looked over the edge, suffered a wave of dizziness and forced herself to look again.

No, it hadn't happened here.

Where, then? she asked herself impatiently.

The trail turned to the right, keeping to the trees. To the left was the end of the lake and the beginning of the waterfall, lake and rock and land falling away from the lip of the hanging valley.

Nausea turned in Alana, and a fear so great that it hammered her to her knees.

The lake. The lake lapping at the edge of space, water churning, thunder bounding and rebounding, darkness and screams. She was screaming.

No, it was the wind that screamed. The wind had come up at dawn and she shivered until Jack came to her. . . .

"Change your mind yet, Jilly?"

She closed her eyes and said nothing, did nothing, helpless, tied to stone.

"That's okay, babe. We've got all the time in the world."

"Untie m-me." Her voice came at a distance, a *stranger's voice, harsh as stone scraping over stone.*

"You going to listen to me if I do?"

"Y-Yes."

"You going to stop crying for that bastard Winter?"

Silence.

"I heard you, Jilly. Last night. Lots of nights. I'm going to break you of loving Winter, babe. I'm going to break you, period. When we get down off this mountain, you'll come to heel and stay there."

Alana listened, all tears gone.

She listened, and knew that Jack was crazy.

She listened, and knew that she would die on Broken Mountain unless she stopped crying and started using her head.

Her mind worked with eerie speed and clarity, time slowing down as she sorted through probabil-

ities and possibilities, certainties and hopes.

And then came understanding, a single brilliant fact: She must get Jack to untie her. Then the second fact: Jack's only weakness was his career; he needed her.

"If you l-leave me on this rock any longer, I'll be too s-sick to sing."

Jack put his hand on Alana's arm. It was cold enough to shock him. He frowned and fiddled with the zipper on his jacket.

"Are you going to listen to me?" he demanded.

"Y-Yes."

Jack untied her, but Alana was too stiff, too weak to move. He hauled her off the rock and set her on her feet.

She fell and stayed down, helpless, tied by a kind of pain that made her dizzy and nauseated. Finally feeling began to come back to her strained joints and limbs. Then she cried out hoarsely, never having known such agony.

Jack half dragged, half carried Alana to the camp, jerking her along, her braids wound around his hand. He dropped her casually by the fire. She lay there without moving, her mind spinning with pain. Eventually the worst of it passed and she could think.

She concealed the fact of her returning strength, afraid that Jack would tie her up again. When he spoke to her, she tried pretending that she was too dazed to answer. He hit her with the back of his hand, knocking her away from the fire. She lay motionless, cold and aching and afraid.

"You listen to me, Jilly. I need you, but there are other ways, other women who can sing. I've been sleeping with one of them. You can sing circles around her, but she comes to heel a hell of a lot better than you do. Don't be more trouble than you're worth.''

Alana shuddered and said nothing.

It seemed hours before the moment came that she had been waiting for. Jack went to get more wood. She came up off the ground in a stumbling rush, running in the opposite direction, seeking the cover of the forest and the mountainside.

That was the beginning of a deadly game of hide-and-seek. Jack called to her, threats and endearments, both equally obscene to Alana's ears as she dodged from tree to thicket to boulder, her heart as loud as thunder.

Storm clouds opened, drenching the land with icy water mixed with sleet. Weakened by cold, her mind fading in and out of touch with reality, Alana knew she was running out of time and possibilities.

Her only chance was to flee down the mountain. She had begun working toward that from the first moment, leading Jack around the lake until he was no longer between her and escape.

Now only the margin of the lake itself lay between her and the trail down Broken Mountain, the lake where water lapped over boulders and then fell down, down, to the rocks below. There was no shelter there. No place to hide from Jack.

Lightning and thunder shattered the world into black and white shards. Ice sleeted down, freezing her.

And then a rock rattled behind her, Jack coming, reaching for her.

Water rushing down, cold, and darkness waiting, lined with rocks, ice and darkness closing around, clouds seething overhead, lightning lancing down, soundless thunder.

Fear.

It was too cold, no warmth anywhere, only fear hammering on her, leaving her weak.

She tried to run, but her feet weighed as much as the mountains and were as deeply rooted in the earth. Each step took an eternity. Try harder, move faster, or get caught.

She must run!

But she could not.

Something had caught her braids, jerking her backward with stunning force.

Jack loomed above her, anger twisting his face, her braids wrapped around his fist. Jack cursing her, grabbing her, hitting her, and the storm breaking, trees bending and snapping like glass beneath the wind.

Like her. She wasn't strong enough. She would break and the pieces would be scattered over the cold rocks.

Jack slipped on the rocks where white pebbles of sleet gathered and turned beneath his boots. He let go of Alana's braids, breaking his fall with his hands.

Running. Scrambling.

Breath like a knife in her side.

Throat on fire with screams and the storm chasing her, catching her, yanking her backward while rocks like fists hit her. She was broken and bleeding, screaming down the night, running.

Caught. Her braids caught again in Jack's fist,

ice sliding beneath her feet, wind tearing at her, Jack lifting her as she screamed, lifting her high and when he let go she would fall as the water fell, down and down over the lip of the valley, exploding whitely on rocks far below.

Clawing and fighting. But she was swept up, lifted high, helpless, nothing beneath her feet, earth falling away and her body twisting, weightless, she was falling, falling, black rushing up to meet her and when it did she would be torn from life like an aspen leaf from its stem, spinning away helplessly over the void.

She called to Rafe then.

Knowing that she was dead, she cried Rafe's name and her undying love for him into the teeth of the waiting mountain.

And Rafe answered.

He came out of the storm and darkness like an avenging angel, his hands tearing her from Jack's deadly grasp.

At the last instant Rafe spun aside from the drop-off, balanced on the brink of falling. With certain death in front of him and Alana at his feet, Rafe whirled and launched himself in a low tackle that carried Jack away from Alana, helpless at the edge of the cliff.

The two men grappled in the darkness, pale sleet rolling beneath their feet, their struggles bringing them closer to the brink with each second.

Rafe kicked away, freeing himself and coming to his feet in a poised, muscular rush. Jack staggered upright, his hair shining palely with each flash of lightning, his face dark with hatred. He leaped blindly for Rafe.

*But Rafe wasn't there. He slipped the attack with
a supple, disciplined movement of his body, leaving
nothing but night between Jack and the lip of the
cliff.*

*Jack had an instant of surprise, a scream of fury
and disbelief, and then he was falling, turning over
slowly, screaming and falling into night.*

*Silence came, and then the sound of Alana's tear-
ing screams.*

*"It's all right, wildflower. I've come to take you
home."*

*Alana shuddered, giving her mind and her body
to the cold and blackness. . . .*

Alana stirred and slowly surfaced from
memories. She was surprised to find that it
was day rather than evening, fair rather than
stormy, and she was huddled on her knees
rather than unconscious in Rafe's arms.

She shook her head, hardly able to believe
that she wasn't still dreaming. Rafe's words
had sounded so real, so close.

She opened her eyes and saw that she had
walked to the treacherous margin of rock and
water and cliff. With a shudder, she turned
away from the edge—and then she saw a man
silhouetted against the sun.

She froze, fear squeezing her heart.

Rafe's face tightened into a mask of pain
when he saw Alana's fear.

She had remembered and he had lost
her.

"Stan was right," Rafe said, pain roughening his voice. "You were running from me,

too. You didn't want to believe that the man you loved was a killer."

"No!"

Alana's voice shook, making a ragged cry out of the single word.

"Yes," said Rafe flatly. "I killed Jack Reeves. And you remembered it."

"It wasn't like that," Alana said quickly. "Stan was wrong. You didn't come up the mountain planning to kill Jack and seduce me and—"

"But Jack's dead," Rafe interrupted. "I killed him."

"You were saving my life!" Alana said, trying to understand why Rafe's face was so closed, so remote.

Rafe shrugged.

"So it's manslaughter, not murder one," he said curtly. "Jack's dead just the same."

"It was an accident!" she cried fiercely. "I saw it, Rafe! I know!"

"Technically, yes, it was an accident," Rafe said, his voice as controlled as his expression. "When I ducked, I didn't know that Jack would go over the cliff."

Alana let out a ragged breath.

"But there's something about the fight that you still haven't faced, Alana." Rafe spoke slowly, clearly, leaving no room for evasion or misunderstanding. "When I saw Jack trying to kill you—after that instant, Jack Reeves was a dead man walking. There was no way I'd let him leave the mountain alive."

Alana's eyes closed, but it wasn't in horror

at what Rafe was saying. It was the pain in him that made her flinch.

"You knew that," Rafe said. "Yet you couldn't stand knowing that the man you loved was a murderer. So you forgot. But not well enough. Somewhere, deep inside you, you knew. You didn't trust me enough to marry me."

"That's not true!" said Alana desperately. "You saved my life! You—"

"It's all right, wildflower," Rafe said, cutting across Alana's urgent words. "You don't owe me anything. You gave it all back to me that night."

"But—"

"When you were certain you were going to die, you screamed, but not for mercy or revenge. You called to me, telling me that you loved me. *And you didn't even know I was there.* In those few seconds you wiped out all the bitterness that had been destroying me since I found out you were married."

"Rafael," she whispered.

"You don't owe me anything at all. Certainly not trust."

Alana looked at Rafe wildly.

"But I do trust you!" she cried.

Rafe's mouth turned down in a sad travesty of a smile.

"I don't believe you, wildflower."

Before Alana could say anything more, Rafe turned toward the trail where his big spotted stallion stood patiently.

"We'd better go," Rafe said. "Bob has prob-

ably found your note by now, and mine. He'll
be beside himself with worry."

Rafe began walking toward his horse. After
a few steps, he realized that Alana wasn't following. He turned back and saw that she was
still sitting on a rock very near the edge of the
cliff.

"Alana?"

She sat motionless, watching Rafe, her eyes
dark.

"I'll need your help," she said distinctly.

With a few swift strides Rafe was at Alana's
side. He knelt in front of her and began running his hands from her knees to her feet.

"Did you wrench your ankle again?" he
asked. "Where does it hurt?"

"Everywhere," Alana said softly. "You'll
have to carry me."

Rafe's head snapped up.

He searched Alana's eyes and her expression, afraid to breathe, to hope. Even when she
had given herself to him in the moonlit cabin,
he had not dared to lift her, to hold her helpless above the ground.

And now she was at the edge of the same
cliff Jack had held her over, held her high
above his head, getting set to throw her out
into darkness and death.

Silently Alana held her arms out to Rafe.

He stood and looked down at her for a long
moment. Then he bent and caught her beneath
her arms.

Slowly Rafe lifted Alana to her feet, waiting
for the first sign of fear to tighten her body.

He held her almost level with him, her toes just off the ground.

She smiled and put her hands on his shoulders.

"Higher, Rafael. Lift me higher. Lift me over your head."

"Alana—"

"Lift me," she whispered against his lips. "I know you won't let me fall. I'm safe with you, Rafael. You aren't like Jack. You won't throw my life away. *Lift me.*"

Rafe lifted Alana as high as he could, held her, watched her smile, felt her trust in the complete relaxation of her body suspended between his hands.

Then he let her slide slowly down his body until their lips met in a kiss that left both of them shaken, clinging to each other.

They rode the same way down the mountain, clinging to each other, whispering words of love and need. Rafe's arms were wrapped around Alana and her hands were over his as he guided the big stallion along the trail.

Rafe was the first one to spot the plane bobbing quietly on the third lake.

"Sheriff Mitchell," Rafe said. "Bob must have hit the panic button."

Alana shrank against Rafe and went very still.

For the rest of the ride she was silent, her hands clinging to Rafe's wrists, her mind racing as she tried to figure out ways to protect the man she loved.

No matter what Rafe says, he isn't at fault for Jack's death, Alana thought. Jack brought it on himself. Rafe doesn't deserve to be punished for Jack's selfishness, his murderous rage.

Yet Alana was afraid that was exactly what would happen.

Sheriff Mitchell was sitting on the porch of the lodge, his feet propped against the rail. When he heard the big stallion's hoof strike a rock, Mitch looked up.

"I see you found her," Mitch said, satisfaction in his voice. "Just like I told Bob you would."

Alana spoke before Rafe could.

"My memory is back. Jack's death was an accident, just like Rafe said. It was icy and Jack fell and I passed out from shock and cold."

Mitch looked at Alana oddly. His homely face creased into a frown.

"That's not what Rafe told me," the sheriff muttered. "He said that Jack tried to kill you, they fought, and Jack ended up dead. Is that how you remember it?"

Alana made a helpless sound and looked over her shoulder at Rafe. He kissed her lips.

"I told Mitch everything when we rode back in to bring out Jack's body," Rafe said. "When we came off the mountain, you were gone."

"But—but that's not how the newspapers explained Jack's death," said Alana.

Mitch shrugged.

"Well," the sheriff said, "I didn't figure that justice would be any better served if we went to the hassle of arraigning and then acquitting

Rafe on a clear-cut case of justifiable homicide."

Alana's breath caught. She turned and looked at the sheriff with hope in her eyes.

"And then there would have been reporters hounding you for all the bloody details," the sheriff drawled, "what with Jack being such a famous son of a bitch and all. You didn't need that. You were having a hard enough time staying afloat as it was."

Alana let out a long sigh of relief.

"So I told the reporters the only truth that mattered," the sheriff concluded. "In my opinion, Jack's death was legally an accident."

Mitch paused and looked at Alana, his gray eyes intent. "Unless you remember it some other way and want to change the record?"

"No," Alana said quickly. "Not at all. I just didn't want Rafe to be punished for saving my life."

Mitch nodded. "That's how I had it figured."

He pulled out a pipe from his jacket pocket, struck a match, and held it to the bowl. He sucked hard a few times, then looked at the lake.

"Well, now," Mitch said, changing the subject with finality, "what's the fishing been like?"

Rafe tilted his head and kissed the nape of Alana's neck.

"You're too late, Mitch. I just caught the most beautiful trout on the mountain."

Mitch grinned around a cloud of pungent smoke.

"Keeper size?" he asked dryly.

Rafe laughed and slid off the big stallion. When he was on the ground, he held his arms out to Alana.

She smiled and let him lift her out of the saddle. For a few moments he held her off the ground, enjoying the sensation of her body pressed against the length of his own.

"Definitely keeper size," Rafe said.

Mitch laughed.

"Unless," Rafe whispered too softly for Mitch to hear, "the trout doesn't want the fisherman?"

Alana kissed Rafe gently, brushing her lips across his mouth as her fingers slid deeply into his thick hair, dislodging his Stetson.

The front door of the cabin slammed open.

"Mitch, when in hell are you going to— Alana! Are you okay?"

Mitch laughed. "Bob, are you blind? She's never been better."

Reluctantly Rafe released Alana so that she could reassure her brother.

"I've remembered," she said, turning to face Bob. "And I'm fine. I'm sorry I worried you."

"Hell, sis, it was worth it!" Bob turned to yell over his shoulder. "Stan! Janice! Alana's got her memory back!"

There was a triumphant whoop from the cabin. Janice and Stan ran out onto the porch. Stan looked at Alana, wrapped securely in

Rafe's arms, relaxed and smiling, obviously not afraid.

Then Stan turned and gave Janice a thorough, hungry kiss.

Bob looked startled.

Rafe simply smiled.

"I think I'd better make a complete introduction this time," Rafe said. "Bob, meet Mr. and Mrs. Stan Wilson."

When Stan finally let go of Janice, she smiled.

"Now we can wash out the blond highlights and get rid of the blue contacts," she said to Stan. "If I open my eyes, I feel like I'm kissing a stranger."

Alana watched, speechless, as Stan removed his dark blue contacts, revealing eyes that were light green.

"Blond highlights?" asked Alana weakly.

"Yep," said Janice, tugging on a lock of Stan's fair hair. "I'm used to my man being a sun-streaked brown, not a California blond."

"I don't understand," Alana said.

"I'm afraid you've been caught in a conspiracy," said Janice gently. "But it was a conspiracy of love. When Rafe told me what had happened to you, I told him to give you a few weeks to remember on your own. Then he called again and told me you weren't sleeping, weren't eating, were having nightmares—"

"How did you know?" asked Alana, turning to Rafe.

"I told you, wildflower. You're a lot like me."

"In short," summarized Janice, "you were tearing yourself apart. Rafe thought that if you came back here, you would see him and know that you were safe, that it was all right to remember what had happened. I agreed, so long as you came willingly. If you came back it would mean that you wanted to remember. That you wanted to be whole again."

"Some travel agent," Alana said dryly. Then, "Oh. You're still a practicing psychiatrist, aren't you?"

"One of the best," said Rafe, his arms tightening around Alana. "Damn near every word we said in front of you was vetted by Janice first."

"Not every word," Janice said crisply, looking sideways at Stan. "I nearly choked my husband when I found out about the fight by the lake."

Stan almost smiled. "Yeah, I know. I don't take orders worth a damn. We've argued about Rafe a lot," said Stan, flashing Alana a pale green glance. "I thought she was too gentle on Rafe after he got back from Central America. And then, when she couldn't put him back together, it took two years for me to coax her into marriage."

Janice looked surprised. "Two years! You only asked me out two months before we were married!"

"Yeah. So much for being subtle. I wasted twenty-two months tiptoeing around, thinking that you held it against me that I was the one who'd been wounded. If it wasn't for me, Rafe would have flown out of the jungle with the rest of us."

Rafe started to say something, but Stan cut him off.

"No way, buddy. I'm not finished. I thought you were being too gentle with Alana to get any results. Hell, I didn't even know you had that much gentle in you! I'm still having a hard time believing that you're the same man I worked with in Central America."

Stan shook his head. "Anyway, I wanted to stir up Alana, to make her think. I didn't believe you'd snuffed good old Jack to get Alana. If you'd wanted to do that, you wouldn't have waited almost four years, and you sure as hell wouldn't have been caught after you'd done it. You're too smart for that."

"Thanks . . . I think," said Rafe dryly.

Alana looked from Stan to Janice to Rafe. Finally she gave her brother Bob a long, considering look. He flushed slightly.

"You aren't mad, are you, sis?"

"Mad?" Alana shook her head. "I'm . . . stunned. I can't believe that you knew about the whole conspiracy and kept it a secret. Old in-the-ear-and-out-the-mouth Bob. I'm impressed, baby brother."

"It wasn't easy. I thought I'd blown it more than once," admitted Bob.

"We didn't tell him everything," Rafe said dryly. "Oh, he knew that he wasn't trying to start a dude ranch, but that's about it. He didn't know that I'd worked with Stan and Janice before. He didn't know that Stan was camouflaged as carefully as any lure I'd ever made. And he didn't know that Janice was a practicing psychiatrist."

"Well," Mitch said, "I'd better get down the mountain before the light goes."

"Can you fly back tomorrow?" asked Rafe.

"Sure. Need something in particular?"

"Champagne. A justice of the peace."

Mitch smiled. "Somebody getting married?"

Rafe looked at Alana, a question in his amber eyes.

"Damned right," she said, putting her arms tightly around Rafe. "This time, the trout is landing the fisherman."

19

A<small>LANA</small>   STOOD   BY   THE hearth in the small cabin, wearing only Rafe's warm robe. She let the song fade from her lips, watching Rafe as he played soft notes on the silver harmonica.

He was stretched out on the bed, eyes closed, sensitive fingers wrapped around the harmonica as his lips coaxed beautiful music from it. He wore nothing but firelight, which clung and shifted with each breath he took. His hair gleamed like winter mink, alive with the reflected dance of flames.

Rafe looked up, sensing her watching him.

"Happy, Mrs. Winter?" he asked, holding out his hand.

"Very happy."

Alana took Rafe's hand and curled up beside him, enjoying the hard warmth of his flesh beneath her cheek.

"Even though you haven't remembered everything?" he asked quietly.

She looked at Rafe's eyes, gold in the firelight, and wanted nothing more than to be loved by him.

"I don't care anymore," Alana said, "because I'm not afraid anymore."

Rafe let out a long breath. Tenderly he traced the satin darkness of Alana's eyebrow with his fingertip.

"Good," he said softly. "I don't think you'll ever remember coming down the mountain. You were bruised, bloody, out of your mind with cold and shock."

His eyes closed, as though he was afraid she would see too much looking into them.

"Frankly," Rafe said in a low voice, "I'd forget it if I could. I loved you so much and I thought you were dying, that I'd come too late."

" 'Come too late,' " Alana repeated. "You say that as though you knew I needed you."

"I did."

"How?" whispered Alana. "Why did you come to the highest lake when I was there with Jack?"

"I can't explain it. I just . . . knew."

Rafe looked at the harmonica for a moment before he carefully set it aside.

"The night before I rode up Broken Mountain," he said, "I kept thinking I heard you calling me again and again. But that was impossible. I was alone at the ranch. Nothing but the wind. Yet by morning, I was wild, half crazy, certain that *you needed me.*"

Rafe blew out a long breath. "I had no choice but to ride up the mountain and find you, Alana. It was irrational, crazy, but I had to do it."

"You weren't crazy," said Alana, trembling. "When Jack tied me and left me by the lake, I called for you all night long. I couldn't help myself."

Rafe's breath came in sharply. He rolled over and faced Alana, touching her as though she were a dream and he was afraid of awakening.

"If only I hadn't fought against it so hard," he said in a low voice. "I should have come to you sooner."

"It's a miracle that you came at all. You hated me."

"No," he said, kissing Alana's eyebrow, her eyelid, the corner of her mouth. "I never hated you. I wanted to, but I couldn't. We were tied too deeply to each other, no matter how far apart we were."

"Yes," she whispered, returning the tender kisses.

"That's why I couldn't ride away from you after we made love," Rafe said, "even though I thought you didn't trust me. Every time the wind blew down the canyon, I heard you calling me. I had to come back to you."

Rafe's fingertip traced Alana's lips. "I love you more than you know, more than I have words to say."

With slow, caressing movements, Rafe unwrapped the robe until Alana wore only firelight and the fine gold chain he had given to her. The elegant symbol of infinity gleamed in the hollow of her throat, speaking silently of love that knew no boundaries.

He gathered Alana close to his body, kissing her gently at first, then with a passion that was both restrained and deeply wild. She gave herself to the kiss, to him, melting in his hands, wanting him, loving him. He listened to the soft sounds that came from her, and he smiled.

"Yes," Rafe whispered, "sing of your love for me, a lifetime of love. And after that . . ."

His lips touched the golden symbol at Alana's throat, and he knew there would always be a song of love that knew no bounds.

Enjoy an excerpt from
DEATH ECHO
the new hardcover by

ELIZABETH
LOWELL

Coming soon from William Morrow

Prologue

Y ou must believe me. St. Kilda Consulting is
our best hope."

Former Ambassador Steele pinched the bridge
of his nose and wished he'd never met the woman
who now sat opposite his desk. "Alara…"

"I'm no longer called that."

Steele blew out a hard breath and wheeled
his chair back from his desk. Very few people
on earth could make him uncomfortable. The
woman no longer called Alara was one of them.

And one of the most dangerous.

"Just as I no longer work for the government,"
Steele said.

"We established that years ago." Alara smiled
almost sadly. Her silver hair gleamed, hair that
once had been as black as her eyes. "In the
shadow world, St. Kilda Consulting has made
quite a reputation for itself. Trust is rare in any
world. Even more so in the shadows."

"You're asking him to break that trust," Emma
Cross said, speaking up for the first time in fifteen minutes.

Steele and Alara turned sharply toward Emma,

telling her what she'd already guessed—they had forgotten they weren't alone.

All emotion faded from Alara's expression. It was replaced by the frightening intelligence that had made her a legend within the nameless, anonymously funded government agencies whose initials changed frequently but whose purpose never did.

"I came in soft," Alara said coolly, "requesting not threatening. I don't have time for games with disillusioned children." She looked at Steele. "America could lose a major population center in less than ten days. We need St. Kilda to prevent that. We will have what we need."

Without looking away from Alara, Steele said, "Emma, summarize the facts as they were presented to us."

Emma's light green eyes watched her boss for a moment. Then she began speaking quickly, without emotion. "As given to us, no questions asked or qualifications offered. Ms. Alara's department or departments have been following various overseas entities. One of those entities is suspected—"

"Known, not suspected," Alara cut in.

"—of stealing and reselling yachts," Emma continued without pause. "One of the stolen yachts was specially modified to hold contraband—chemical, biological, and/or radioactive. Motives, whether the actors are state or nonstate, weren't part of Alara's presentation, which is going to make finding and stopping who or whatever is the enemy before time runs out is just this side of impossible." She looked at Alara.

"No surprise the bureaucrats and politicians want to dump this steaming pile on St. Kilda's doorstep."

Steele almost smiled. Emma Cross had a pretty face and a bottom-line mind.

"The excuse for said dumping," Emma continued, turning back to Steele, "is that St. Kilda has an agent who has been investigating missing yachts for an international insurer. The yacht, *Blackbird*, which I have been tracing, is a dead ringer for the refitted and purportedly dangerous yacht pursued by Alara's department. Or departments. The person, group, or entity responsible for theft of the nameless yacht wasn't identified. At all."

Alara's still-black eyebrows rose, but she said nothing about Emma's coolly mocking summary. The older agent simply sat in her crisp business suit and pumps, looking like an employee of a middle-management team, back when women were called secretaries rather than administrative assistants.

"Satellite tracking and other intel confirm that a yacht believed to be the *Blackbird* will be off-loaded from the containership *Shinhua Lotus* at approximately fifteen hundred hours Pacific Coast time," Emma continued. "According to St. Kilda's investigation, an unknown transit captain will pick up the boat in Port of Seattle. We have no assurance that the yacht aboard the containership is the same one that originally was loaded aboard the *Lotus*. We won't have that assurance until someone finds a way to get aboard either the containership or the yacht. I'm sure our would-be 'client' has the resources to covertly conduct that search."

"Had," Alara said. "Past tense."

"You have a leak," Emma said bluntly.

"Always probable," Alara said. "St. Kilda has carefully and repeatedly distanced itself from any traceable connection with any U.S. intel agency. The targets won't be looking for you. They sure as bloody hell are looking for us. We don't have anyone on the ground who isn't being followed."

Emma kept her mouth shut because she hated agreeing with the other woman. Nothing personal. Just past experience. The officers and agents she had worked with all over the world had been decent people, at the lower levels. The farther she went up the food chain, the less trustworthy the bosses were. Again, nothing personal. Just the Darwinian facts of survival in a highly politicized workplace whose rules changed with every headline.

"Do you have anything else you can tell St. Kilda?" Steele asked.

"Not at the present time," Alara said.

Emma made a rude sound.

Steele didn't bother.

"You aren't required to help," Alara pointed out.

"But it sure is hard to do business in the U.S. when everyone who works for St. Kilda is audited quarterly," Emma said, "when St. Kilda personnel are stopped at the border, or their passports are jerked, or their driver's licenses are revoked, their spouses fired, and every business that approaches St. Kilda is warned not—"

Steele held up his hand.

Emma swallowed the rest of her argument and waited. Steele knew how harassment worked. Good old Uncle's bureaucrats could hound St. Kilda to death. Literally.

"That's the price of living in a society you can't fit around a campfire," Alara said to Emma. "Cooperation is required in reality if not in law. Ambassador Steele knows this. Why don't you?"

Emma hoped her teeth weren't leaving skid marks on her tongue. She really wanted to unload on the older woman.

Because Alara was right.

"Reality is a bitch," Alara said. "When all else fails, you can count on that." She glanced at her watch. "In or out?"

Steele rolled his chair to face Emma. "You're off the hook on this one. Be prepared to brief another St. Kilda employee in less than an hour."

"No," Emma said. "I'm in."

"I don't want someone whose head isn't in the game," Alara said.

"No worries." Emma's smile was thin as a knife. "I've learned to use my head, not my heart. I'm in unless Steele says otherwise."

"You're in," Steele said,

"Nine days, which began counting down at midnight," Alara said, coming to her feet. "When the time is up, civilians die. If we're lucky, the number will be under a hundred thousand." She looked at Emma with cold black eyes. "Be smarter than your mouth."

1

Emma Cross gripped the round chromed bars of the pitching Zodiac's radar bridge as it raced over the Puget Sound, twenty miles beyond Elliott Bay. St. Kilda Consulting had assured her that the boat driver was capable. But Joe Faroe hadn't mentioned that the dude called Josh didn't look old enough to drink.

Was I that young once?

Yeah, I must have been. Scary thought. You can make some shockingly dumb, entirely legal decisions at that age.

I sure did.

Josh must have, too. His eyes are a lot older than his body.

She had seen too many men like him while she worked as a case officer in places where local wars made headlines half a world away, innocents were blown to bloody rags, and nothing really changed.

Except her. She'd finally gotten out. Tribal wars had been burning before she joined the CIA. The wars were still burning along just fine without her. World without end, amen.

Until Alara had dropped into St. Kilda's life.

She has to be wrong, Emma told herself. *God knows it wouldn't be the first time intel was bad.*

But if she's right…

The thought sent a chill through Emma that had nothing do with the cold water just inches away.

Nine days.

Automatically she hung on as the Zodiac bounced and skidded on the wake of a ship that was already miles behind them, headed for Elliott Bay's muscular waterfront. She pulled her thoughts away from what she couldn't change to what she might change.

Emma tapped the driver and shouted over the roar of the huge outboard engines. "Shut it down."

He eased off the throttle. The boat slid down off plane and settled deeply in the steel-colored water. Like a skittish cat, the inflatable moved without warning in unexpected directions.

"You okay?" Josh asked.

"As in not wanting to hurl?"

He smiled crookedly. "Yeah. As in."

"I'm good."

He gave her a slow once-over and nodded. "Sure are."

"Faroe told me about you, darlin', so thanks but no thanks."

Josh looked at her eyes for a moment, nodded, and waited for his next order. No harm, no foul.

Emma wished she could say the same about her job.

Shading her eyes against the bright afternoon overcast, she looked west, toward the Strait of

Juan de Fuca. Swells from the distant Pacific Ocean, plus choppy wind waves, batted at the twenty-foot-long Zodiac, lifting and dropping the rubber boat without warning. Some of the waves had white crests that streaked the gray water.

"We good?" she asked. "That wind's kicking up."

"No worries. We can take three times the blow, easy."

Land looked real far away to her, but she'd learned to trust expert judgment. For all the pilot's fresh-faced looks, he was utterly at home with the inflatable and Puget Sound.

"Let me know if that changes," she said.

Even as Josh nodded, she switched her attention back to the western horizon. Ten minutes earlier, she'd spotted her target when it was only a dark blob squeezed between the shimmering gray sky and the darker gray sound.

Now the target was a huge ship plowing toward them like a falling mountain. Dark engine smoke boiled up from funnels behind the bridge deck. The deck cargo was a colorful collage of steel shipping containers stacked seven high. The boat was close enough that she could make out the white bow wave it pushed up before it.

"That her?" Josh asked.

She lifted binoculars, spun the focus wheel, and scanned quickly. On the Zodiac's shifting, uncertain platform, staring through unstabilized binoculars was a fast way to get seasick.

The collage leaped forward and became a random checkerboard of colors, a toy for giants playing an unknown game.

"Meet the container ship known as the *Shinhua Lotus*," Emma said, lowering the glasses. "Standard cruising speed close to thirty knots. One hundred and eighty thousand horsepower. Her hull is steel, a thousand feet long. She's stacked with more than fifteen thousand steel freight containers. One hundred and sixty thousand tons of international commerce at work."

"Gotta be the most boring job in the world."

She glanced quickly at him. "What?"

"Driving that pig between ports. Tugs do all the fun stuff close in. The ship's captain mostly talks on the radio."

She looked at the little boat that had carried her out to meet the *Lotus*. Twenty feet long, six feet wide and powered by two outboard engines. She touched the fabric of the Zodiac's inflated side tube. It was only slightly thicker than the rubberized off-shore suit she wore. All that supported the boat was the breath of life, twenty pounds-per-square-inch of air pressure.

And one of the biggest ships ever built was bearing down on them, bearing bad news in the shape of a yacht called *Blackbird*.

She lifted the binoculars again. The huge ship overwhelmed her field of view. Everything was a fast-forward slide show. Stacks of shipping containers in various company colors. The windshield of the bridge deck. The hammerhead crane next to the forward mast.

The black-hulled yacht perched in a cradle on top of stacks of steel boxes.

Hello, Blackbird. *So you made it.*

If that's really you.

"How close can you get to the *Lotus*?" she asked.

"How close do you need?"

She pulled a camera from the waterproof bag at her feet. Unlike the binoculars, the camera had a computerized system to keep the field of view from dancing with every motion of the boat.

"I have to be able to see detail on a yacht on top of the containers. A two-hundred-millimeter lens is the longest I have."

That and intel satellite photos, courtesy of Uncle Sam. Too bad I don't really trust Alara.

For all Emma could prove, the photos St. Kilda had been given could have been taken on the other side of the world a year ago. Or three years. Or twelve. Not that she was paranoid. It was just that she preferred facts that she'd checked out herself. Thoroughly.

"Two-hundred-millimeter lens." Josh whistled through his teeth and narrowed his eyes. "And the lady wants details."

"What's the problem?"

He held up one finger. "That great pig up ahead is throwing a ten-foot bow wave." A second finger uncurled. "The Coast Guard patrol boats would be on us like stink on shit. After Nine Eleven, they lost their sense of humor about bending the rules."

No news there for Emma. "You saying it can't be done?"

"Depends. How bad do you want to swim or go to jail?"

"Not so much, thanks." She let out a long breath and reminded herself that impatience was a quick way to die, and she was chasing nothing more dangerous than luxury yachts. At least she had been, until Alara appeared like a puff of darkness. "I can wait until the tugs are nudging that 'great pig' against a dock."

"If you're working on a really short clock," Josh said, "I'll be glad to take a run at the *Lotus* right now." He grinned suddenly. "It beats my usual gig—hauling seasick tourists out to chase whales."

She thought about it, then shook her head. "It's not life or death."

You wish.

She laughed silently, bitterly. That was why she'd quit the CIA and taken an assignment from St. Kilda to investigate yacht thefts. No alarms with this job. No adrenaline exploding through her body.

No blood.

No guilt.

And best of all, no corrupt politics.

Guess again, she told herself. *Then get over it.*

"Back to shore?" Josh asked.

"Not yet. Keep the *Lotus* in sight while you give me a sightseeing tour of the famous and beautiful Elliott Bay."

"Legal distance maintained at all times?"

"Until I say otherwise."

Standing on top of seventy-foot high stacks of containers, with only the unforgiving steel deck below to catch him, Mackenzie Durand wrestled with the cargo sling that would lift the yacht off the *Shinhua Lotus*. He looked up to the glassed-in cab of the deck crane, where the operator was waiting for directions.

Hope the he knows what he's doing, Mac thought as he held up his right hand and made a small circle in the air. Sign-language for giving more slack to the cable that held the lifting frame.

The operator dropped the frame six inches at a time until Mackenzie's hand clenched into a fist.

The cable stopped instantly.

Damn, but it's sweet to work with professionals, Mac thought as he began positioning the sling on the yacht's black, salt-streaked hull. The man in the cab might be a miserable son of a bitch who beat his wife and was an officer in the most corrupt labor union on the waterfront, but when he was at the controls of his pet hammerhead crane, he could be as sure and gentle as a mother cradling a nursing baby.

Mac manhandled a wide strap into position just

ahead of the spot on the hull where twin prop housings on the *Blackbird* thrust out like eggbeaters. Lift points were crucial in controlling a vessel that weighed almost thirty tons.

Besides, if anything went wrong, he was going to be splat on ground zero. He'd been there, done that, and vowed never to be there again. He'd been the lucky one who survived.

At least he'd told himself he was the lucky one. After a few years, he even believed it. During daylight.

At night, well, night was always there, waiting with the kind of dreams he woke from cold, sweating, biting back howls of fury and betrayal.

Long ago and far away, Mac told himself savagely. *Pay attention to what's happening now.*

When he was satisfied with the position of the lifting strap, he signaled the crane operator to pick up cable. The frame went from slack to loaded. The aft strap was in front of the propellers and the forward strap was even with the front windshield. Both straps visibly stretched as the overhead cable tightened.

Just before *Blackbird* lifted out of its cradle, Mac clenched his fist overhead. Instantly the crane operator stopped bringing in cable.

Mac checked everything again before he scrambled up the ten-foot ladder that stood against the swim step at the stern of the yacht. When he was aboard the *Blackbird*, he gave the crane operator a palm-out hand signal with fingers spread.

Take a break, five minutes.

The operator nodded and reached for a cigarette.

A *Lotus* deckhand appeared and took the ladder away from the yacht's swim step.

Mac popped the hatch in the rear cockpit and went down below. He had been a professional transport skipper for five years. He was regularly dropped on the deck of a boat he had never seen before and was expected to take command of it immediately. Since he didn't plan on going down with any ship, he had developed a mental checklist as rigorous and detailed as an airline captain's.

He liked the idea that if he died, it was his own screw-up, not someone else's.

The first thing Mac did was snap on the battery switches. Each of the eight batteries was big enough to power a hybrid automobile. A quick check of their status showed they had retained enough charge on the ten-day trip from Singapore to start the yacht's engines and operate its various systems.

Next, he opened the seacocks that supplied saltwater to the cooling systems of the two shiny new Caterpillar engines that drove the boat. Oversized engines, a special order that made for a cramped engine room.

Gotta love those yachties with more money than sense, Mac told himself.

Quickly but thoroughly, he checked the hose clamps on the through-hull fittings to make sure none had vibrated loose at sea. Cooling water was good. Gushers of saltwater in the bilge weren't.

The through-hull fitting that normally supplied cooling water to the generator had been left open to drain rainwater or ocean spray out of the yacht during the voyage. Mac closed the seacock so the small ship wouldn't sink minutes after it touched the waters of Elliott Bay.

He checked the through-hull fittings for the septic and water maker systems, then the fuel lines that fed the two six-cylinder diesel engines. He had been assured there was enough fuel aboard to make Rosario, sixty miles to the north, but he was suspicious by nature.

It had saved his life more than once.

A shipping crew in Singapore, where the yacht had begun its voyage, could make hundreds of dollars by shorting the fuel tanks. Mac didn't want to come into the Rosario rigging yard at the end of a tow line.

The sight gauges for both fuel tanks showed less than an inch of fuel.

Ah, human nature. All for me and screw you.

His first stop would be the fuel dock on the Elliott Bay waterfront. The good news was that the diesel fuel in the feed lines from the tanks looked clear. With quick, economical motions he checked both fuel filter housings for water.

All good. At least the greedy sucks put in clean fuel.

What there was of it.

He looked carefully around the engine room. Salt water was as corrosive as acid to metal parts and systems. Even with the best of care and maintenance, time and use and the sea would mark the yacht. But right now, she was bright and clean, shining with promise.

Mac loved taking a new boat on its first real cruise. It was like meeting a really interesting woman. Challenging. That was where the reward came—getting the best out of himself and an unknown boat. Or a woman.

No one else at risk, no one else to die, no one else to survive alone and sweat through nightmares the same way.

When Mac had finished his checklist, he climbed back up out of the engine compartment and went inside the salon to the helm. Plastic covered the upholstered furnishings. The teak dining table and polished granite of the galley counter were protected beneath cardboard and shipping blankets, as was everything else except the wheel. But the opulence of the yacht's fittings was evident in the bright brass lamps and the oriental style carpeting on the salon floor.

Mac opened the teak panel that concealed two ranks of electrical circuit breakers and meters. He noted a scratch on the inside of the door. Cosmetic, not a problem. He checked each carefully labeled meter and breaker, going down the ranks, engaging breakers and energizing the circuits he expected to need.

The last two breakers he threw were marked Port and Starboard Engine START/STOP. When he engaged them, two loud buzzers signaled that the Caterpillars in the engine room were ready to go.

With a final check of the batteries, he went back through the salon, into the well, and up the narrow six-step stairway to the flying bridge. He checked the switch settings on bridge controls, then lifted his hand and twirled his fingers in a tight circle.

The overhead crane operator smoothly picked

up five feet of cable, lifting the yacht up and out of its cradle. The fresh afternoon breeze off Puget Sound tried to turn the boat perpendicular to the container ship, but the operator had anticipated the wind and corrected for it. The overhead crane arm swung the yacht toward the huge ship's outside rail.

For a second Mac felt like the boat was adrift, flying. This was the part of the job he didn't like, when he had to trust his life to the crane operator's skill.

He looked out over the waterfront toward the Seattle skyline beyond. The restless sound, the rain-washed city, the evergreen islands. The beautiful silver chaos of intersecting wakes— container ships, freighters, ferries, tugs, pleasure boats zipping about like water bugs.

One of the water bugs seemed to be fascinated by the process of unloading the yacht. Mac had seen the Zodiac while he waited for the *Lotus* to be nudged into its berth. The little rubber boat had weaved through the commercial traffic, circling ferries and tugs, taking pictures of everything, even the Harbor Patrol boat that had barked at it for getting too close to the *Lotus*.

Sightseers, Mac thought, grateful he no longer lived a life where the little inflatable would have been an instant threat. *Sweet, innocent civilians.*

He did a quick check of the water near the container ship, where he would soon be dropped into the busy bay. A small coastal freighter, freshly loaded with two dozen containers destined for local delivery, steamed west toward the San Juan Islands. Two Washington State ferries, one inbound to Seattle and the other headed across to Bainbridge Island, were passing one another a few hundred yards to the north. A City of Seattle fireboat was making way toward its station at Pier 48, and a dozen pleasure craft of varying sizes were crisscrossing the riffled waters in the afternoon sunshine.

The black rubber Zodiac with two people aboard lay about a hundred yards offshore, bobbing and jerking in the wakes and chop. The open craft had a shiny stainless steel radar arch and the logo of a local water tour outfit. The captain and single passenger wore standard offshore gear to protect them from wind and spray. The passenger was busy with the camera again.

The round black eye of the long-distance lens made the fine hairs on Mac's neck lift.

Too many memories of sniper scopes.

He shook off his past and watched as the crane operator delicately lowered the yacht into the water until Mac signaled for a stop. The operator held the boat in place in the cradle, afloat but not adrift. Mac checked his instruments once more, then touched the switch that locked the batteries into series and hit the port start button on the console.

Beneath him, he felt as much as heard one 550-horsepower engine rattle and cough. He held the switch closed while he glanced over his left shoulder toward the stern quarter of the boat.

Black smoke belched, then cleared and belched again. The stuttering sound of engine ignition suddenly smoothed out into a comforting, throaty rumble.

The starboard engine started more easily and leveled out instantly. He went to the stainless steel rail aft of the bridge and checked. Both exhaust ports were trailing diesel smoke. Beneath it, he could see the steady flow of cooling water.

Good to go.

He signaled thumbs-up to the crane operator. The yacht slipped down a few more inches until the water held the boat. Moments later the slings went slack. Then the operator let out enough cable to ease the lifting frame far enough aft that the yacht was free.

The big power pods took over as Mac put the engine controls into forward. She felt solid. Clean. Good. A grand yacht doing what it had been designed to do.

Mac idled away from the container docks. He purely loved the first instants of freedom, of being responsible only for himself. Grinning, he glanced over his shoulder to check the wake.

The black Zodiac was moving with him. No faster. No slower. Same direction. Same angle.

The hair on Mac's neck stirred again in silent warning.

This time he didn't ignore it. He went below, got his binoculars, and took a good, long look from the cover of the cabin.

You're being paranoid, the civilian part of himself said.

The part of him that had been honed to a killing edge ten years ago just kept memorizing faces, features, and boat registration numbers.

At Avon Books, we know your passion for romance—once you finish one of our novels, you find yourself wanting more.

May we tempt you with . . .

- **Excerpts** from our upcoming releases.

- Entertaining **extras**, including authors' personal photo albums and book lists.

- Behind-the-scenes **scoop** on your favorite characters and series.

- **Sweepstakes** for the chance to win free books, romantic getaways, and other fun prizes.

- Writing **tips** from our authors and editors.

- **Blog** with our authors and find out why they love to write romance.

- **Exclusive content** that's not contained within the pages of our novels.

Join us at
www.avonbooks.com

An Imprint of HarperCollins*Publishers*
www.avonromance.com